The Girl Who Left

Jenny Blackhurst lives in Shropshire where she grew up dreaming that one day she would get paid for making up stories. She is an avid reader and can mostly be found with her head in a book or hunting Pokemon with her son, otherwise you can get her on Twitter @JennyBlackhurst or Facebook. Her favourite film is Fried Green Tomatoes at the Whistle Stop Cafe, but if her children ask it's definitely Moana.

The girl who left

JENNY BLACKHURST

CANELO

First published in the United Kingdom in 2022 by

Canelo
Unit 9, 5th Floor
Cargo Works, 1–2 Hatfields
London, SE1 9PG
United Kingdom

A CIP catalogue record for this book is available from the British Library.

Print ISBN 978 1 80032 926 3
Ebook ISBN 978 1 80032 925 6

This book is a work of fiction. Names, characters, businesses, organizations, places and events are either the product of the author's imagination or are used fictitiously. Any resemblance to actual persons, living or dead, events or locales is entirely coincidental.

Look for more great books at www.canelo.co

Printed and bound in Great Britain by Clays Ltd, Elcograf S.p.A.

1

Chapter One

Kathryn

'*Where is she?*'

The room smells of stale sweat and overpowering after-shave. A steady hum of conversation surrounds us of people making the most of every minute until the bell rings. And yet this is the only question I ask. The only question I ever ask. *Where is she?*

At the table next to us, a solid man covered from head to toe in tattoos weeps openly at the sight of his baby daughter. The mother, a sallow-faced youth, sits uncomfortably chewing her nail, too young to be in this situation, too immature and unsure of herself to be raising a miniature woman on her own. I have a momentary glimpse of the future, a future in which this baby girl sits in the exact same spot as her mother once did, enduring her half an hour visit to a boyfriend who doesn't care about her enough to stay out of prison. *The Circle of Life*, I think sadly.

I'm not expecting an answer to my question, I'm just giving the old man in front of me half a chance to speak before I get up and leave, just like I did last month, just like I will next month. For the briefest moment, I allow myself to look directly at him. *I will not cry*, I tell myself stoically. *He means nothing. He is nothing. I will look at him.*

As always, he is clean-shaven for our visit, although a beard might better hide the gaunt grey features that have taken the place of the youthful, tanned face I can't seem to forget. His face seems to have slackened over the years, melted, as though he has been sitting too close to a candle. I don't – can't – look into his eyes. I don't want to see the nothing that is behind them. I know there is no life there, no future. He murdered that the day he murdered Elsie Button.

Everyone has to have a purpose in life. Some are more commendable than others. Alan Turing founded computer science, Martin Luther King had the world's most important dreams, Lizzo was 100 per cent *that bitch*. I sometimes wonder if anyone else in the whole world has the specific purpose in life that I have. To find out where the body of five-year-old Elsie Button is buried.

Plenty of people have made it their life's mission to find missing people, missing children. I'm not unique in that fact. What makes my purpose in life different is that the man I'm trying to force a confession from is Patrick Bowen, infamous child killer. My father.

The bell rings and the silence at our table solidifies around us. Despite the fact that I have made this journey twenty-six times in twenty-six months, since the day I decided I would try to get the answers to our past from Patrick himself, each and every time I still feel the sting of disappointment when the man sitting across the table from me makes no attempt to answer the only question I ever ask him. *Where is she?*

Taking a deep breath, I stand, shoving the grey Formica chair so fast it topples backwards. A few people turn to look at us, but I'm taking no notice. I'm certain I hear Patrick take a breath of his own and for a split second

2

I freeze, my body half turned from him, waiting for the words I have waited so long for.

He is going to tell me this time. This is it, right now. This is why I have put myself through hours of torment, why I have allowed myself to imagine taking the news to Elsie's family, to give them some reprieve from the twenty-five-year nightmare they have endured. I haven't spoken to them in years, haven't even told them I'm here. Will they thank me for my interference? Or will it be fresh hell from the family that ripped their lives apart?

Patrick lets out the breath without saying a word and I feel my shoulders sag in defeat. Just for that one second I'd had hope…

Determined not to let him see my disappointment, I lift my chin and, staring straight ahead, I join the queue of leavers without a backwards glance, steeling myself for the thought of going through all this again next month. *Where is she?*

–

The air outside is warm and clammy and I drag in a deep lungful of it, willing myself over and over not to cry. I've done this so many times before and walked away without a second glance – why should today be any different? I haven't cried since the first time, two years ago now, but it feels like both yesterday and a different lifetime. That day, I went home and sobbed until my eyes were tiny slits and my head felt as though I'd taken a baseball bat to the side of it.

I know why today is different. Today, just like that first time, I honestly thought he was going to answer the question I've asked him every single time I've visited that godforsaken place. I heard that intake of breath and for a minute all the hope I had at my first visit came flooding back to the surface, making me feel ashamed now that it had obviously never been buried very deeply to begin with.

Tomorrow marks the twenty-fifth anniversary of Elsie's disappearance. I had thought that might make a difference somehow, but it hasn't. My father is as silent on her whereabouts today as he was on the day he confessed to her murder.

Lasciate ogne speranza, voi ch'intrate.

Abandon hope, all ye who enter.

Chapter Two

Kathryn

When the doorbell to my tiny flat rings that evening it barely registers with me and I make no move to answer it. I'm used to just ignoring it around this time every year. I make a mental note to disable it before bed.

Despite changing my name legally by deed poll, moving another two times since our first escape from Anglesey to Liverpool and ending up in Manchester, the reporters and other assorted ghouls turn up as if there's a tour bus that drops off on my doorstep every 18th June. They seem to have started early this year.

I had considered getting a nice big dog, but a dog is for life, not just the 18th of June, and as much as I'd love something to cuddle up to at night, I haven't exactly proved myself responsible enough to take care of another human being.

When I ignore the third ring of the doorbell, my phone begins to buzz and the word 'Jordan' flashes across it with a picture of my brother's goofy grinning face. My brother rarely rings me, despite us being in contact constantly. He prefers to WhatsApp me – I think so he can see when I've read the message. Which is why now I automatically assume there's something wrong. Is this it? Is this the day Patrick has been killed in prison?

'What is it?' I ask. 'Is he dead?'

'What?' Jordan sounds confused. 'Is who dead? No one's dead.'

Something that feels strangely like relief floods through me and I tell myself it's only because he alone holds the answer I need. *Where is she?*

'Then what's wrong?'

'Don't you answer your door anymore? I've been ringing the bell for ages. Miriam had to let me into the front.'

'Shit, sorry, Jay.' I hang up and go to let him in.

I open the door to a male, stretched-out version of me. Where Jordan is tall, slim with a shock of dark red hair and bright blue eyes, I am short and you-say-plump-I-say-curvy, but with the same trademark Bowen hair-eye combination. The same hair and eyes as our grandfather, and Patrick. He's holding a bunch of flowers and a bottle of wine – the flowers are for me and the wine is for him. As I let him in, he gives me a quick hug and makes his way through to the kitchen, which – given that my flat is the size of a postage stamp and still costs over half my wages (thanks, city life) – isn't very far away.

'Fuck me, I'm knackered,' he announces, unscrewing his bottle of wine and pouring himself a tumblerful.

'You say that every time I see you, but I'm yet to work out what it is you actually do for a living that is so utterly exhausting. You are still fannying around on computers, right? You didn't join the fire service or train as a bricklayer in the six days since I last saw you?'

He flicks me the V and takes a swig of his wine.

There are seven years between us and yet Jordan and I have always been close. He's my big brother, my protector and the one man in my life I've always been able to rely on. I sometimes wonder if we'd have the same bond if Patrick hadn't murdered my best friend when I was five years old.

'So, tomorrow's the day,' he says.

'Is it? I hadn't noticed.' My attempt to sound nonchalant fails with my brother. He raises his eyebrows.

'Is that why you're ignoring your doorbell?'

I flick the kettle on and join him at the breakfast bar. 'No, I looked through the peephole and saw it was you.'

'Have you called Mum?'

'And say what?' I ask. 'Happy "your-husband-murdered–a–child–iversary"?'

'Even for you that's below the belt,' Jordan says, but I know he doesn't mean it. He gets me – sometimes I think he's the only one who does. After all, there are very few people in life who can say they've been through what we have. Actually, thinking about it, there's probably more than you'd expect – after all, people commit murder all the time, and a good percentage of them must have families. Maybe I should start a Facebook group. If I did, I wonder if the others like us would be more like me or like Jordan? Because, despite our shared experience, we grew up to be very different people.

'Have you called her?' I challenge.

He nods.

Of course he has.

'She's fine, thanks for asking. She asked how you were. She worries about you.'

'She's my next of kin. If anything had happened to me, she'd know before you.'

The kettle finishes boiling and I get up to make myself a coffee, grateful of the chance to avoid his eye. There are two topics that are usually off limits between me and my

7

big brother – our mother and Patrick. He's flouting the rules because of what day tomorrow is, but if I let him carry on he'll start on the 'she only worries because she cares' stuff.

'You know she only worries because she cares about you.'

I sigh, a huge, exaggerated sound, and put my mug down harder than intended. Jordan flinches.

'I am thirty years old. She doesn't need to worry about me. In fact, of the two of us, I'd say it's you she needs to worry about.'

Jordan's tumbler freezes on the way up to his lips. He raises his eyebrows. 'Me? I'd love to hear your deductions on that one, Sherlock.'

'Okay.' I raise a finger. 'One; you were old enough to actually understand what was going on twenty-five years ago –' Jordan had been thirteen years old when Patrick was arrested for the murder of Elsie Button. Yes, that was her real name. Cute as a button, people used to say, and they were right. With white-blonde hair and the tiniest of frames, she was a complete contrast to the muddy-faced ginger girl I was at the age of five. 'And yet,' I carry on, 'you have never shown even the smallest psychological effect. Which either makes you the most resilient thirteen-year-old on the planet or a psychopath. And two –' I push on before he can object to being labelled a psychopath, raising a second finger '– you have the world's most beautiful wife, a well-paid job which, unlike your feckless sister, you have managed to hold on to most of your adult life, and yet you remain completely childless, which I'm certain smacks of some deep-seated issue with the death of a child in your distant past. Three, and this one's the most convincing in my humble opinion, you are – simply put – too bloody perfect to be true. Therefore,' I wave my arm with a flourish, 'you are, of the two of us, the most Bundy-like. Bundy-esque?'

'Bloody hell, Kat, thanks a bunch. I turn up to make sure you're not hanging from the rafters and you insult me and label me a serial killer in the making. I'm really not sure why I came over here brandishing flowers in the first place.' He tries to sound grumpy but my brother never gets mad at me. Exasperated, yes. Mad, no.

'Because I'm the wayward younger sister who causes the family no end of shame and concern. DUI, assault, anger issues – I'm a liability. Freud could have written a volume about *me*.'

'You forgot delusions of grandeur,' Jordan snorts. He drains his glass of wine and refills.

'Why didn't Verity come?'

Jordan looks sheepish. 'We had a fight.'

'A fight?' Jordan and Verity never fight, or not that he's ever admitted to me. They are one of those sickening couples who still dance together at weddings and get up early on Sundays to wander around car-boot sales.

Verity is an artist and a collector; their house is full of interesting knick-knacks that all have a 'story'. Everything I own was bought from IKEA all on the same day. Verity is also a spoilt bitch, but we all have our flaws and she makes my brother happy so I am the last person allowed to judge. Especially since I have never managed to find a man I trust enough to settle down with and not turn out to be a monster.

'It's a friend's fortieth and we were invited to this meal thing, she wanted me to go with her. Don't worry, she's picking me up afterwards, so I don't have to sleep on your sofa.'

9

'Why didn't you go?'

'I wanted to check you were okay. I know you'll probably go away first thing in the morning, so I just wanted to make sure you were all right.'

You would think that after twenty-five years we would be allowed to forget what Patrick did. Okay, maybe not forget entirely, but at least be able to get on with our own lives. I was nearly six at the time, in a couple of months I turn thirty-one and yet I have had to move jobs countless times when people find out who I am related to, which is why I now work in temping jobs, never staying long enough to progress up the ladder, and why I will never trust a man enough to bear his children.

The temp things works for me, especially because it means I can book leave at the same time every year – the anniversary. Every year, I leave my flat on the morning of the 18th and drive as far out of the city as I can, until the high-rise offices and flats transform into cottages and eventually coastlines, and when I return there is always a small pile of business cards behind the door with reporters' details on them. Jordan gets the odd couple, Mum too, but it turns out I'm the main attraction. After all, Elsie was my best friend. We went into the woods together and only one of us came out, or so the story goes. The fact that her body was never found is the reason the story has survived, I think, and every few years a new documentary is made about the day she disappeared.

'Well look, I'm fine,' I hold out my hands and point to my coffee mug in evidence. 'Not a criminal charge in sight. Ta-da! My therapist even thinks I'm brave enough to do some hypnotherapy.'

I slide the leaflets my therapist had given me across the counter where they have been untouched since.

Jordan snatches up the top one, his face darkening. 'What is this bullshit?'

I let out a low whistle. 'Geesh, calm down. I haven't said I'll do it.'

'Well you shouldn't,' he says firmly, slamming the leaflet back down on the counter in front of me. 'It's absolute rubbish and will only make you feel like shit. Promise me you won't go near it, Kat, promise.'

'All right, Jesus, I promise,' I say, picking up the leaflets and dropping them into the bin. 'Satisfied?'

'Very,' Jordan replies, still looking pale. 'Well, my wife and her friends are going to be boring the pants off each other for hours yet. So grab your blankets – I do believe you have a DVD of *The Goonies* somewhere in your film collection. Don't forget the popcorn, Kitty Kat.'

–

Jordan is picked up by a placated Verity at eleven thirty – placated by the fact that he hands her the bunch of flowers he'd brought round for me the minute she turns up. As she rings the door buzzer, Jordan turns to me and says, 'This pop psychology thing you do? Do me a favour and don't do it in front of Verity. She doesn't get this,' he signals between the two of us, 'and she can't have kids.'

So that's why you've stayed with her, I almost say, but instead I say, 'Okay. Sorry.'

'For being a bitch? Or that we can't have children?'

'The bitch thing,' I shrug. 'The kids thing is probably for the best.'

Jordan stares at me for a second, then laughs. 'Sleep tight, little one.'

I put on *Misfits*, my go-to entertainment at the moment when I want my brain to switch off and I don't feel like lying in silence waiting for it to happen. Despite telling Jordan I'm fine – and believing it – I can't help running over my meeting with Patrick this morning, the moment he took that breath and I honestly believed he was about to tell me what he'd done with Elsie Button's body.

I open the vodka at midnight and drink until I fall asleep at three.

Chapter Three

Maggie

Maggie uttered a curse word her mother would not be proud of and shoved a hand over the naked man's mouth.

'Shut it,' she hissed. 'Not one word, understand?'

He nodded, his wide eyes terrified.

She lifted her phone to her ear. 'What?'

'Sorry to bother—'

'But you have,' Maggie cut him off. 'So get to the fucking point.'

'Right, um, yeah, sorry. I thought you should know, there's been a kid reported missing in Pentraeth. I'm on my way over, you know how it is with these things, it could go either way: found in ten minutes playing at a mate's house or dead in a ditch. Just thought you should know.'

'Fucksake,' she hissed, lifting herself off the man underneath her and reaching for the bra hanging from the bedpost. 'Get every available unit to the house and road-blocks at the bridges. Search and Rescue on standby. I'd rather go for overkill than be the one who let a kid disappear. Today of all days. Better let the DCI know too. I'm on my way.'

She flung the phone on the bed and sighed.

'What's going on?' Sergeant Rob Murray asked, his now flaccid cock still exposed as he lay spreadeagled on the bed. He reached over to pick up his cigarettes from the bedside table. 'Missing kid?'

'Ever thought of becoming a cop?' DI Maggie Grant asked, her eyebrows raised. 'Yeah, Pentraeth.'

'Isn't today—'

Maggie snatched the lit cigarette from his fingers, her shirt open and her trousers yet to be found. They were probably on the stairs where she'd discarded them as soon as she'd walked into Rob's place three hours ago in response to his early morning booty call. They'd already fucked once so she was less annoyed than she would have been at being interrupted, but still pretty pissed off; her day off nearly never coincided with his wife's early shifts. She took a drag and let the smoke fill her lungs. Exhaling, she pointed the cigarette at him.

'Don't say it. Don't even say it. God, if the press catches wind of this before the kid is found they will be all over it faster than your erection dropping when you hear your wife come home.'

Rob pulled a face. 'Funny. Real clever. So you're just gonna leave me here like this?'

Maggie handed him back the cigarette and buttoned her shirt. Running a hand through her cropped blonde hair, she retreated into the en suite bathroom and checked her make-up in the mirror. Rob's wife, Angelica, had some pretty expensive-looking creams and perfume. All paid for on Angelica's wage, no doubt – Maggie knew how much Rob got paid, after all. She picked up one of the perfumes and gave herself a couple of squirts. Still only half dressed, she opened the bedroom door and blew Rob a kiss.

'If this doesn't resolve quickly, you'll be called in,' Maggie warned him. She spotted her trousers on the stairs and her handbag by the front door. 'See you at work.'

She'd parked her car three streets away, so she used the walk to call for an update. Her DS answered on the first ring.

'How goes it?' she asked, her phone pinned to her ear as she fumbled in her handbag for chewing gum.

'Missing child is a five-year-old girl by the name of Abigail Warner,' DS Bryn Bailey answered.

'Warner? I know them?'

'Probably not,' Bailey confirmed. 'They've only been here two years and they seem straight. Mum is a mess, dad on his way home – he works on the trains and was just approaching Wolverhampton when his wife got hold of him. He's getting a taxi back rather than wait for the next train.'

Maggie reached her car and pulled her keys out of her jacket pocket. Sliding onto the driver's seat, she chucked the phone onto the passenger seat knowing that it would connect to the car's speakerphone any minute. When it did, Bryn was saying '—wen place.'

'Right, fine. Text me the address and I'll meet you there.'

'Didn't you hear me?'

She hadn't heard him the first time, but she sure did the second.

'Holy fuck,' she swore into the air. 'I hope this is some kind of joke.'

'No joke, ma'am,' Bailey replied. 'I sincerely wish it was.'

–

When Maggie pulled up outside the cluster of houses, there were already three police cars lining the street. Pentraeth didn't have 'estates' in the way towns in England did, no uniformed streets lined with dwellings. Rather, there were clumps of houses springing up and huddling together against the biting sea wind that seemed to permeate even the inland towns, even in the summer, and then just space in between. The Bowen home stood apart from these clusters, as ostracised as its former owners, although today it was once more very much the centre of attention.

Bailey had worked fast – she could see her officers in high-vis jackets moving in and out of gardens, knocking on doors, peering under tarps, parting bushes. Every time one of them left a house, the occupier trailed after them to join the search. Blue and yellow marked vehicles were parked at intervals along the road and the air was full of the shouts of the little girl's name. She looked at her watch. Ten forty. She'd made it in twenty minutes.

DS Bailey opened the front door and stepped out before Maggie had even opened the gate. The house was surrounded on three sides by six-foot hedges, giving the illusion of privacy, when, of course, nothing was private on this island. The Warners would find that out soon enough.

'No sign of her,' Bailey said, his voice low. He glanced at the closed front door as though someone might hear him.

'No shit Sherlock.' Maggie scowled at him. 'You think I'd take a look at this circus and wonder if she was still missing?'

Bailey opened his mouth to speak, then thought better of it.

'What time was the call?' Maggie asked.

'Nine fifty-seven. PCs were on the scene at ten twelve. They called the office en route and I arrived at ten twenty, I called you and two more PCs for back-up. They've been doing door-to-door around the streets; neighbours have started helping search.'

'How long had she been missing before the mum called it in?'

'Her work call ended at nine thirty, she thinks it took her a couple of minutes to realise she couldn't hear Abby.'

'Call started at…?'

'Nine.'

'Jesus, an hour and three quarters and no one's spotted her yet? Doesn't look good. Anything else before I go in?'

'I've done the usual prelim questions – I don't think she's hiding anything.'

'Bollocks.' Maggie snapped. 'Everyone is hiding something. We've just got to figure out if her something is connected to her daughter being missing.'

-

Bryn watched DI Maggie Grant walk into the Warners' home without knocking and let out a sigh. If there was ever a woman who could make your balls jump up inside your body, there she went. Bryn knew that some of the other officers thought she was hot, but he would feel safer sticking his cock in a shark's mouth than put it anywhere near Maggie Grant. The front door reopened and her thunderstruck face appeared. Bryn started, realising he had been stupidly watching the closed door, sucking in those few moments of reprieve when he should have been following his boss inside. He did an idiotic little quickstep up the path after her and was certain he saw her roll her eyes.

'Mrs Warner,' Bryn heard Grant say as she stepped in and closed the door. 'I'm Detective Inspector Grant.'

Caroline Warner hadn't moved from where Bryn had left her on the sofa, staring straight ahead at the wall, but she stood now and took the hand Grant offered her.

'Have you found her?' she asked, her urgent voice barely above a whisper. 'I wanted to go out looking – I should be looking for her, but he said…' She shot a glance towards Bryn, who opened his mouth to explain. Predictably, he didn't get the chance as Grant began to speak over him.

'DS Bailey is right, Mrs Warner. We've got a lot of people looking for Abby right now. The best place for you is right here helping us.'

It was amazing really, how she could go from ice queen to gentle and compassionate – if Bryn's daughter was missing – God forbid – Maggie Grant was actually exactly who he would want in charge of the investigation.

'I don't know if DS Bailey has told you,' she continued, 'but both my team and your neighbours are already out in force. As an extra precaution, I've set up stop-and-search at both bridges – just as a precaution, as I said. We're doing everything we can to get Abby home safe. In the majority of cases like this, the child has wandered off and is home in no time. In the unlikely event that isn't the case here, unfortunately,' Grant put her hands on Caroline's shoulders and looked into her eyes, no hint of the hardness she reserved for officers who messed up, and suspects, 'I have to ask you some difficult questions and time is of the essence, so I can't afford to skirt around these. And I know we've only just met, but I need you to trust that everything I'm doing and everything I'm asking is to help find Abby. Can you do that? Will you trust me?'

Caroline Warner nodded – Grant had done her job and had the mother's full cooperation, for now at least. Bryn had to hand it to her, Grant knew what she was doing.

'Okay,' DI Grant glanced over at him as though only just remembering he was there. She gave him a tight smile – he wondered if it hurt her face. 'Could you get us some drinks please? Coffee for me and—'

'Tea,' Caroline whispered. 'I'll have a tea.'

DS Bailey smiled back, trying not to let his resentment of being demoted to the tea boy show on his face. 'Of course,' he said. 'I'll be right back.'

–

Bailey disappeared into the kitchen, a weird kind of grimace on his face. Maggie assumed he was annoyed at being demoted to tea boy, but she needed to get Caroline Warner on her own for a few minutes. She had clearly gone past the hysterical stage and was in shock, not surprising of course. Maggie took her arm and guided Caroline to the sofa. She didn't have kids but that didn't stop her being able to well imagine the terror of not knowing where your five-year-old child was, not knowing if they were hurt or in trouble, or if you had potentially seen them for the last time ever. Helplessness, intense fear, you didn't need to have had children to know those feelings. Maggie sat down next to Caroline, her knees touching the other woman's, and rested a hand over hers.

'You've given DS Bailey a list of all Abby's friends, we have officers and volunteers tracing the route to all of their houses to see if she went to play and maybe took a wrong turn. Is there anyone else we need to add to that list? A family member she might have gone to visit?'

Caroline shook her head slowly. 'We don't have any family here. Or many friends to be honest, we haven't lived here long.'

'Okay,' Maggie nodded. 'If you think of anyone else she might have gone to see, just let us know straight away. Has Abby mentioned speaking to anyone new recently? Someone you haven't heard of before, a new friend? Or have you seen anyone hanging around?'

Caroline cringed and looked as though she could be sick. The implications of what she was asking were clear; that someone could have been grooming her daughter to take her away. 'I don't... No, I don't think so. I've never... never had to think in that way.'

Most parents didn't, until they did.

'No, of course,' Maggie said, 'and the chances are that's because there's no one or nothing to think about. These are just standard questions we have to ask.'

Bryn walked in and placed mugs in front of them.

'We found that bracelet, in Abby's room,' he says. 'It's been bagged and tagged.'

'What bracelet?'

'When we had a look around Abby's room, there was a bracelet Caroline didn't recognise, and a five-pound note in her jewellery box. We're waiting to ask her dad if he knows anything about them, but Caroline didn't think he would – he doesn't tend to buy her gifts for no reason and it isn't a birthday present.'

Maggie cringed. If someone had been buying Abigail gifts... the word 'grooming' was always on the cards.

'Wait,' Caroline held up a hand. 'There might be something else. I saw a car out of the window before I, um, before I answered the phone. About seven thirty. I hadn't seen it here before, I only noticed it because it was badly parked. It was across there,' she gestured out of the window to the street opposite. 'I thought they were visiting at the Greens' across there.' She looked panicked, her hands gripped tightly together, her fingers turning her wedding ring around over and over. 'Do you think they could have… it could be them?'

'I don't think we should jump to any conclusions,' Maggie soothed, her heart thumping slightly faster. 'Abby was playing in the back garden – no one in the front would know she was there and if the owner of this car had any intentions of taking her, there are better places to park. But I'll take the details and ask one of my officers to check them with your neighbours. If they were visiting one of them, we'll identify them in no time.'

'And if they weren't?'

'Let's just take this one step at a time.' Maggie flinched as the front door opened and slammed shut again. 'It looks like your husband's home.'

Chapter Four

Kathryn

There's a thumping inside my head and my eyes feel as though they have been superglued shut. It takes me longer than it should to work out that the thumping isn't just coming from inside my head, it's coming from the front door. A fuzzy memory of me disconnecting the buzzer surfaces; obviously someone has got past the front door and up to my flat. Pieces of the puzzle start to fly into place: it's Elsie's anniversary. I took the buzzer down because of reporters.

I pick up my phone and see several missed calls from Jordan, one from Mum and an answerphone message.

'Kathryn?' the banging on the door stops and I hear Miriam's concerned voice. That completes the trio of the only people who I have let close enough to contact me today. She sounds frantic. What the hell has been going on? Did I forget to warn her what today was? There had been no point in trying to keep my identity a secret from my neighbour, even if she had been polite enough not to enquire why reporters would turn up at my door every few months – Miriam isn't polite enough by the way – the intrusive fuckers actually went round to her house and offered her a thousand pounds to try to get me to talk about what it was like to be the daughter of a murderer.

Bless her, Miriam chased the first lot off with a mouthful of obscenities and the threat of pepper spray, then came straight round to get the entire sordid story from me. Miriam is sixty-four years old and basically guilted me into telling her everything with a story about how she can go weeks without speaking to a soul and yet she'd still seen off her only visitors that month with a threat to life if they came back. I happen to know that Miriam has two daughters with a menagerie of children who visit her once a week each, but instead of arguing, I invited her in and told her everything. It felt good.

Phone still in hand, I open the door to my friend, who pushes past me and slams it behind her. She's in the kitchen before I can stop her. The bottle of vodka, now only a quarter full, sits there accusingly. Miriam looks at it, then at me. She pulls two glasses from the cupboard and pours me a Coke and a glass of water.

'Drink these. Where's your Ibuprofen?'

'Bathroom,' I say. Resistance is futile with Miriam.

She scurries off to fetch the drugs and I look at my phone again. Miriam arrives back just as I'm dialling the answerphone.

'Listen, your brother has been trying to get hold of you—'

I hold up a finger to signal that I'm on the phone, but she doesn't stop.

'Put that down a second, this is urgent. He phoned me—'

I give up trying to listen to the EE voicemail service and hang up. 'What did he phone you for? I didn't even think he'd still have your number.'

'He worries about you, Kathryn, it's what big brothers do. Anyway, listen, it's about your mum. You mustn't panic, but she's in hospital. You need to call Jordan.'

In hospital? My first thought is a heart attack, today of all days. Five missed calls.

You're a fuck-up, Kathryn Starling. When are you going to grow up and be dependable for once in your life?

I groan and put my face in my hands, but Miriam's having no self-pity whatsoever. She pokes me in the shoulder. 'Come on, you need to call.'

Jordan picks up on the first ring. Only it's not Jordan, it's Verity.

'Oh thank God, Kat. I'm really sorry, sweetie, but you need to come to the Princess. It's your mum. Jordan's in with her now.'

'What is it, V? What's happened to her?'

There's a hesitation, as if she's weighing up whether to tell me over the phone versus whether to let me drive all the way there with no clue what I'm driving into. Eventually though she lowers her voice and says, 'They think she took an overdose. She's in a coma. Please be quick.'

–

Miriam makes sure I don't look like I've just woken up with a hangover and when we get downstairs, she stands by the driver's side of my car and holds her hands out for the keys.

'You what?'

'I'm driving.' Her fuchsia pink lips are drawn together in a line. 'You've been drinking.'

'Last night,' I counter. 'I'm fine now.'

'You'd bet your previous driving conviction on that, would you?'

'Fine.' I hand her the keys. 'But I *am* fine.'

She raises her eyebrows and makes a *hmmm* sound but doesn't say any more, thank goodness.

The hospital is a ten-minute drive, but at the speed Miriam is going, we'll be there in six. All of a sudden I remember why I don't get in cars with her anymore.

'Shit, Mum called me earlier today.' With the phone call to Verity, I'd almost forgotten. 'Jesus, I wonder—' I stop short of saying I wonder if I could have stopped her. The thing about Miriam is, although I love her like, well, like a mother without the baggage of having married a murderer I suppose, she does tend to be very... honest. So if she thinks for a second that I might have been able to stop Mum taking an overdose if only I hadn't been passed out drunk, she'll tell me so. And I'm not sure I want to hear it confirmed by someone else.

Just eight minutes later Miriam pulls up outside the hospital doors and skids to an abrupt halt. I swear to God I'd have been safer driving drunk than I am in the car with this woman.

'Go on, I'll park up and meet you in there.' She gestures for me to get out and I realise that worrying about the state my car might be in when I go back to it is an inappropriate reaction.

'Thank you,' I say as I slam the car door behind me. I leave my coat in the car but pull my cardigan around me, tie my red hair into a ponytail and hope I don't stand out enough for anyone to recognise me. It's unlikely – even when they print stories about Patrick and my family in the papers, they use old photos of him and Elsie and they never use pictures of me. You can find them on the internet, I'd imagine, but my face hasn't been splashed over the front of the nationals. I guess there are laws about printing photos of children who aren't missing or murdered and it's not really necessary for the world to know what I look like – not in the public interest. My mum's photo was printed a couple of times. I remember that was when she stopped taking me to school and Jordan put me on the bus every day and made sure I got to class.

Verity is waiting in reception for me and gives me a sympathetic look. She moves in for a hug, but I pretend not to realise and dodge it – despite having changed my clothes and brushed my teeth, on Miriam's orders, I don't want her to smell drink and report back to Jordan. He worries enough about me as it is. I thought I'd managed to make it look natural, but she frowns for a second, then gestures to a set of double doors.

'She's through here. Jordan is with her.'

Mum is in a private room, lying in the hospital bed hooked up to all sorts of monitors. She looks so frail and old that I want to rip everything off her and just hold her in my arms. I say a silent prayer that it isn't too late for that.

'Kat.' Jordan gets up immediately and there's no dodging the bear hug he wraps me in, but when we break apart, he makes no comment about how I smell. 'Where were you? Miriam said your car was outside. I thought you'd be halfway to elsewhere by now.'

I might have been had I not made my way through half a bottle of vodka last night, but I choose not to tell him that. He worries enough as it is.

'My phone was on silent, so I didn't see your voicemail. What happened? Did she do this on purpose? What have the doctors said? Is she going to be okay?'

Jordan sighs and he looks as though he's aged ten years since last night. 'The neighbours heard a crash. They knew what day it was, so I think they'd been keeping a bit of an eye on her – you know Joyce next door, she's a bit like your Miriam.'

Joyce next door is nothing like 'my Miriam'. Where I managed to move in next door to a sixty-four-year-old Rottweiler with her faculties fully intact and the driving skills of Lewis Hamilton on crack, Mum set up camp next door to a fifty-seven-year-old knitting circle manager. To say Joyce is old beyond her years is an understatement. I've only ever seen her shuffling to the recycling and back, holding up a hand as if it were made of lead. She's been a good friend to Mum though, a better friend – it seems – than I am a daughter.

'When Mum didn't answer, Joyce let herself in and found her on the floor in the bedroom, called 999. The paramedics pumped her stomach, but she was unresponsive. She's been like this ever since. I tried calling you but, wait – did you say voicemail?'

'Yeah, I didn't get it because my phone was on—'

'I didn't leave you a voicemail, Kat. I didn't want you to find out like that.'

I pull my phone from my pocket. 'Mum called me again,' I say, pulling up the call list. 'While I was asleep. Maybe she…' I hit the voicemail button and the ever-chirpy EE answerphone woman welcomes me. I have one new message. First new message…

I shove it onto speakerphone. We both cringe as Mum's voice rings out across the room. It's so strange to hear her so clearly when she's lying in a coma next to me.

'Kathryn, it's Mum.'

She always says this, as if after thirty years I might not recognise her voice.

'I had to call you. I wanted to speak to you, but I'm glad you didn't answer because this is quite hard to say and… Oh dear, I'm not even sure I can say it, and what if you'd answered and wanted details from me and I just can't give them to you.'

Tears prick at my eyes. She sounds so distressed. Why couldn't I have been there for her? Why do I always have to let people down?

'Anyway,' her resolve is back and she sounds calmer again. Jordan squeezes my hand. 'I have to say this because I think it's time I let go of the past, let go of everything. Don't you worry about me, dear, I have to do this, for everyone. I just, I don't want you to hate your father anymore. He had his reasons for doing what he did, for taking the blame like that. He had things he wanted to make up for and now no one knows what really happened. And I had no choice but to go along with what he wanted and I just think now that it was such a *mistake* and I wish I could just turn back time… Oh god, I think I need to lie down. If I could just think clearly—'

The message ends and the EE woman happily informs me that I can listen to my message again by pressing one.

Instead I hang up and look at Jordan, who has gone as white as the wall behind him.

–

'What does she mean *about taking the blame like that*?' Verity demands, looking from one of us to the other. 'What could anyone need to make up for that would make them take the blame for killing a child?' Her voice is getting more and more high-pitched with every sentence, and Jordan looks like he'd gladly take the blame for Elsie's murder himself if she would only quieten down.

We're in the day room at the hospital and although we're the only ones actually in here, there's no door, so doctors and nurses are passing continuously. Children's garish pictures adorn every wall – if they are supposed to make people feel better, I think they miss the mark somewhat, especially the one that looks like a clown who has been shot in the chest. Or maybe it's supposed to be a doctor – still, they are the stuff of nightmares if you ask me. The mismatched chairs and ancient TV complete the asylum feel. If we have to spend much longer here, I'm going to lose my mind.

'I'm sure you're a lovely girl, but there's a partially deaf man in Scotland who didn't quite hear you,' Miriam says in the way that only Miriam can. 'And your voice is starting to grate a little.'

Verity shuts up as completely and beautifully as if my elderly neighbour had slapped her in the face. Sometimes I could kiss that woman, but I'm too afraid I might be the one getting slapped.

'She was drunk, upset, delirious,' Jordan says quietly, placing an arm around Verity's shoulders, but his eyes are fixed on me. 'She didn't know what she was talking about. This doesn't mean anything.'

'No, of course it doesn't,' I agree almost immediately.

Too immediately it seems. Jordan's eyes narrow.

'It doesn't,' he says, his voice hardening.

'That's what I said, it doesn't.'

'So why have you got that "what does this mean" look on your face?' he asks.

'I haven't,' I insist. 'Because it doesn't mean anything.'

'Right.' Jordan nods.

'But what if—'

'Kat.' His tone is warning.

Verity and Miriam are looking between us as if we are speaking in tongues.

'Look, Kat, there's something else you should know. It doesn't mean anything…'

'Nothing does, apparently,' I retort. I look between Jordan, Verity and Miriam, but suddenly they are not so chatty. They look even more serious than before. What can be more serious than what's already happened? 'What? What is it?'

Jordan looks me in the eye and reaches out to put a hand on my arm, but I pull back. What's going on? What do they know?

'There's been another abduction, Kat, in Pentraeth. Another girl is missing.'

Chapter Five

Maggie

Maggie couldn't help but feel relieved when the Family Liaison Officer had turned up at the Warners' home and she could get out of there. Not that anyone was calling it the Warners' home – it was forever cemented in the minds of the people of Anglesey as the 'old Bowen house' and Maggie knew that's what tomorrow's papers would say too. It was inevitable the connection would be made, even twenty-five years apart. The chances of two abductions from the same back garden were so slim that Maggie was having a hard time convincing herself they were unrelated. If it hadn't been for the fact that Patrick Bowen was firmly behind bars and had never shown any signs of being related to Harry Houdini, she would be looking for ways of linking them herself. It wasn't like the house was on a major highway, easy to spot a child playing and pull them into the back of a van while barely slowing down. She knew there were places in America that were hotspots for child trafficking, but this was Anglesey for God's sake. Everyone knew everyone on this bloody island, for better or for worse.

Speaking of worse, Maggie shuddered at the memory of Abigail's father arriving home an hour ago. Of course it was natural that he would be worried, frightened, but she hadn't quite expected to see him so angry. He'd flown into a rage at his wife the moment he'd seen her, his words and body language so aggressive that Maggie wondered what would have happened had she and Bryn not been there.

'So the father will be the first one we look at is it, ma'am?' Bryn said from the seat beside her.

Maggie almost jumped – it was like he'd read her mind. Until then, he'd been so quiet and she so lost in thought that she'd almost forgotten he was there. They were almost back at the station and she would be expected to have a plan.

'Temper like that usually he would be,' she admitted. 'But he's got an alibi, hasn't he? Working on the train?'

'Only his word for that actually,' Bryn said, and Maggie's head snapped to look at him sharply. ''Twas his wife who said he was at work and she'd had trouble reaching him. I've already got someone at the station checking with National Rail to see if he was where he said he was.'

Maggie was impressed. She turned the car into the station car park. 'Good work. Be a bloody stupid lie, easy to check. Criminals aren't always masterminds though, far from it most of the time. Aw shit, looks who's here already.'

The 'who' was Jeremy Taylor, local newshound – if you could call him that when the biggest sniff he got was the occasional domestic incident or drink-driving conviction. Most of the news articles in north-west Wales were political, how much was being spent on which roads, et cetera. Old Jimmy T must have near pissed his pants when he heard the words 'missing child'.

Maggie looked at her watch. It had been just over an hour since the first call, nationals would be on their way before long, if not already. A pretty blonde girl abducted from the same spot a near identical girl went missing from twenty-five years to the day. Give it an hour, there would be a Netflix script.

'No comment, Jim,' Maggie said as she opened her car door.

'Come on Maggie...' He froze at the look she gave him, 'DI Grant. You're going to need the media and you know it.'

Maggie sighed. He was right. They were going to need the press if Abigail wasn't found by about an hour ago.

'Fine. Come in, wait in reception. I'll brief the press officer, he'll be with you as soon as we've put something together. Have you already put something on social media?'

Jimmy looked guilty.

Maggie took a deep breath in.

'Nothing we can do about it now, might as well use it for good. Follow up on it saying volunteers are not to go to the house, they should go to the Memorial Hall – Search and Rescue are using it as a base, they are there already.'

Jimmy nodded, trying to look helpful and professional all at once. The result was constipated toddler. He followed a few feet behind Maggie and Bryn, trying not to give the DI any reason to change her mind.

They entered the station and Maggie nodded to the duty officer.

'Are the rest of CID here yet?' she asked.

'Upstairs waiting for you, ma'am,' he said. 'They've commandeered Investigation Room One. It's the biggest. Any news, ma'am?'

Maggie threw a look towards Jeremy Taylor, who had seated himself far enough from the desk as not to be a nuisance, but close enough to hear everything that was being said.

'He's the only news at the moment,' Maggie replied. 'Make sure he behaves himself. Don't speak to him unless it goes through the press office. Speaking of which, can you page whoever's on duty in press and tell them to meet me in I One?'

'Yes, ma'am,' the duty officer replied. 'I take it this is a big one then?'

Maggie didn't answer. From the look on her face, she didn't need to.

Chapter Six

Kathryn

Jordan showed me an article on his phone and all I could do was stare in silence. Two girls, practically identical in looks and age – Elsie and I had been in our sixth year, although neither of us had had our birthdays yet – go missing from the same small island on the same day? Even twenty-five years apart, it was newsworthy. Parallels were going to be drawn.

What does it mean? That she disappeared from the same place, on the same date. That she has the same blonde hair and button nose. *Little Elsie button nose.* It certainly doesn't mean Patrick is innocent. Does it?

It's harder to get into Strangeways than it is to get an audience with the queen – It'd be quicker to commit a serious crime and go through the courts than try to get a spontaneous visiting order. So I'm shocked and a little suspicious when the governor tells me to 'come on down' and he'll sort it out.

'Why?' I ask.

'Sorry?' Governor Evans asks. 'Wasn't it you who just rang me to ask for an emergency visit? Now you're asking why I want you to come to the prison?'

'Yes, sorry, I'm just surprised it was so easy, that's all. Why am I allowed? It's not normal visiting hours.'

'You've just told me your mother is in a coma,' Evan explains. 'I'm classing that as urgent. We're not totally heartless. If he wants to see you, I'll have him brought to a visiting room for an emergency visitation.'

Right… if he wants to see me. Will he refuse the visit? Even if he doesn't refuse, will he sit there and say nothing, like he's done once a month for two years? Does he even care if my mother lives or dies?

And that's the question, isn't it? The one I've wondered for my entire adult life. Can a man who is capable of killing a five-year-old-girl also be capable of loving another? Can evil and good exist inside the same person? And I don't mean multiple personality, or dissociative identity, or whatever the DSM calls it these days. I suppose what I really mean is… was Patrick ever really capable of loving any of us? Or were the long walks to the brook and the fishing trips and pushing me on the swing until I thought I was going over the bar – was that all an act?

I might just be about to find out.

–

For the first time in two years, the man who walks in to see me doesn't look calm and composed. He doesn't stare steadfastly ahead, determined not to look at me or say a word. Instead, his eyes fix on me as if he is seeing me for the first time ever.

'What is it, Kat? What's the emergency?'

That he can still call me Kat after all these years, as if I was only five years old just yesterday and nothing had ever gone wrong between us, shoves a knife into my chest. For so long I've wanted to hear him speak to me, to tell me there had been a mistake and he was going to fix it like he always did, that everything was going to be okay. And only now, when everything is less okay than it has ever been, does he speak.

I falter for a second, forgetting everything at the shock of hearing his voice. The cold grey walls of the visitors' room seem to converge, making the space tighter and more claustrophobic than ever. My vision swims.

'Kathryn?' he repeats, snapping me back into myself. 'What's going on? Is it Jordan?'

'Mum,' I manage to croak. 'It's Mum. She tried to… She's in a coma. We think she…' the words 'tried to kill herself' are almost impossible to say. It's almost impossible to acknowledge, that I have one parent in prison for murdering a child and another in a coma after attempting suicide. *How is this my life?*

'Oh God.'

Patrick puts his head into his hands and sinks into the uncomfortable-looking plastic chair. I can't even bring myself to sit down, such is my agitation.

'Is she going to be okay?'

I shake my head. 'They don't know. We don't know. It's too soon to say.'

His head and shoulders begin to shake and a strange noise comes from underneath his hands. Is he crying? Oh Jesus. The breaking of his composure is hard to watch, this man who didn't shed a tear when he was sentenced to life for the murder of a five-year-old child crying like a baby now.

After the longest, most uncomfortable silence of my life, he sits upright, wiping his face on the sleeve of his top.

He made that choice, I tell myself. *He is a monster. This man is a monster.*

37

'What have I done?' He looks up at me and the words are so hushed that I'm not sure I heard him properly.

'Excuse me?'

'This is all my fault.'

Oh God, this was a bad idea. I should have let Jordan come because now the anger raises up inside me and I can't help myself.

'All. Your. Fault?' I repeat, slowly, my voice sounding incredulous. 'You're damn right this is all your fucking fault! You think Mum would be lying there in hospital now if her husband wasn't a murderous child-killing bastard?'

He flinches as if every one of my words is a dart aimed at him, but he doesn't reply, only making me more mad.

'Only Mum seems to think it's all her fault,' I continue. I'm on a roll now, there's no stopping me. 'I'd let you listen to the answerphone message she left me, but you're in prison so you can't. It went something along the lines of "please don't hate your father for taking the blame like he did, he wanted to make up for something and I shouldn't have let him and you're better off without me".'

Patrick's face slackens. He looks old and grey and exhausted. His eyes drop to the table as though he's trying to decide what to do next. Then his resolve tightens and he looks back up at me, the old dead-eyed Patrick of my monthly visits.

'I don't know what she's talking about,' he says, his voice flat. 'She must have been drunk, or delusional.'

'Don't be ridiculous,' I snap. 'She knew exactly what she was saying. Did she do it, Patrick? Did she kill Elsie and make you take the blame? What were you making up for?'

The only time he reacts to my words is when he hears me call him Patrick. That I haven't called him Dad since I was old enough to realise what he'd done is probably news to him. Now he's back to his stony silence.

'Aren't you going to say anything?' I push. 'Do you even know what day today is? Do you know another girl is missing on Pentraeth?'

This, he reacts to. His head snaps to attention. 'What?'

'Oh yes, another five-year-old girl, just like little Elsie. Looks just like her too. And here's the thing, none of us were with Mum today. So she could have gone back, couldn't she? Back to the island where it all happened and just snapped, then, unable to handle the guilt anymore, tried to end her own life.' Even as I'm saying it, I'm thinking how ridiculous it sounds, the idea of Mum driving to Anglesey in the early hours of the morning to kill a child.

'That's... impossible,' Patrick mutters, but he doesn't sound sure. He doesn't look sure of anything anymore. 'Where's Jordan? I need to speak to him.'

Of course, he doesn't want the information from his daughter the monumental fuck-up, he wants the perfect son to come and tell him I'm making up nasty lies. Even from prison, he seems to know his children well enough.

'He wanted to come, but I said I wanted to do it,' I say. 'I wanted to be the one to tell you because I wanted to see your face when you lied to me. Are you lying, Patrick? Are you covering for your wife?'

Patrick shakes his head and I want to believe that Mum isn't to blame so much. I've already lost one parent, I don't want to lose the one I've got left, the one who picked up the pieces and rocked me to sleep when I missed my daddy, and went to all of Jordan's football matches because his dad couldn't be there. And losing her to suicide is one thing, but finding out she had been the monster all along, that's something else entirely.

'I'm going back there,' I say, surprising myself. 'To Anglesey. I'm going back to find out the truth.'

Patrick shakes his head more furiously now. 'No. You cannot go back there, Kathryn. After what happened – after what I did,' he says these words firmly so I get the point. 'It wouldn't be safe for you. That's why you had to leave – our family is not safe on Anglesey anymore.'

'Mum's in a coma,' I say, my voice harsher than I intended it to be. 'And another little girl is missing. Our family isn't safe anywhere until the truth is out.'

'Let the police deal with it,' he begs. 'Let them find her.'

I move up close to him and he flinches backwards as though he thinks I might hit him. I'm not sure I won't. The anger inside me is a hard knot, twisting inside my chest. Instead I point a finger into his face.

'If you know anything that can save this girl, you need to tell the police now,' I say, my teeth gritted together. 'Because whatever happened to Elsie Button, this family has some atoning to do, and I'd say now is a good time to start.'

He takes another breath – another goddamn breath just like he had when I saw him yesterday – Jesus, was that only yesterday? – and I think he's about to speak. His head hangs, his eyes dropping to the table in front of him and he retreats into his silence once more.

'You bastard,' I mutter, and I go to the door and hammer three times for the guards to let me out. 'I hope you rot.'

Chapter Seven

Maggie

'Okay, everyone,' Maggie said as she entered Investigation Room One – more because she felt she should than because she needed to: the room had fallen silent as they had seen her approaching through the frosted glass. 'You all know the situation. And you also know that it's unlikely Abigail Warner will be found by us standing around talking about her. So I'm going to keep this, well, brief, I suppose.'

A couple of the officers gave an obligatory smile.

Maggie turned to the huge whiteboard, which was depressingly still mostly white. Someone had helpfully written a timeline on the left-hand side, noting the time Abby went missing to the time they were on scene. An arrow next to 7:30 a.m. noted the car that had been seen outside the house. There was a huge map of the area, the Warners' house circled and three radius circles marked.

'For anyone who doesn't know, five-year-old Abigail Warner has been missing for between two and a half and three hours,' she said, trying not to sound like she was giving a lecture at a university. 'She was last seen by her mother in her back garden.' She pointed to the Warner home. 'Her back garden leads onto this small patch of trees which comes out on Raleigh Street over here. We've got officers on both streets knocking on doors, and volunteer searchers combing the streets. I've asked Jeremy Taylor to direct further volunteers to Memorial Hall, where Search and Rescue are already kitting up and setting up their grids. Obviously, first stop is the Nod.'

Afon Nodwydd was the small river that ran through Pentraeth, small but wide and deep enough for a child to fall in and not be able to get out. And Anglesey was home to some of the most fascinating wildlife, especially near the river. Red squirrels, brown owls, otters if you were lucky. There was an undeniable draw to a small child.

A few of the faces looked staggered at how fast this was escalating. They had missing children calls on the island all the time, but usually they had been located by the time the police even turned up: kids on a crowded beach who had wandered off for more sand, parents letting go of their hands for a minute and little Timmy going to look at the big boats. They didn't lose kids for hours here – not for a good many years, anyway.

'It's a small, quiet street where everyone knows everyone else,' she continued. 'The Warners are fairly new to the area and Mrs Warner reported seeing a car there this morning she didn't recognise. Like I say, they are new and keep to themselves so we don't yet know if this is anything to be concerned about and certainly nothing to mention in the media yet. Who is working on the car?' she asked.

Ted Rollins from Traffic put his hand up. Maggie shuddered silently. Seeing Ted always reminded her of the one time she'd tried to make friends within the police force. She'd ended up puking in the toilets of some shite bar in Cardiff, while Ted's wife sat next to her sobbing about their sex life – or lack thereof. Both of them had been too mortified to ever speak to one another again and Ted had remained suspiciously quiet about the whole incident. She suspected it had more than a little to do with his fear that if he told everyone about her inability to hold her drink she might tell them about his inability to hold his erection. Not that she would ever be so unprofessional. Probably. Anyway, now every time she saw him, she couldn't help but picture the time he actually did come and was so relieved he cried. That was not an image anyone – even his wife – wanted in their heads.

'Nobody else saw the car at that time, but one did recognise the description. Said it sounded like Doctor Roberts from the local surgery. I relayed the information back so that door-to-door could check if Will had been visiting any of them this morning.'

'Excellent, thanks. Can somebody speak to the doctor and see if he was in the area? That would save us a lot of time trawling CCTV for his car. Speaking of which – who's on CCTV?'

A young girl entirely too thin and pointy – even her grey-blonde hair was cut in a sharp asymmetric bob – held up a hand. Maggie had never seen her before, but the way the girl looked at her made Maggie feel like the Grand High Witch, expected to turn someone into a mouse at any point.

'I don't think we've met?' She tried to put on her least scary voice, but from the look on the girl's face, she wasn't particularly successful.

'PC Stagg, ma'am,' the girl spoke. 'I was asked to help with the research effort.'

Which meant scrolling through hours of mostly pointless CCTV in the hope that a camera somewhere had captured Abigail Warner holding hands with whoever might have taken her. Preferably with a perfect licence

43

plate number and holding a map with a circle around where they intended to go next. Maggie hoped that no one had told the poor girl she'd been handed the shit work – this was probably the highlight of her career.

'Do you have anything to report at this time, PC Stagg?'

Stagg held up a sheet of paper. 'I have a list of all the places that might have CCTV within a twenty-mile radius. I'm just calling them all to try to get access to their tapes.'

'Anywhere that looks promising?' She was fully expecting a no, hardly anywhere within the village had cameras, there was just no need for them.

'Actually, the laundrette on the corner had CCTV installed after a few kids vandalised them last year. It points straight at the entrance to the road – they said they would email it to me as soon as they can figure out how to download it.'

'Don't wait for that,' Maggie said instantly. 'Bryn, radio one of the officers on the ground to go over and look at it straight away.' She turned back to the girl, who looked petrified. 'Are there any other cameras pointing directly at the place a young girl might have been abducted from?' She knew she sounded harsh, but she didn't care. This was what you got for putting children onto the research jobs. It was mainly endless loops of old Doris taking her dog for a walk, but occasionally there was something important that could be missed.

The girl shook her head and Maggie thought she saw tears pricking the corner of her eyes.

'Okay – if you find anything like that you bring it straight to me or DS Bailey – okay?' She tried to sound a bit more motherly, feeling a stab of guilt that the entire room was focused on this girl and her evident humiliation. 'Don't worry about if you think it might not lead anywhere, we've got next to nothing to go on as it is.'

She straightened up and addressed the room again.

'According to Mrs Warner, there wasn't anyone who would wish to harm Abby, but we all know that's bullshit. If you hear anything – anything at all – I don't care if it's gossip and rumours about the man who runs the corner shop, about Jeff, your next-door neighbour who suddenly packed up and ran away, or about the Archbishop of Canterbury swooping in and grabbing her; cults, trafficking rings, your friendly village paedophiles – I want to hear it. I can't make that clear enough. I don't want us blindsided on this one because we dismissed something as rumour or hearsay. Village people usually know more than the police within hours, and if we're not careful, via the wonderful medium of Facebook and Twitter, so will the rest of the country.'

There were sage nods around the room, but no one spoke.

Maggie was ready to dismiss them when a hand shot up. She'd thought it was too good to be true, but they'd just waited until the end, when she let her guard down.

'Is there any indication this has anything to do with Elsie Button, ma'am?' Everyone else looked down at their shoes as though they hadn't just egged on the new boy to ask the question that might set her off. Cowards.

Maggie sighed. She supposed it was to be expected. She was going to have to address it sooner or later. 'Patrick Bowen admitted to killing Elsie Button twenty-five-years ago,' she said. 'So unless he has mastered the art of walking through walls in his time in prison, there is no way this can be related to the tragic murder of Elsie. With any luck, Abigail will turn up before we have to answer these questions in the media, but should anyone in this room speculate publicly that these two unfortunate incidents are related, they will be finding out how difficult it really is to walk head-first through a wall. My office wall. Is that clear?'

There was a sea of nodding heads – nothing could be clearer. Except Maggie knew that this wasn't the only time that question would be asked today, or in the days to come, if Abigail Warner wasn't found soon.

Chapter Eight

Kathryn

My heart is still pounding from the confrontation with Patrick and my head is still pounding from the alcohol that is working its way out of my system. Miriam was right, I probably shouldn't be driving yet, but it's the middle of the day and unless I crash into something or someone, I'm unlikely to get pulled over. I just need to get Mum's stuff, get back to the hospital, then I should go home. I've been to give Patrick the news, I've done my duty. Now my place is with Mum.

So why can't I resist letting in the little voice that tells me something is seriously wrong? I mean, my father is in prison for murder and my mum is in a coma, so obviously something is wrong, but this little voice – actually it's getting bigger by the second – is saying something is seriously wrong with this situation. There's too much I don't know, too much I've never asked. Like why, for a start. Why did Patrick kill Elsie? Had he ever shown any signs of being attracted to children? The thought makes bile rise up in my throat, but maybe it's a question I should have asked before now. Was his first illegal act really the murder of my best friend? That's not usually how it goes, is it? I mean, even when people say they can't believe it, he was the nicest man, et cetera, et cetera, we eventually find out that they had boxes and boxes of child porn, or thousands of indecent images downloaded, or they were addicted to illegal sites or they pulled the wings off flies as a child. But not Patrick Bowen. He progressed straight from reading his daughter a bedtime story to killing her best friend and hiding the body so well no one ever found it. An accomplished first-timer, no? Some might call him an overachiever.

But even if the voice is right, even if there is something off about the whole situation, I'm not sure what it expects me to do about it. Especially if it means finding out my mum is to blame for what happened back then.

–

Joyce is waiting in the window when I arrive at Mum's house. Urgh. It's not that I don't like Joyce, she's lovely to Mum and they get on really well, but how the bloody hell do I explain any of this? 'Oh yes, not to worry, Joyce, my mum just tried to end her life because she may or may not have been hiding a terrible secret – yes, Joyce, more terrible than my father killing a child – but I'll tell her you were asking after her when she wakes up and, oh, thank you, Joyce, yes she'd love some clotted cream fudge, I'm sure.'

I do not, in fact, say anything of this ilk. Instead, I manage not to make any clever remarks when Joyce says how sorry she was to hear of Mum's 'unfortunate accident' and nod sagely when she says she's sure she will be okay, and to let her know if there's anything she can do.

'Thank you, Joyce, that's very kind,' I say, edging my way towards the door. 'I'd better get these things though – if she wakes up and she doesn't have her dry shampoo, well, you know what she's like.'

Joyce doesn't seem to know what to say to this, given that she doesn't, in fact, 'know what my mum is like'. She doesn't really know anything about her. Mum has been the same as me in that respect: make no friends, attract no attention. Except I failed on the 'attract no attention' part, what with the drink driving and the antisocial behaviour. Mum did much better and has managed to bring no attention on herself whatsoever in the last twenty-five years. Until today.

Inside, the house is spotless, as I expected it to be. No need to let cleaning standards slip, even if you are planning on ending your own life. There are no dishes in the sink or on the drainer, nothing to suggest a life almost ended here this morning.

Upstairs, it's a different picture. The covers from Mum's bed are on the floor and there is an empty bottle of whisky upended on the bedside table. The paramedics took the empty pill pack with them – standard procedure – but one single white tablet remains on the floor next to the bed. Should I leave it there? It's not a crime scene, is it? I'm torn between tidying away evidence and putting the room back to normal for when Mum comes home. Because she will come home – I have to keep telling myself that.

See, this is why Jordan should have come, he would know whether or not to tamper with the scene. I've always been bloody useless at making grown-up decisions.

I leave it as it is for now and open Mum's wardrobe to look for a bag. There's one up on the shelf. It looks like it hasn't been used in years and as I pull it down, a thin cloud of dust puffs into my face. I cough, waving a hand in front of my face and furiously batting at myself to make sure it hasn't covered me in spiders. The bag hits the ground with a thud much louder than it should have made and when I

49

pick it up to shake off the last of the dust, it's clear there's something inside. Hardly surprising; my mum is definitely the type of person to pack away her winter wardrobe on the eve of the spring solstice like clockwork.

It's not her winter wardrobe, I discover when I open the bag. Annoyingly, it looks like about ten years' worth of paperwork, which feels unusual for Mum; although I'll admit that this is probably the first time I've been in her bedroom since I was a child, she hasn't ever been a hoarder.

I start pulling out the papers. They all look like bank statements and my heart plummets into my stomach, thinking I'm about to discover that Mum is up to her armpits in debt with no way of me helping her out. In actual fact, I realise, as I scan over the statements, that Mum has more than enough money in the bank. She's not got millions of pounds in there, I certainly don't think she's been running drugs or money laundering, but she's comfortable enough, thank goodness.

As I'm shoving the statements to one side, one sum catches my eye. It's on every single statement, a payment each month of £2,000, from Clayton, Wilson and Lamb. The name of Patrick's solicitor. Weird – I thought we were supposed to pay them, not vice versa.

I check the rest of the statements; on the older ones, the amount is bigger, on the more recent ones, it's gone down to £500, but it's still there, a regular transfer. Perhaps it was some kind of trust, set up by Patrick, with his solicitors as the trustee. I'd never even thought to ask where Mum got her money from – we've never been the kind of family to talk about money; as long as she's not drowning in debt, it's none of my business. She hasn't ever worked but I guess

I always assumed the sale of the house and her pension was enough to get her by.

I tidy the papers into a neat pile and remind myself to bring round a box to store them in. I unzip the side pocket of the bag and pull out a thick manila envelope, tatty and ancient-looking. It smells musty, like when you put the books to your nose in an antique shop and inhale deeply. I'm not surprised to pull out handfuls of photographs – every household has them, don't they? Photos that you pledge one day will make it into an album but they never do. Except I haven't seen my mum pick up a camera since Patrick was arrested – we had more than enough of the press pointing them at us to not want to point one at each other.

If you've ever been involved in a tragedy, you know that your life is split down the middle in a clean line. Events are either Before, or After. The photos I'm holding in my hand are Before.

Surprisingly, I don't find them too painful. They are full of a time I don't remember – I don't really even recognise the people in them. I know it's my mum, Jordan, Patrick and I, but they don't bring back sudden and awful memories. We look happy and that hurts a bit, that all that joy had to be taken from us.

One photo in particular catches my eye – it's of five men standing together as though they have been instructed to 'line up'. There's Patrick in the middle, a wide grin across his face. One side of him are two men I don't recognise: one about the same age as Patrick, one slightly younger. They look like they're messing around, because they are laughing a genuine belly laugh, not a smile put on for the camera. The man on the other side of Patrick is looking at them in a kind of disapproving amusement and the man on the end – the only other one I do recognise – is gesturing at the photographer to get on with it and take the photo, but again, he looks happy, jovial. If this man could tell the future, he wouldn't be within a million miles of Patrick Bowen, because this man is Rowley Button – Elsie's dad.

The last thing in the envelope isn't a photo, it's a browning piece of paper that looks as though it's been folded and unfolded a million times. There are tiny holes appearing along the creases and I have to be careful not to rip it. Printed on the inside is a message to my mother.

Dear Jill, it reads. *You can't write to me anymore; they read everything you send in and everything I send back, it's not safe. You say this is hard for you to understand, but I don't regret what I did. You must be strong for the children and forget I exist. Move on with your lives and stay away from the island. Kevin will take care of you, if you need anything call him. Don't trust anyone else.*

I love you now and always. Be strong my love.

Patch xxx

There is another letter folded up inside and I expect this too to be from Patrick, but it's not. It's a different handwriting, larger, angrier letters. It reads:

> I know they are all lying to me I just don't know why. I'm going to find out the truth about what happened to my daughter you bitch. And when I do you will be in prison with your bastard husband.

This letter isn't signed, but it's obvious who it's from.

I look again at the photo of the five men, my eyes resting longer this time on Rowley Button, his large hands, capable of writing such threatening words. Without really knowing why, I shove the photo, and a few others, along with the letters, into my handbag and start filling Mum's bag.

Chapter Nine

Maggie

'Go on then, go git it.'

Maggie watched the bright yellow tennis ball sail in a perfect arc through the air and smiled as Dolly Annabel – absolutely not her owner's choice of name, she knew, but most definitely his daughter's – sprang forwards after the speck of yellow, the brown mass of curls that passed for ears bouncing as she bounded gleefully. Dolly reached the spot where she expected the ball to be and started searching through the grass. Once upon a time, she'd have caught it in mid-air; she was getting old.

'Yer gettin' old,' Maggie's predecessor, retired DI George Fisher, called after his dog. 'But then aren't we all,' he muttered.

'Speak for yourself,' Maggie said. Her voice startled him, and he turned, frowning when he saw it was her. 'I hope you're not tarring me with your grumpy old brush.'

George turned back to face the field again. He gestured to the wide-open space that backed onto his home. 'I come out here to get away from insults, you know. I'm surprised Linda hasn't taught the bloody dog to have a go.'

'I bet she's working on it,' Maggie said with a smile. She pictured his petite, dark-haired wife, who was probably cooking him something tasty at this very moment. The

Fishers' relationship was the one everyone aspired to, but Maggie thought the idea of committing to one person the way they had was terrifying.

'What do you want, Maggie?'

Dolly bounded back towards them, much more delighted to see Maggie than George had been.

'I came to tell you that there's a girl missing.'

'I'm retired.'

'Yes, I do remember. I can hardly forget, what with the amount of times in a day I'm told how George did things. I just thought you'd want to know.'

'Flattery does not suit you.' George reached down to wrestle the ball from Dolly Annabel, who – after making a good show of trying to keep it – let go with an excited bum wiggle. George loaded it up and tossed it through the air again. Dolly shot off after it and George turned back to Maggie. 'So why do you think I'd want to know?'

'Because I haven't forgotten what today is – no one here has, and I know you haven't either. And the girl is missing from the Bowen house.'

Maggie saw George's whole body go rigid. She hadn't even intended to visit George Fisher, except that he was an old colleague and the Elsie Button disappearance had been his case. Plus his house was on the way to her next stop.

'I'm on my way to Memorial Hall, there's a massive search effort underway already and it's only going to get bigger. We're about to have police and press descend on the island and I thought I should warn you.'

'You know what will happen to the island if this girl isn't found?' he asked. His eyes seemed to darken; he looked every inch his sixty years. 'The rumours of the bogeyman living in the woods behind the house, the suspicion, the fear in everyone's eyes. And the grief that settles in the air once all the searchers and media have gone away, like a dust cloud that can't be washed away no matter how many people send thoughts and prayers.'

Maggie nodded. 'I know.'

She gestured behind him, where Linda Fisher, George's wife of thirty-five years, was approaching them. As expected, she was wiping her hands on her apron as she walked.

'Maggie Grant,' she said, slipping her arm through her husband's. Dolly Annabel jumped up at her mum, yipping and yelping. Linda batted her down with affectionate exasperation. 'I hope you're not trying to seduce my husband away back to your force.'

Her words were teasing, but Maggie knew she was deadly serious. Linda had made no secret of her joy the day George retired.

'Couldn't if I wanted to,' Maggie replied. 'I'm just here to give George some bad news, I'm afraid.'

'About Jill Bowen?' Linda placed a hand on his shoulder and squeezed.

George's head snapped to look at his wife. 'What about Jill?'

'It's why I came to find you. Jordan just called, he needs you to call him back immediately. Jill is in a coma. He said she tried to commit suicide this morning.'

Chapter Ten

Kathryn

I've been waiting for the doorbell to ring. So when it does, I'm not surprised to see my brother standing there, his face like thunder. After the short but sweet answerphone message I left him after seeing Patrick – three words, *I'm going back* – I'd expected him sooner.

'I thought we'd agreed to let this go,' he says, pushing past me and through to the living room, where my suitcase is open on the floor.

I screw up my face, throwing in the jumper I'd been folding. 'I don't remember agreeing to that.'

'We agreed that what Mum said never meant anything. That she was drunk and delirious, remember? That it *didn't mean anything*.'

'That was before I spoke to Patrick,' I say, and Jordan still, after all these years, flinches at the fact that I refuse to call him Dad. 'He doesn't want me to go back there, Jordan. You should have seen him. He's hiding something – he knows exactly what Mum meant in that phone call and he—'

'Kathryn, no!' Jordan practically screams at me and I take a few steps back in horror. I don't think my brother has ever screamed at me before. His face looks twisted with fury, he doesn't even look like my Jordan. 'Don't you see? Our dad killed Elsie. He admitted it. Why would he do that, why would he leave us just to protect someone else? Whoever has this new girl, it's nothing to do with what happened back then. Why can't you just leave this alone and get on with your life?'

'Because this is my life!' I shout back. 'This, this *thing* that happened to us, it's with me every day, wondering why he did what he did, hoping against hope that one day I'd find out what happened to her. It's the reason I can't hold down a job, the reason I can't keep a relationship! It hangs over *everything I do*. It's okay for you, just cracking on with your perfect life—'

'Okay for me?' Jordan steps forward as though he's going to strike me. Let him, if that's what it takes. Let him hit me so I can feel like I'm not the only screw-up. He doesn't though – of course he doesn't. Instead, he crumples into my armchair as though someone has punched him in the stomach. 'How can you think that? You were only five when Elsie disappeared. You had no idea what it was really like. How angry people were, at all of us. Running away in the middle of the night, leaving my friends – not that any of them wanted to be my friend after Dad was arrested. Overnight, we were the people you read about in the papers – we were the monsters. So we moved, but it didn't stop.'

'What do you mean, it didn't stop?'

Jordan sighed. 'People found out who we were. We moved three times in six months, Kat. Don't you remember?'

I don't, although some of what he's saying makes sense. I remember the house we moved to when Patrick went away – that's what Mum always used to refer to it as – Daddy 'going away'. Only the memories I have, sometimes they differ. Sometimes the kitchen is long and thin, a sickly green colour on the walls – other times, it's wide with walls the same colour as unpainted plaster. There's an old electric fire with a fake marble surround, but then it's gone, replaced by a three-bar heater that always smells like burning wool. Different houses – it makes sense, although I don't remember moving between them.

'I guess, well, not really. It was twenty-five years ago, Jordan, and I was five years old.'

'Exactly,' Jordan says, his face softening. 'You get to just forget. I was nearly fourteen and all of a sudden I was the man of the house. I had to listen to Mum crying at night, I was the one who had to put you to bed and read you stories because she'd had too much wine and fallen asleep in front of the TV. I still have the scar where Rick Barnes threw a metal protractor at my eye when he found out my dad was a "fucking filthy paedo". That was the second move, by the way.'

'Jordan, I'm sorry, I—'

'You didn't realise. No, Kat, you never do. Because you've only ever been determined to see how it affects you and your life. *Poor little Kathryn can't keep a job because she's got such a tragic past. Sorry, judge, I was only drink driving because my father killed my best friend when I was five.* Not a thought about how hard the rest of us tried to put those years behind us – oh no, you've been determined to carry this around like a fucking albatross for years and I'm not going to be dragged down with you.'

I open my mouth in shock but nothing comes out. I can't remember a time when Jordan has ever spoken to me like this before.

He gets up to leave and I grab his arm. 'Please, Jordan, don't just storm off. I'm sorry, I get that I've been selfish and I'm sorry. I don't know how you've managed to put all of this behind you and become so well adjusted and perfect, I wish I could be like you, I just—'

His face darkens. 'Believe me, Kat, I'm not perfect. There are things you don't understand, things you can't understand. Sometimes the past should just be left in the past. I just want you to *let this go.*' His eyes search mine and he knows it's useless. We know each other so well and now I realise why. Jordan was the glue who held our family together. And now the only thing he wants from me, I can't give to him. 'But you won't.'

'I *can't*,' I correct. 'I'm sorry, but I just can't. I have to know the truth. It's the only way I can get on with my life.'

Jordan sighs. 'You're not safe there, Kitty Kat. You never will be. The Bowens haven't been safe on that island since Elsie Button disappeared.'

Chapter Eleven

Maggie

Bryn let out a low whistle as they approached Memorial Hall. 'I'll say one thing about this place, they react fast to a call to arms.'

He wasn't wrong. At least fifty people were gathered on the car park of the hall, all dressed for what looked to be a hike up Snowdonia rather than a scout around the local area. Search and Rescue were nowhere to be seen, but the door to the hall was open.

Maggie parked the car, took a deep breath and got out, grabbing the large stack of paper from the back seat. She cleared her throat and silence dropped like a curtain.

'Thank you all so much for coming,' she said, holding up her warrant card. 'I'm DI Maggie Grant, in charge of the investigation, but I am not in charge of the search for Abby. The Search and Rescue Team have all the appropriate training and in situations like this we defer to them. Whatever they say goes. We are, of course, still hoping that Abby has just wandered off, but even so, she might be hurt. There are a limited number of radios available to us, so we will be sending you out in teams. If you find Abby and she appears to be stuck somewhere or injured, please use your common sense and assess the situation before trying to help her. Radio in and help will be with you immediately.' She waved the stack of paper in the air. 'This is the latest picture of Abby. Ask everyone you see if they have seen her. If they want to join the search effort, direct them here to be given an area. It's the best way of making sure everywhere gets searched, rather than the same area multiple times. Hand these out between you.' She passed the stack to the nearest volunteer, a small woman with short, dark brown curls and an athletic build. She looked as though she'd taken the day off training for the Olympics to come and help search. 'And await further instruction from the search coordinator, who will come and give you a full statement and answer any questions. All okay?'

The group nodded almost in unison.

Maggie motioned to Bryn, who followed her towards the entrance to Memorial Hall, where two men were struggling with the double doors and a table.

'Here,' Maggie said, immediately locating the bolt at the top of the doors and stretching up to release it. The door gave way with a jerk and the man closest to her looked embarrassed.

'Didn't see that one,' he muttered.

God, I hope these two aren't in charge, Maggie thought with a pang of despair. 'DI Maggie Grant,' she said. 'Who's in charge here?'

The man jerked his head to indicate inside. 'Scott Marshall. He's in there.'

A search marshal called Marshall? Cute.

Cute was hardly the word. Scott Marshall was drop-dead gorgeous. Maggie didn't think she'd ever seen someone that attractive who wasn't on the TV or in a catalogue. His dark hair was unbrushed and he was sporting three-day-old stubble against tanned skin. His eyes were a turquoise shade that made her feel uncomfortable to look into; he'd probably been told so many times about his piercing eyes that he would know exactly what she was thinking.

Maggie didn't trust beautiful people, there was no way they could go through life not knowing they were abnormally attractive. It would be impossible for it not to colour their every experience. Maggie knew this, mainly, because she had always been hot. Not beautiful, like Scott Marshall, where it almost felt embarrassing to look at him for too long, not supermodel stunning, but attractive enough that quite often men wanted to sleep with her, and it had coloured every part of her life.

Scott was standing with a group of people all dressed in searching gear, leaning over a map. He had a pen and was marking a route, oblivious to her arrival.

'Scott Marshall?'

He said something to the young lad next to him, who nodded and took over from pointing at the map in front of them. 'That's me,' he said, giving her a quick once-over. She wondered if she met with his approval, which made her bristle. She didn't like being scrutinised. 'Are you the officer in charge?'

'DI Maggie Grant,' she held out a hand which he shook. 'Are you ready to take charge of the volunteers? They're forming quite a motley crew outside.'

'I've sent a couple of guys out there with a table to start co-ordinating non-specialised searchers. They will be logged in with a timestamp and put into groups, that way if anyone runs into any trouble, we'll know if a group doesn't return. I've already spoken to Aled – he's volunteered with us before and has promised to get some of the locals who know the areas well to head up groups. We don't want a missing child to turn into ten drowned adults and a child still missing.'

'Sounds like you've been thorough.' Maggie nodded her appreciation. Nice to look at and good at his job. Scott Marshall was ticking boxes. 'Can you make it clear that anything that might be considered evidence stays in situ and DS Bailey here will take charge of recovery.'

'No problem. Anything else we should know?'

'If it looks like you're going to find a body, send the volunteers home. The people here have been through enough.'

Chapter Twelve

Kathryn

My throat gets tighter with every mile I get further from Manchester and closer to Anglesey, the place of my birth and my family's undoing. You can tell you're entering Wales when everything gets greener and the walls begin to change from harsh manufactured bricks to a beautiful natural stone. Houses start to look as though they have been grown from the ground itself rather than built. The Welsh countryside feels so magical that if you saw a fairy or a group of elves holding a meeting around a toadstool you wouldn't be particularly surprised. Brooks trickle, swell and then subside along the road, the water sprites making each journey with you, popping up occasionally to let you know they are still there. Sweeping mountains of slate drop away to rolling hills home to ogres or Hobbits or whatever else you can dream. In Wales, you are the closest you can get to myth and legend, you can reach out and touch it.

I listen to podcasts as I get on the road and leave the city behind – true crime, of course – but I avoid any that cover Elsie's murder. Although every podcast out there has done at least one episode on it, there is one dedicated entirely to the case. I've listened to it three or four times by now, but not today.

People have different theories about what happened to Elsie that day in the woods – and believe me, it's been talked about a *lot*. I used to spend hours trawling through websites dedicated to true crimes looking for theory after theory about where Elsie might be. Some people think Patrick is innocent, set up by the corrupt police because they had no clue what had happened to her, others think he threw her into the sea, buried her in the woodland, chopped her up and fed her to pigs, I've read it all. I've even seen theories that she is still alive, sold to traffickers – because there are so many of those in Anglesey you can't move for them – or snatched by gypsies. The way people talk about her as if she wasn't a real child with a family should shock and disgust me, but, more disturbingly, I understand it. In the same way that Jordan and I joke (between ourselves – only ever in private) about the 'murderversary', others dehumanise the situation because if they thought for a second about Elsie as what she was, a beautiful, innocent five-year-old child, they would have to accept the true horror of the situation. That it wasn't your TV villains, your child traffickers or the monster that hides in your cupboard, it was a man, a real flesh-and-blood man, with a wife and two children who killed Elsie Button and disposed of her body God knows where. And if it was our dad who did it this time, it could be your dad next.

That's why we had to leave Anglesey, in the end. Because people just couldn't come to terms with the fact that we had no idea Patrick was a monster. Mum must have known, they said. She must have known what he was and still she let Helen and Rowley Button bring their daughter over to play. They refused to believe that monsters can look normal on the outside, like your next-door neighbour or – as Patrick was – your friendly local butcher. Oh, I forgot to mention that the police had a field day with that. Yes, Patrick was a butcher, and yes we were used to seeing him covered in blood. For years, I couldn't sleep thinking about how the police found bloody burned rags in the back room of the butchers, or how her urine-soaked underwear had been shoved in with our household washing in the hopes they would be mistaken for mine. I read all this online many years after we'd left Anglesey, along with the fact that it had been my mother who had found them and turned him in. Her own husband. I've never been able to bring myself to tell her how much respect I have for her for doing that, because we don't talk about Elsie, and we sure as hell don't talk about Patrick. Now I might never get chance to tell her.

I was only five when we left Anglesey and the memories of a five-year-old are notoriously unreliable, most of them are gone completely. I have no idea if the warmth I feel towards the country is because it was once my home, or because after living in an urban jungle for so long, anything green feels like another world, but there are no more pangs of recognition or flashes of memory. My inner five-year-old is silent, she shrugs her shoulders, I don't know, maybe I've been here before, maybe not.

My podcast on the case of Asha Degree finishes and I flick over to the news – luckily it's in English because my Welsh is rusty to say the least.

'Police in Anglesey today are searching for missing five-year-old Abigail Warner. Abigail was last seen playing in her back garden in Pentraeth at around nine a.m., according to frantic Facebook posts by her mother appealing for anyone who might have seen her leave. Abigail has shoulder-length blonde hair and blue eyes and is wearing a My Little Pony T-shirt and blue denim

dungarees. North Wales police say they are not currently making any connection between this disappearance and the murder of five-year-old Elsie Button exactly twenty-five-years ago to the day. Elsie's killer was found, but her body was not. Despite this, Patrick Bowen is currently serving a whole life sentence for her murder. If you have any information about Abigail's whereabouts please contact North Wales Police.'

The description makes me shudder. Blonde hair, blue eyes, five years old – it could have been a report from the day of Elsie's disappearance.

Across the Britannia Bridge on the other side of the road, a lone police vehicle sits in a lay-by, stopping and searching cars as they attempt to leave the island. This is the only sign, far out here, that anything is wrong. A speck of mould on the outside that hints that there may be something rotten within. They're looking for Abigail. A lump rises in my throat. I never ever planned to come back here. Especially not like this.

I see four more *Heddlu Gogledd Cymru* cars on the ten-minute drive from the bridge to Pentraeth, then I pull off the road sharply and sit back in my seat, heart thumping furiously. It's as if a carnival has arrived in the usually quiet village: red and blue lights flash out of sync, groups of people dressed in hiking gear huddle over maps, pointing in one direction or another. Search parties. The stench of fear hangs over the village – they hope she's alive, they fear she's dead. Microphones have sprung up everywhere, glossy women and suited men talking over the thrum of voices into camera lenses, addressing the rest of the country. I thought I knew what a media circus looked like before, but this is something else. I hadn't planned this far ahead, for this many people. How could I not have realised that a missing five-year-old would attract so much attention?

A helicopter hovers over the coast, searching. I feel unreasonably guilty, like I'm walking into Nothing To Declare when I do in fact have something massive to declare. I am the daughter of Patrick Bowen, convicted child killer. I am not welcome here.

But it's been twenty-five years. I have a different name, I am a different person. Even if I was recognisable, no one is expecting me to be here, no one is looking for me. I can blend in; there are so many out-of-towners here already, people who have driven to the island to help in the search. I am anonymous.

Well, I would be, if I didn't look quite so much like a bloody townie. I have pumps on, for God's sake, pretty little ballet pumps and a light denim jacket. I've thrown jeans and jumpers in my suitcase but I don't even own any decent walking jackets or boots. If I don't want to stand out quite so much, I need a change of attire. Good, something to do, something to focus on in my spaghetti muddle of a brain. Find an outdoors shop.

My best bet is Bangor, back over the Menai, only this time I'm on the side of the roadblock. A police officer gestures me to pull in and I stop the car alongside him. My heart thuds – have I been recognised already? *Don't be stupid*, I think. *He's just doing his job. Be cool.*

'*Diwrnod da,*' he says when I wind down my window.

'Good day,' I reply. 'Do you need to check the car?'

He smiles. 'Nice to get someone so co-operative. Are you here to help with the search?'

'I was,' I say. 'Until I realised how stupidly dressed I am. Last thing you need is an idiot townie in inappropriate shoes, right?'

'I wouldn't like to comment,' he replies, but his smile widens. 'I'll take a look, if that's okay? Seems a waste not to now you've pulled in.'

'Sure.' I get out of the car, my heart pounding. I feel stupid – there is no little girl in my footwell, so why do I feel like such a massive criminal? He peers into the back seat and I open the boot – may as well be thorough, get him a nice big tick on his clipboard.

'Perfect, thanks. There's a Trespass in Bangor up there, should get you kitted out nicely.'

'Thanks. *Hwyl.*' Shit. Where did that come from?

He looks at me with good-natured suspicion. 'A Welsh-speaking idiot townie?'

'Family in Wales.' I put the car into gear before he can ask where my relatives are from. If this is any indication of my undercover abilities, I won't be putting my application for MI6 in any time soon, I think as I pull onto the bridge and away from the bemused officer.

Chapter Thirteen

Maggie

'Grant.' Maggie answered the phone as curtly as possible. She'd always wondered why the cops on TV did it, having spent her life answering with 'hello' like the rest of the population, and then, in her first year as DI, what felt like a million years ago, her DCI had given her a tip. 'If you answer with your last name, it reminds the caller that your time is more important than theirs. Unless it's someone higher, then you answer with Sir, that reminds them that you know how important their time is. It's all about psychology, Grant. Keep answering with hello and you'll have them asking how you are, and what you did at the weekend.'

'Sorry to bother you, DI Grant, it's Lesley Thomas.'

It took Maggie a moment before she realised that Lesley Thomas was the Family Liaison Officer she'd left to look after the Warners just a few hours ago. God, this was already turning out to be a long day.

'Lesley, is everything under control there?'

'I… I don't think so. Mr and Mrs Warner, well, they're fighting a lot. And she is insisting on going out to search while he's just on the phone all the time and stops talking as soon as I get near. I heard him mention a lawyer.'

It wasn't unheard of for the families of missing people to ask if they needed a lawyer, but it was extremely rare for it to be in less than twenty-four hours. They were usually too busy making frantic lists of everywhere their loved one might possibly be.

'How many times did we search the house?'

'First officers on scene searched once when they arrived. I think DS Bailey had a quick look around when he got here.'

It was bit soon to do a full forensic search yet, but Maggie made a mental note to have the team on standby. She desperately hoped it wouldn't come to it, but should it turn out that harm had come to poor Abby, then it was almost better if it was the parents, even better if it was an accident. God, she hated that years of policework had made her think this way, but after this was all done, the people here were going to need a way to process what had happened, and some situations were easier to swallow than others. The friendly local butcher being a paedophile and a murderer was one of those 'hard-to-digest' ones. A parental accident was far more palatable.

'*Iawn*,' she said to Lesley. *Okay*. 'I'd been planning to come over to update them anyway. If we've got nothing by this evening, the press office wants them to do a press conference. What do you reckon?'

'I think the mum shouldn't be a problem. The dad might be a different matter. He's on edge.'

'His daughter is missing.'

'Of course,' Lesley sounded as though she was trying not to remind her that she did this a lot more than Maggie did. 'I mean in a different way to normal. It honestly feels a lot like he's hiding something.'

'Most people are,' Maggie remarked. 'I'll leave DS Bailey here and come on over now.'

–

The house was surprisingly quiet on the outside. There were only four other houses on the street and their occupants were presumably out searching. The media hadn't fully descended yet and those who had were back at the Memorial Hall where the best shots were to be had. In Maggie's experience, the press would really rather not shove camera lenses through open curtains to take pictures of distraught parents if they could get something equal or better. Most papers would have a heart-wrenching picture of Abigail Warner on the front page.

Maggie nodded to the PC at the front door. 'Any disturbance?' she said. Before she finished her sentence, she could hear shouting coming from the inside of the house.

'You mean apart from the disturbance in there?' he asked, jerking a head at the window. 'Nothing out here. A few people coming over to ask if they can help, I've been sending them to the hall. A woman came over with a fucking lasagne, as if they're going to be tucking into a three-course meal when their daughter is missing. She brought garlic bread. Garlic bread for Christ's sake?' He rolled his eyes.

Maggie had stopped listening as soon as she heard the shouting start. She made out the word 'watching' and 'fucking mother'. She could hear Lesley's soothing voice and a man – Mr Warner – snap back 'none of your business'. She'd better get in there.

Maggie rapped on the front door, loud enough to punctuate the raised voices. Immediately they stopped.

She heard an inside door open and footsteps, then Lesley's relieved face appeared in the doorway.

'Thank God you're here,' she said, opening the door wider. 'Although I'm not sure he won't just yell at you too.'

When you'd been in the middle of a riot in Cardiff city centre at two a.m. you tended to cease to be afraid of middle-aged train conductors. Then again, she'd also learned not to underestimate anyone, so she kept her mouth shut.

'Who is it?' Caroline Warner's tear-streaked face appeared at the sitting-room door. When she saw Maggie her eyes widened. 'Have you found her?'

'Not yet,' Maggie said, moving towards her and putting a hand on her arm. 'There are hundreds of people searching – your neighbours, a specialist team. We've got… Well, why don't we go through to the living room and I'll tell you both.'

Caroline hesitated, as if she was reluctant to let Maggie come in contact with her husband. Sensing she had no choice, she moved to one side and Maggie followed her in.

John Warner looked Maggie up and down as if she'd brought dog shit in on her shoes. So that's how it was going to be, was it?

'Mr Warner,' Maggie said. She kept her voice warm, no indication that she'd heard the row from outside. 'How are you coping? Is there anything you need? Anything I can get for you?'

'Apart from the obvious, you mean?' he snapped.

Lesley slipped past them both into the kitchen, clearly glad of the excuse to get out of the way.

'We're working very hard on that, I promise you. I was just saying to Mrs Warner—'

'Caroline,' Abby's mum said, her voice agitated. 'Please. It sounds... Just please call me Caroline.'

'Of course,' Maggie replied. 'I was just saying that your neighbours have turned up in droves to help. We have a Search and Rescue Team co-ordinating the search right now and I've requested a hundred extra officers to help search tonight. I want you to be reassured that there is nothing more we could be doing right at this moment to find Abby.'

'Abigail,' John Warner said.

'Excuse me?'

He looked at her as if she was stupid.

'He hates it when people shorten her name,' Caroline supplied.

Maggie nodded and bit the inside of her lip. 'Right, I apologise. I'll make sure people know. The reason I've come here is to ask if you would be willing to make a televised appeal, if we haven't found Abigail in a couple of hours.'

'Yes,' said Caroline at the same time as John said 'No.'

Both Maggie and Caroline looked at him.

'Can I ask why you'd prefer not to?' Maggie enquired.

Caroline looked away from her husband in disgust.

'I just don't think they help,' John said.

'He thinks you'll get a psychologist to watch if he's looking up when he's trying to remember something or shaking his head when he says he wants her home. Says you always pin it on the dad.'

'That's a myth. The only time those things are used is on TV after you've been arrested to make it look like we

75

knew it was you all along.' Maggie knew as soon as she said it that she was being petulant and unprofessional.

John's eyes widened and he shot his wife an 'I told you so' look.

Caroline shook her head.

'She thinks you're a dick,' Caroline told him.

'Oh, yes, I'm the dickhead. *I'm* the dickhead! I forgot!' He threw his hands in the air, his voice getting increasingly erratic. 'I'm the one who left her for an hour while I had a "work meeting".'

'What does that mean?' Maggie asked, pointing at him. 'That inverted comma thing you did when you said work meeting. Are you saying it wasn't a work meeting?' She looked over at Caroline, who couldn't meet her eye.

'I don't see what difference it makes,' she mumbled.

'It makes a big difference, if we're being lied to, Caroline.' Maggie tried to keep her voice even. This woman's child was missing, she didn't want to upset her any more than she had to, but… A thought occurred to her. 'You told us the call was half an hour. He just said an hour. How long was Abigail missing before you noticed?'

'Go on, tell her the truth,' her husband taunted.

The door leading to the kitchen opened and Lesley walked in carrying two mugs. This had the infuriating effect of Caroline clamping her lips shut, as though to keep her words in. Lesley placed the mugs down and, sensing now wasn't the time, went back into the kitchen.

'Caroline, if you made a mistake earlier, when you told us about this morning, we just need to know the truth so we can alter our timeline,' Maggie said, trying to stay patient. 'You're not going to be in trouble. You were in shock, everyone makes mistakes at times like those, believe me. We just need to know the truth now.'

Caroline began to sob. 'Do you know what people are already saying?' she began, her voice a raspy whisper. 'On Facebook, in the comments on the news articles? They're asking what I was doing, why no one was watching her. She was in our back garden! No one expects their child to go missing from their garden. Those people saying I'm a bad mother, where are their children while they are tearing people's lives to pieces on Facebook? Probably on their Xbox or iPad, that's where. At least my daughter was getting some fresh air, not constantly on screens!' She was almost yelling now, getting increasingly worked up by the faceless trolls and their vitriol.

'You should stay away from those sites,' Maggie said. 'Those people are vultures, picking the bones off other people's tragedies.'

'I tried to tell her that,' Lesley said, coming back in with another two mugs. She placed one in front of Maggie. 'The kind of people who make nasty comments on stories about missing children aren't the kind of people whose opinions you want anyway.'

'And what do you think they're going to say when they find out that I wasn't on a work call?' Caroline snapped. 'That I was playing online bingo when my daughter was snatched from outside our own home? They'll think even worse of me than they do now.'

Maggie heard John make a snorting noise and ignored him. She had to remain calm and not let Caroline see her own frustration at having been lied to.

'And what time did you last see Abigail, Caroline? That's what's important now. That we have the correct information to find her. When we find her safe and sound, all this will go away.'

Caroline was still sobbing, but she nodded now. 'She went out to play at eight thirty. That's when I logged in to BadgerBingo.'

Maggie felt her head begin to throb. 'So it was an hour before you realised she was missing?'

Caroline nodded. Maggie held in her sigh.

'But I could hear her, I'm sure I could!' Caroline said. 'In the back garden, she was definitely in there for a bit...'

'How long, would you say?' Maggie urged.

Caroline shook her head. 'I don't know,' she said. 'You know when you realise it's gone quiet but you don't know how long it's been quiet for? It was like that. One minute it was half past eight and I was four pound up, next it was nine thirty and I was twenty pound down and I realised I hadn't heard Abby – Abigail – in a bit.'

John openly let out a disgusted scoff and shook his head. 'It's one thing when your little habit impacts our finances, but another when you put it before our daughter.'

Caroline looked at Maggie, her eyes wide with fear. 'Will they take her away from me? When we find her, will social services take her away?'

'That's a really unlikely outcome,' Maggie said. 'Is there anything else you're not telling us?'

Caroline looked at her husband, almost as if there was something else she wanted to say. Then she fixed her eyes on her feet and shook her head.

'No,' she said. 'Nothing else.'

Chapter Fourteen

Kathryn

It's nearly six-thirty by the time I pull up outside the third B&B. It turns out when there's a national news story, beds fill up pretty fast and at this one I don't even bother taking my case in, that's how hopeful I feel about getting a room. There's an actual doorbell that rings when I open the door and I'm immediately assaulted by the smell of incense in the air – sage, I think. Odd statues, some carved from wood, others stone, adorn every available surface and gilt framed pictures depict raven-haired women wielding daggers and men wrapped in serpents. In stark contrast to the pagan icons, the decor is chintzier than I thought possible: net curtains on the windows, floral wallpaper, the lampshades even have tassels. I'll bet a tenner the bedspreads smell musty, like my grandmother's house.

Did I mention I have a grandmother? Just the one – Patrick's parents died when I was a baby – thank God, I suppose. They never lived long enough to see their only son become a murderer. My mother's mother is in a nursing home in Ruthin, where Jordan visits her most Sundays. I can't remember the last time I visited and as I approach the desk of the B&B, I make a silent promise to go and see Nonna as soon as I leave Pentraeth.

The woman behind the counter looks to be in her fifties. She's small – maybe five feet – and her shoulder-length hair which shines silver is cut in a straight lustrous bob, a thick fringe almost over her eyes. She looks ferocious and practically barks at me as soon as I reach the desk. 'Press?'

'Excuse me?' I stutter, taken aback at her harsh manner. You'd think someone with as many florals surrounding her would be a bit less spiky.

'Are. You. With. The. Press.' She spits each word as though they contain poison and her eyes are narrowed at me.

'No,' I shake my head vehemently. 'I'm here to help with the search.'

She crosses her arms across her chest. 'Can you prove you're not with the press?'

'Can you?'

Her eyebrows relax, her shoulders drop and her snarl transforms into a wicked grin. 'Fair enough. I suppose I can't – although the odds on me being undercover as a bed and breakfast owner a few years past her prime are low. I take it you're looking for a room?'

'You're not full? Everywhere *else* is packed.'

'That's 'cos everyone else is taking those bottom-feeding reporters. I'm not. Nasty business, this little girl going missing. We don't need the whole country watching us trying to guess which one of us did it like it's an Agatha Christie novel.'

I picture Abigail Warner's mother and father, huddled on their sofa waiting for any news about their baby girl while reporters try to get a look through the windows and shudder.

'Maybe they just want to help,' I say, but it sounds weak to my own ears.

'You weren't here last time, love,' the woman says and I feel the heat spreading through my cheeks. 'Exactly twenty-five years ago it was, and they still won't leave us alone. I'm Nora. Just you, is it?'

'Yes, thanks.'

I sign the forms and then go out to get my things from the car, heaving my suitcase in behind me.

Nora is waiting to hand me a key. 'Stairs are narrow,' she says, eyeing my bulging case with suspicion. 'How long are you expecting to be staying?'

'I always pack too much.' I grimace at the mess my case will be in thanks to my rushed packing skills. 'Don't worry, I'll get it up there. Then I'd better go and join the search. Do you know where they're based?'

'Memorial Hall,' Nora says. 'Police are coordinating the search from there. It's been about nine hours now – they need all the help they can get.' She glances at my thin denim jacket. 'You might want to put something warmer on though. Drops really cold here at night, being so close to the sea and all.'

'They say she went missing from her back garden, not the front. Do they think someone has taken her?'

Nora hesitates. I'm an outsider, not someone to be taken into confidences. She'll know though, what the local feeling is – women like her in this kind of village always do. She just won't want to tell me yet. 'No one knows what to think, love, we're just hoping she's found before dark.'

'Yes, of course. That's why I'm here. To help.'

Nora opens her mouth, bites her lip, then closes it again. Then, 'Do I know you from somewhere, love? You have family local?'

'I live in Manchester,' I say, truthfully. 'Perhaps you've seen me on TV, when I present the news, being the super sneaky journalist that I am.'

Her eyes narrow, but then she gets the joke and smiles. After a few seconds' pause, she leans in close – although there's no one else here to overhear us – and whispers, 'Here's the thing. You might not know, on account of you *not being local* and all, but Abigail Warner and her family live at the old Bowen house. She was playing in the woods behind there. The exact same place poor little Elsie Button was snatched from twenty-five years ago this very day.'

Chapter Fifteen

Maggie

The Pit was the spare office, so called because it was located in the basement of the building, and also because it was the office used by senior officers when they needed to visit. Maggie knew that going down there felt like being thrown to the lions. Which is why she was unsurprised to see PC Fisher looking so terrified when Maggie called for her to come down.

'Someone said you asked to see me? PC Fisher?' Her name came out as a question. Poor girl had only been on the job for nine months, Maggie knew, and had probably been shocked as all hell to get the message that a DI wanted a word with her in the dragon's lair.

Maggie took a deep breath in through her nose, blew it out through her mouth and nodded. 'I did. We've not been properly introduced, but I know who you are, of course, and I know who your father is. I take it you know why I wanted to see you?'

Fisher shook her head. 'No, ma'am. I mean, obviously something's going on, the whole office is buzzing. I've been doing the collection for old Robinson's retirement so I've been going round the support staff. They—'

'It's a girl,' Maggie cut her off. Nerves obviously made Fisher chatty. 'Missing from Pentracth. Five years old, today of all fucking days.'

'Wow. Who is it?' Fisher asked. 'I know most of the families on the island...'

'Abigail Warner. The family is relatively new to the island. They've got—'

'The old Bowen place,' PC Fisher finished for her. 'The Warners are living in the house Elsie Button disappeared from twenty-five years ago today. Shit.'

'Thank you for that astute summary,' Maggie said, trying not to smile at the young woman's succinct assessment. 'You see my dilemma, I suppose?' She ran a hand through her short blonde hair. 'A missing child is newsworthy on any day, especially a little blonde girl, but today – well, it's not just a story, it's a bloody urban legend. We've already had to alert the media – we've shut off both bridges, but that's not going to be helpful if whoever has her has already left. But I suppose you're wondering what any of this has to do with you.'

PC Fisher opened her mouth to answer, but Grant continued without waiting for a response.

'I asked you here because I need a favour.'

Chapter Sixteen

Kathryn

Abigail Warner and her family live at the old Bowen house.
Abigail Warner and her family live at the old Bowen house.
Abigail Warner and her family live at the old Bowen house.

The words run through my mind on a loop as I zip up my new hiking jacket against the biting cold. It might be the middle of June, but the wind is brutal on an island in the evening. I set my Google Maps to Memorial Hall, the epicentre of the search party. *The old Bowen house. My old house.*

There is something about the way Nora said the words 'not being local' that sticks in my mind all the way there – it almost sounded like she didn't believe me. Could it be possible that she knows who I am?

She's just a slightly batty lady, I tell myself. *Just a harmless crackpot who was winding you up. You're used to dealing with those – you've lived next to Miriam long enough.*

The thought of Miriam gives me a longing for home – home where it's safe and where I can choose when I pick at scabs that should have healed a long time ago. Being back here on Anglesey – as lush and green as it is, with more space to breathe than Manchester could ever dream of – it still feels more like I'm digging a rusty knife into an old wound and I don't know how deep it goes.

I've barely left the end of the road when I come across the first police car. It's parked straight across the road, blocking any access for cars and its occupants, a man and a woman, are leaning on the outside. As I pass, the woman calls over, 'Excuse me? Do you know about the missing girl? Can I give you this?'

I stop and she approaches me, hand outstretched, waving a piece of paper which I take. The words 'MISSING GIRL – ABIGAIL WARNER, 5' are printed across the top in bold red capitals and underneath there is a picture of her, Abigail. It's a different one than I saw when Jordan called me this morning; in this one Abigail is wearing a party dress and holding a gold foil balloon in the shape of a five. You can see in this photo just how tiny she is – the balloon is almost the same size as her – you couldn't see that before, not when the shot was close up. It strikes me that they must have done this for Elsie, printed out posters of her little cherub face grinning into the camera. When the whole time she was already dead – probably before they even started looking. The thought hits me like a blow to the chest and I wonder if this concerned-looking police officer already secretly suspects it's too late for Abigail.

'I'm just about to join the search, actually,' I say. 'Have you had any information yet? Anyone who's seen her or anything?'

The PC hesitates long enough for me to know the answer is yes, but nothing they'll release to the public.

'No, nothing,' she says. She shoves a stray strand of dark hair out of her eyes. 'It'll be dark soon, poor thing'll be terrified. Thanks for coming to search. Memorial Hall's down that way.' She points down the road across from a church, although it's not strictly necessary. Unless they moved Glastonbury to a small field in Pentraeth, it's quite clear where the search efforts are being run from.

'Thank you,' I say, and make my way towards the search.

Clusters of people huddle around maps in groups of about ten. There's got to be fifteen groups here at least, and I can see more in the fields surrounding. Newscasters litter the car park, each positioned at the optimum angle to report with the action behind them. Police officers move between the groups of people, sending them off every few minutes. Abigail's name can be heard drifting across the island as people call out like a record stuck in a groove.

As I approach the entrance, a stern-faced man in a uniform greets me as if he's a bouncer on a nightclub door. 'Are you here to search?'

I nod my yes, waiting for him to tell me if my name's not down I'm not coming in.

'Do you have any local knowledge or search and rescue experience?' He is brusque and businesslike and makes me feel like I'm on a job interview. He looks at me, taking in my brand-new coat and walking boots that have clearly never seen a field. I think he already knows the answer.

'No,' I reply. 'And no. I'm not from here.' I resist the urge to add, 'Honest, guv.' 'Do I still qualify?'

He doesn't smile. 'We're making sure we mix people with no specialist knowledge with locals, and preferably a specialised search unit as well, now that night is approaching. Name?'

It hadn't occurred to me for a single second that I might have to give my name here, to the police. I imagined showing up and being pointed to a field – nothing like this Gold Command level organisation. 'Verity Austin,' I reply, giving Verity's maiden name like I did at the B&B. I hope he doesn't ask for ID, Nora didn't.

Fortunately, he just writes it on his clipboard list and points to a group at the far end of the car park. 'Join that group over there for me, Verity, someone will be across to talk about search areas and what to do if you find anything, okay? And thanks for coming out to help.' The words come out in a monotone as if they have been said roughly two hundred times today – which likely they have.

As I join the cluster of people who are to be my fellow search team, an enthusiastic-looking PC bounds over from behind me and practically jumps into place at the head of the group.

'Okay guys, thanks for coming out and helping us look for Abby this evening. She's been missing over nine hours now, so you can imagine she must be feeling pretty scared, cold and hungry if she's out there somewhere on the island. Your priority is what we refer to as the preservation of life, but we're also looking for any clues as to where Abby might have been today, so if you see anything at all, I want you to stand in place and your team leader will use their radio,' he gives his radio a jiggle for those of us with no search and rescue or general life experience, 'to call an officer to let us know. It's important you don't pick anything up, or touch anything. Is everyone okay with that?'

The group nods like Churchill dogs.

The PC claps a hand on the shoulder of a weathered, rugged-looking man and when he looks up and straight at me, I feel heat flood my face. I don't know how, but I recognise this man.

'This here is Aled,' the PC says, oblivious to the fact that I must have gone from flushed red to white in seconds and am now praying I don't throw up. 'He's your local knowledge, and your team leader. Anything he says – listen. If there's anywhere you think is too dangerous to search, Aled will mark it on the map and one of my fellow officers will take a look-see for you.'

Aled looks like he would rather eat his own intestines than mark an area as 'too difficult' for him to search, and there's no way he'll be calling PC Enthusiasm to 'take a look-see' for him.

'Great, right,' the PC says, as if Aled has answered him. 'So you guys can make a start now. Good luck.'

He bounds off and the group all instinctively look to Aled for our direction. I'm less certain now that I recognise him – with his wild black hair and weathered face full of stubble, he could actually be a culmination of every Welsh stereotype I've ever seen on TV. He couldn't have a bigger 'I'm the baddie' vibe if he was wearing a wax fisherman jacket and holding a hook. True to stereotype, he turns without a single word and stalks away, leaving us looking between ourselves bewildered. He hasn't paid me any attention, for which I'm grateful.

There are nine of us in total: three women in their forties who look like they could use an excuse to get out of the house, four blokes maybe early fifties, me and Aled.

'Aled, wait up!' a voice comes from behind me and I turn to see another woman of around my age bounding towards us.

Aled hesitates for a second, looks at the woman and turns to go again.

She stops beside me, leans over with her hands on her knees to catch her breath. Her short black hair is shot through with bright red and she runs a hand through it now, looks up and rolls her eyes at me. 'He's always like that,' she says, straightening up. 'Come on – he won't wait for us.'

I take this as my cue to buddy up with her. She's clearly from around here – her thick Welsh accent and the way she referred to Aled as if they were old friends give that away – but she's not dressed for either rambling or the cold. In fact, she looks like she came off a night drinking cider in the park and accidentally fell into the search. She has a stud in her nose, dark eye make-up and bright red lipstick, and she's wearing a black T-shirt with a question mark emblazoned on the front, a leather jacket and black combat trousers. Her Doc Martens at least look suitable for walking.

'Who is he?' I ask, walking faster to try to keep up her pace.

The rest of the group take our lead and follow Aled out across the field. He doesn't stop to glance at a map or break his stride to check where he's going and I'm getting out of breath already. My new friend isn't.

'Aled Evans,' she replies. 'Local farmer. He knows Pentraeth, whole of Anglesey actually, like the back of his hand. Not that it'll make much difference.'

'What's that supposed to mean?'

'Well, Abigail isn't in these fields,' she gestures around us, 'and she isn't going to be found by any of us traipsing around shouting her name. She's been taken, hasn't she?'

'What makes you think that?' I ask, even though it's exactly what I think as well. Five-year-old girls don't just wander off for nine hours without anyone finding them. Pentraeth is so small, I'm surprised there's still anywhere to search after nine hours.

'She went missing from the old Bowen house, do you know where that is?'

'No,' I lie. 'I'm not from around here. What's a Bowen house?'

'Patrick Bowen,' she says, stopping and raising her eyebrows at me. 'Surely you've heard of him? Killed that little girl here twenty-five years ago today. Today! Tell me that doesn't mean something?'

Believe me, I wish I could. She doesn't actually wait to see if I think it means something though, just carries on talking.

'…and she disappears from the house he lived in? Too much weird to be a coincidence. The police have managed to keep their address a secret from the press so far, but it'll break any time now and the conspiracy theories will start rolling in.'

'What kind of conspiracy theories?'

We've apparently reached our allotted area because Aled stops abruptly and turns to face us. He looks somewhat confused to see that my new friend and I are the only ones directly behind him. He waits, his face a thunder cloud, for the stragglers to catch up. When they reach us, he lets out a massive sigh.

'This is our area. You might want to use your phone torches, night pulls in pretty quick on the island. Spread out in a line, eyes to the floor, if you see anything, shout nice and loud.' He looks as though he shares my partner's opinion that this is a waste of time.

Still, we obediently form a line behind him and pull out our phone torches.

'What kind of conspiracy theories?' I ask again, trying my best to sound casual.

'Well, there will be those who think the house is cursed, you know, and old Bowen went mad like Jack Torrance. Those ones will think the dad did it is my guess. Then there's the "it's a coincidence, completely unrelated" people who will cling to the fact that it's some nutter visitor. Third, you'll have the people who will think it's the same person and Patrick Bowen is innocent.'

I swallow back the bile that has risen in my throat. *And Patrick Bowen is innocent.* 'And which of those people are you?' I ask, my eyes still fixed on the floor.

New girl looks up at me sharply. 'Well I'm not crazy,' she says pointedly. 'So I don't think the house is turning its occupants into psycho child killers.'

'Of course not.'

'But it's a bit unreasonable to think that the original killer from twenty-five years ago has waited this long to take another child – right? I mean, they would have to be getting on a bit now, so even if Bowen was wrongly convicted why wait this long to snatch again? Buuuuut, it's a hell of a coincidence – same house on the anniversary. I don't know, I don't really believe in coincidence.'

'What about a copycat?' I ask. It's not the first time the thought has occurred to me, that someone might have decided to copy what Patrick did to Elsie, saw that it was the anniversary coming up and chose that date to take Abigail. Even child abductors have to have a role model.

'Most likely,' she responds, and she actually looks fed up by the thought. 'Even if it is the most mundane of all of the theories. But can you imagine if Bowen really is innocent? Twenty-five years in prison for a crime he didn't commit?' She sounds incredulous.

Actually, I can't. My entire life has been defined by who Patrick is – or rather what he did. It's the reason I never applied for the jobs I wanted, the reason I avoided school and never settled down with anyone. Because who wants to shack up with the daughter of one of the most evil men in Britain? Who wants that kind of baggage dragged down the aisle with them? So now even entertaining the idea that Patrick might not have been responsible for killing Elsie – it might actually be harder to swallow than the current reality. And the idea he might have been covering for the only parent I have left...

I'm about to change the subject when she grabs my arm and stops me short, almost pulling me over. She points excitedly at the grass, then shouts out to Aled at the head of the group.

'Stop! Stop, Aled, I've found something!'

Chapter Seventeen

Maggie

Maggie left the Warners under the care of Lesley, not for the first time mentally congratulating herself for not training as an FLO. She would rather face a pack of press than sit with the parents of a missing child any day of the week. Since Caroline's revelation that she had been playing Bingo when their daughter disappeared things had been even more volatile in the house than they had been before, if that was possible.

Bryn's head was buried in his phone, but he looked up as she approached her car.

'How are they?' he asked as she slid into the driver's seat. Maggie raised her eyebrows. 'Okay, fair enough.'

She started the car just as her phone began to ring. 'Shit,' she muttered. 'It's Murray.'

'Just pretend I'm not here,' Bryn said, holding his hands up.

'Ma'am?' Maggie said.

'DI Grant.' The low tones of Superintendent Angelica Murray rang through the car. 'The Chief wants an update. What's the latest?'

Maggie tried desperately not to picture her boss's husband trapped beneath her thighs just that morning. 'The Warners aren't doing well. Turns out the mum was indulging in an online bingo addiction during the hour Abigail was outside alone. No news from the search teams yet.'

'It's perhaps time to bring in the parents.'

'It's a bit early yet, I think,' Maggie countered.

There was a silence on the other end of the line.

'You could be right. But if you're wrong, I'm not taking the shit for you. Still think it's too soon?'

Maggie gritted her teeth. God she hated that bitch. 'Yes, ma'am. There isn't enough to suggest that the parents have done anything wrong yet, and we don't want to risk the public assuming they have. They might stop searching, the media will create a shitstorm… it's too soon.'

'Fine,' Murray said. 'Call me as soon as you get any news. I don't have to tell you how vital this is. We don't need Anglesey to be labelled as the child abduction capital of Wales.' She hung up without waiting for a reply.

Maggie looked at Bryn, who was staring, slack-jawed, at the centre console where the call had come from.

'And you thought I was a massive bitch,' she said.

Bryn's cheeks coloured.

'I never thought that,' he objected.

Maggie raised her eyebrows again but said nothing. She knew what people thought of her, but whatever people skills she was lacking, she knew one thing that separated her from the likes of Angelica Murray – and it wasn't her ability to make her husband climax. It was that she actually cared about whether Abigail Warner was found alive – not so that it looked good on her or the force, but because Abigail was a five-year-old girl with her whole life ahead of her. Because she deserved her four thousand weeks on the planet, and because Maggie had to be able to look herself in the mirror every day and know she was doing this job for the right reasons. And the day that she lost sight of those reasons would be the day she quit.

'I didn't,' he mumbled, but left it at that. 'Do you really think it's nothing to do with the parents?'

Maggie chewed at the loose skin on her lip. It was the question that had been in the corner of her mind ever since Bryn had called her this morning to tell her there was a child missing. Could it be the parents? Statistically, it was much more likely to be something to do with them. Stranger abductions were mercifully rare, even more so in a place like Anglesey where everyone knew everyone and strangers may as well come with a beacon over their heads.

'She might still have wandered off,' Maggie said. She sighed. 'But, yes, it's probably the parents. But if that's the case, then she's dead, isn't she? So holding back another twenty-four hours on taking them in for questioning isn't going to put her safety at risk the same way it would if she were out there lost and scared. We need people to still have hope so they keep looking.'

'And us,' Bryn said, his voice quiet. 'We need to still have hope too.'

Maggie looked at him and realised that they had worked together for nearly a year and yet she knew barely anything about him. She knew he had kids, but she didn't know how many, or their ages.

'Yes,' she replied, turning her eyes back to the road. 'We have to have hope too.'

Chapter Eighteen

Kathryn

All I can do is stare at the crumpled white square while all hell breaks loose around me. Aled is shouting into his radio, the other searchers run over to see what it is, but the girl holds them back from trampling what might be evidence. Police officers carrying torches run towards us and we're pushed backwards. One of them pulls an evidence bag from her pocket and lifts the tissue into it with a pair of tweezers. One of the women next to me gasps as we see the deep red bloodstain smeared across it.

'Fuck,' she breathes. 'Do you think that might be…?'

'Could be anyone's,' I reply quickly, and it could be. Not everything will be related to Abigail Warner's disappearance. There will still be litter and fly tipping and regular junk hanging around. And yet finding a bloody tissue while looking for a five-year-old girl feels particularly portentous.

'Who found this?' The police officer turns to look at us and grins. 'All right, Beth?'

'All right, Mel. I found it. Do you think it's hers?'

'No idea. You, um, you didn't touch it?'

Beth snorts. 'Is that supposed to be a joke question?'

'Right, sorry.' Mel glances at me. 'Who's your friend?'

'Verity,' I say, holding up a hand. 'Verity Austin. I've come to help with the search.'

If she notices that I sound like a drone pre-programmed to state my name and purpose on demand, she doesn't show it. I'm going to have to practise sounding less suspicious if I want to stay here more than five minutes.

'Well, cheers for this,' Mel holds up the evidence bag. 'I'd better get it to the powers that be. Everyone's scared shitless of getting something wrong on this one. Don't want it to be me. Cheers, Aled,' she calls. 'If everyone could just walk carefully back the way you came – we're going to be sending the forensic team to head up this section now. If you want to carry on the search, please go back to Memorial Hall and we'll allocate you a new area.'

Aled looks as though he's just been told to walk to the other end of Anglesey. Glaring at Beth and I as if we planted the bloody tissue ourselves, he turns and storms past us. The rest of the group trudge wearily after him, not wanting to be left behind.

'Are you going to keep searching?' Beth asks me as we follow our group back across the field.

I shrug. 'I guess. I'm staying here so I may as well.'

'Where have you come from?'

'Manchester.'

Beth lets out a low whistle. 'You have come a way. How come? You know the Warners?'

'No,' I say, a little too quickly. Why else would I have come all this way? 'My, erm, my sister went missing, a long time ago. When I heard about Abigail, it was like I couldn't help myself. I barely remember getting in the car but…' I put my arms out and shrug. *Give me a frigging Oscar.* 'Here I am.'

'Oh,' Beth raises her eyebrows in a 'this is awkward' gesture. 'I'm sorry about your sister.'

'Thanks.' I say, then to steer the conversation away from me. 'You lived here your whole life?'

'Most of it.'

'So you were here when this happened before? With the other girl?'

She nods, looks at me out of the corner of her eye. 'Moved here just after. Why?'

'It's just like you said, it's weird, right? That it's the exact same day. If it's a copycat, they could be from anywhere, they might have come here especially to do this, on the anniversary.'

'Jeesh, that would be one sick son of a bitch.' She falls quiet as if searching for something to say. She seems nice and all, but I've already said too much really.

'Well, it was nice to meet you,' I move to walk away as politely as I can.

'Wait!' she says, as though something has just occurred to her.

When I turn back, she looks dubious, like she's unsure whether to speak.

I raise my eyebrows. 'What?'

She gives her head a little shake as though her mind is made up but there's still a bit of it that disagrees. Before I can turn to go again, she blurts it out. 'Do you want to go for a drink?'

I don't go for drinks with people because that leads to making conversation with them, and becoming friends, and that's the thing I'm truly afraid of. But tonight feels different. Frankly I don't want to be on my own – there's only so much any one person can take of solitude and this feels like my breaking point. I want to say yes, I want to sit and chat like a regular person. So I do.

Chapter Nineteen

Kathryn

The Old Lion and Tap is very much a local pub for local people. It feels like one of those old movies, where the main characters walk in and all heads turn to face them. Luckily, I'm with Beth, and when people notice it's her, everyone gives a nod of greeting. A few smile and give her a little wave, and the barman has poured her drink before she even gets to the bar.

'Who's your friend, Beth?' he asks, not even looking at me.

'You could ask her your bloody self, couldn't you, Dai?' Beth says with a wink. 'Name is Verity, she's here to help search for the missing kid.'

'Horrible business.' Dai shakes his head. 'We've had searchers in and out all night.'

'Anyone find anything interesting?' Beth asks casually.

'No.' He finally turns to look at me. 'What are you having?'

'Diet Pepsi please,' Sensible Kathryn says before Reckless Kathryn can order something stronger. I want to keep my head clear.

We take our drinks over to an empty table in the corner, far from the maddening crowd. Not that we have to worry about anyone hearing us, from the snippets of conversation I can make out around the pub Abigail Warner, and by default Patrick Bowen, is all anyone is talking about. We're not exactly going to stand out discussing child abduction in here today.

'How long you plan on staying then?' Beth asks. She pulls a hair tie out of her pocket and pulls her hair back into a short ponytail, the stubby ends sticking out. You can't see the red streaks as much and it makes her look older. I wonder how old she is? 'Not till she's found, surely? That could be, well…' She looks embarrassed at almost having said that Abigail might take weeks to find, or might never be found. At this early stage, no one ever wants to say that out loud, like even the words are a curse. For now, the police will staunchly insist they are looking for a little girl, not a body.

'I hadn't really thought about it,' I admit. 'I suppose I'll just stay for a few days, until they stop needing help. They won't search forever, will they?'

'I reckon about a week,' Beth says, taking a sip of her drink. 'Until they stop the volunteers searching. The case won't close then — the case won't close until they find her I suppose, but any longer than a week and they'll know that it's a body they're searching for. They won't want a volunteer searcher finding that. To be honest, in these cases, they usually have a suspect within a few days anyway.'

'It only took them a few days last time,' I blurt out without thinking.

'Yes,' Beth says, and she looks at me curiously, as though she's getting suspicious of how much I know. I need to be careful; I'm assuming she won't recognise me from the lanky, ginger, tomboyish five-year-old I used to be — I don't recognise her after all, we wouldn't have known each other for long even if we'd met – but there's no saying her memory isn't better than mine. I glance around the pub, nothing is familiar to me, not a single fixture or face. A long time has passed.

I catch the eye of Dai behind the bar and he quickly grabs a cloth, pretends to be mopping up a spillage that I'm certain doesn't exist.

Paranoid, I tell myself. *As always.*

You see, my life is always like this. Whereas another woman – a normal one – might think that Dai, who looks to be in his mid-thirties and isn't wearing a wedding ring, might be giving them the once-over, checking their finger for a gold band, eyeing up the slightest bit of cleavage on show or the curve of a thigh, that's not the way my mind works. Wherever I am, whatever the circumstance, I'm waiting for the words 'your dad killed that girl, didn't he?'

And now here, back where it all happened, back where anyone might recognise me at any moment, that feeling of paranoia is present every second. The shadow of Patrick Bowen follows me around, pervading every moment of my existence. And so when Dai turns slowly and picks up the phone, speaking into it quietly and moving his head slightly so I can't make out the words, I'm certain he's talking about me.

'Maybe it was all a bit too fast, back then,' Beth says, and my moment of paranoia at her tarring me with my father's deed is gone, just like that. The pub looks lighter, Dai looks like he might be on the phone to a girlfriend. It's like a horror film where the shot slows down for a second, the eyes of the people surrounding the lost hitchhikers flash red, then suddenly everything is back to normal, the villagers no longer threatening and the hitch-hikers are left to wonder if they imagined the whole thing. 'Maybe they didn't look any further because Bowen was so easy. Maybe he confessed because the evidence was damning and he wanted to spare his family a trial and the police took the path of least resistance.'

'And let a child abductor go free?' The idea is too horrific to comprehend. If Patrick confessed to spare us the ordeal of being interrogated ourselves, then whoever killed Elsie Button might still be out there and might have abducted Abigail Warner. And if that's true, well the Bowen family might not have Elsie's blood on our hands after all. But if Patrick, or anyone to do with him, kills Abigail, we'll be covered in hers. The idea is awful, but not quite as awful as him having confessed to protect my mum.

'God, let's hope not, eh? I'm just going to pop to the loo, back in a minute.'

As she gets up, I see Dai watching her. When she's out of sight, he puts down the glass he's holding and walks over to our table. My heart is pounding. I knew from the minute I walked in that this man wasn't a friend of mine.

'I like your hair,' he says, reaching out to touch a strand of my red hair.

I flinch and pull back.

'Um… thanks?' I say, not knowing how to react. What is he—

'Not Welsh, are we?' he asks. 'The red hair and all that.'

'No, Manchester.' I try to make my accent thicker, but I've never adopted the Manchester accent so much as diluted my Welsh one.

'You look like you could be from round here, is all.'

'Plenty of gingers in Manchester,' I give an uncomfortable laugh and look to the door to the toilets. Where is Beth?

'People on this island have long memories,' he says, as if I haven't spoken. 'And there's some things – or some people – we'd rather forget. Do you catch me?' His eyes narrow at me and I can sense the vehemence behind them. My knees feel like they might give way and my heart is thumping.

'I think so.'

'Good.' Dai steps back as he sees Beth come through the toilet door. 'Better to go back to where you came from then, isn't it? Before people start searching their memories and someone gets hurt.'

Chapter Twenty

Maggie

With the help of the volunteers, Memorial Hall had been arranged for the press conference to be held. Caroline and John Warner had agreed to speak in front of the camera – Maggie wasn't sure what she'd said that had managed to convince John that there wasn't a psychologist watching his every eye movement, but it might have been her subtle hint that it suggested more if they didn't show their faces.

A long table had been set up at one end of the hall – or rather three tables slid together and covered with a white sheet – to resemble the top table at a wedding. Only the 'guests' would all be seated in rows facing her and the Warners. The press had been allowed in now to set up their microphones, all jostling for the best position, trying to predict which side Mrs Warner would be sat on. It was the mother who everyone always wanted to hear from. The father would be watched like a hawk for signs that he might be concealing a dark, terrible secret, but the mother would be the one in pain. And the public thrived on seeing the pain. It's the way humans are, the nature of the beast, so to speak.

Maggie had desperately hoped it wouldn't come to this, but a five-year-old didn't stay missing for nearly twelve hours of their own volition. With so much land already searched, the hope that Abigail had wandered off, fallen over and was waiting to be rescued was fading fast. The word 'abduction' was moving around the room in hushed tones.

The Warners were waiting in Lesley's car around the corner, away from prying eyes until everyone was seated and in place. Maggie didn't want John getting cold feet at the last minute.

'You want me to start sitting them down?' The voice from behind her startled Maggie and the blush came easily to her cheeks when she saw it was Scott. *Fucksake, Maggie*, she thought. *Stop acting like a bloody schoolgirl.*

'Please,' she said. 'How's the search going? Will you be able to continue through the night?'

Scott nodded. 'Weather's good. No real massive hurdles to overcome. Any locals who want to keep searching, and any officers, we'll be glad of the help. Anyone not from round here we'll politely suggest they get some rest in case we need to search again tomorrow.'

Maggie nodded. 'Nothing else submitted into evidence?'

'Just the handkerchief. No results yet but could be anyone's.'

'Right, okay. You get these lot sat down then and I'll call Lesley and tell her to bring the Warners. Um, please. Thanks.'

Cursing her inability to act like a grown-up around a pretty man, Maggie slipped outside to call Lesley.

'Ma'am?'

'Five minutes to get everyone sat here, then we're good to go. Everything okay?'

'Yes, ma'am.'

It was a testament to how keen the press lot were to get the party started that they were seated in less than five minutes. Maggie had laid out name cards on all the seats, supposedly picked at random, but, of course, she'd put the ones who would give her the least amount of trouble at the front.

She took her place at the table and a hush fell over the room. Cameras clicked and flashed, journalists stopped recording soundbites into their video cameras. Maggie remembered how daunting this had been the first time she'd had to do it. She'd tried to remember that feeling every time since, just so she mentally noted how much harder it must be for two people whose daughter was missing. John Warner was right to be afraid that people would be judging, picking apart every tear – or the lack of tears – every slip of the tongue – and God forbid they accidentally referred to Abigail in the past tense. Armchair detectives all over loved it when people did that, catapulted them straight to the top of the Number One Suspect list.

'Right, everyone,' Maggie spoke into her microphone and looked at the sound guy, who stuck a thumb up. 'You've all done this before, you know the rules. Anyone who hasn't, you'd better acquaint yourselves with them quickly as the Warners are on their way. Don't shout questions at them, let them do their appeal and we'll take questions afterwards. I'll decide if the questions are to be answered. Don't just reword questions we've refused to answer, this is not my first rodeo.' A message buzzed from Lesley, *Here*. 'And you can start rolling, it looks like we're ready to go.'

The camera operators positioned around the seated journalists all swivelled their cameras towards the door and a dozen small red lights appeared. The Warners emerged from the entranceway, Lesley helping Caroline in. She looked suitably distraught, Maggie thought, and terrified. Mr Warner looked slightly combative and Maggie wondered what was going through his head. There didn't seem to be any love lost between the couple, he wasn't supporting his wife and was almost walking a full step in front of her down the aisle to the table. She understood that he was unhappy about what he saw as Caroline's negligence but his wife had no idea that her daughter was in danger in their own back garden, why would she? Maggie thought the issues probably went far deeper than a bit of online bingo.

Maggie stood to let them through and gave Caroline a warm smile. She didn't smile back, just gave a weak nod.

'Ladies and gents,' Maggie started, her voice loud and authoritative. She was good at this, she'd held more than her fair share of press conferences and she knew the camera enjoyed her. She saw Scott Marshall watching from the back of the room. 'As you know, we are here today to appeal for any information anyone might have regarding a five-year-old girl who went missing from her garden in Pentraeth early this morning. The girl's name is Abigail Warner. Abigail is 120 centimetres tall and around 45 pounds with light blonde hair that she was wearing in ringlets. Abigail is believed to be wearing a My Little Pony T-shirt and light denim dungarees, with yellow tights with either sunflowers or daisies printed on. Mrs Warner?'

They had agreed that Caroline would be the one to do the speaking. Maggie wondered for a second if she would be able to manage it, but she lifted her head and spoke clearly.

'Abigail is a beautiful little girl, full of love,' she read from a piece of paper in front of her. 'Not having her with me feels like I'm missing an arm, or a leg. It's hard to breathe knowing that wherever she is she is sure to be scared and missing her mummy.'

Maggie noted the use of 'I' and 'mummy' rather than 'we' and 'mummy and daddy'.

'Please, please, if you know where Abigail is, please bring her back to us. She is only five years old and she needs to be back at home where she belongs.'

Caroline looked at Maggie, who nodded her approval and turned back to the journalists.

'Questions? Yep, you start.' She pointed at Jim Taylor, pretending not to know his name. She didn't like to show favouritism, but it also helped to keep the local journos on side – not every story was national news.

'Jeremy Taylor, *Local Echo*. Do you have any leads in the case so far?'

Maggie shifted in her seat and leaned towards her microphone. 'We are trying to locate the owner of a car that was seen on Sidney Betts Close this morning. I'd prefer not to release details of the car at the current time but would urge anyone who was on Sidney Betts Close around seven thirty this morning to come forward so we can ascertain if they saw anything helpful. Please don't decide for yourself what you think is helpful – if you were in the area, come and speak to us.'

'What about the tissue that was found in the field covered in blood?'

Maggie raised her eyebrows. Jim was pushing his luck. 'An item was found on the field that may or may not relate to this case. It certainly wasn't "covered in blood", but it has been sent to the lab in case it yields any helpful data. Next question. Yes, you please.'

'Mike Gilbert, *The Sun*. Do you believe the answer to Abigail's disappearance lies locally? Might someone you know be responsible?'

Maggie took a breath to give a standard answer, all routes of enquiry to be heard, et cetera, etc., but Mr Warner was already speaking.

'We just hope,' he said, 'that if anyone had anything against either of us that they would leave a five-year-old out of it.'

His response was like catnip to a room full of journalists. Cameras clicked, pens hit notepads at the speed of light and follow-up questions came at them like John Warner had just opened a set of floodgates.

'Do you know who has Abigail?'

'Who do you think might have something against you?'

'What would you say to whoever has her?'

Caroline looked at Maggie, her eyes desperate.

Maggie held up a hand and let the furore die down.

Caroline started to speak. 'We don't know who has our daughter, but somebody might. If anybody knows anything about where she is, please, please come forward. I'm dying inside without her.'

Maggie started to stand up, indicating the press conference was over. But before she could usher the Warners out of the room, a question came from the back.

'Have you spoken to Patrick Bowen? Do you think this has anything to do with Elsie?'

Maggie cleared her throat and stood up straighter. She looked for the speaker but couldn't make out who had asked the question amid the camera lenses pointed at her. 'There's no need to speak to Patrick Bowen, he has been in prison for twenty-five years on a full life term. Whatever has happened to Abigail has nothing to do with what happened here twenty-five years ago.'

She indicated to Lesley to help the Warners out of their seats and left to the sound of shouted questions about copycats and accomplices that she hoped wouldn't make their way onto tonight's news at ten.

Chapter Twenty-One

Kathryn

He knows who you are.

By the time Beth has come back from the toilets, Dai is back behind the bar and it almost feels like I've made the whole conversation up. Did he just threaten me? Or was he just talking about strangers in general? He did say something about people's memories, but already I can't remember exactly what – it had happened so fast. He's not even looking at me now. I feel like I'm going crazy.

I make some excuse for why I can't stay in the pub and Beth, although she looks surprised, offers to walk me back to the B&B. I seem to have become her personal project, for which I'm actually quite grateful.

The road that had been crammed with cars an hour earlier is now almost completely deserted. It seems that everyone in Anglesey has gathered at the Memorial Hall to hear the press conference where Abigail Warner's distraught parents will make an emotional plea for her safe return. I can't think of anywhere I'd rather be less, the grief and despair hanging so thick in the air that you can't help but breathe it in, swallow their pain.

I saw the police officer in charge of the investigation going in there, a tall woman with cropped white-blonde hair and too-bright lipstick. She looked like she would single-handedly rip the balls off whoever had taken Abigail and I wondered whether she was the best person to appeal for him to come forwards. I wonder how old she is, if she was around when Elsie went missing. She couldn't have been more than a teenager. Maybe I know her, too.

As we are walking, Beth nudges me.

'Look,' she says. 'That's where Abigail lives, the other side of those trees.'

It seems so out of the blue that I'm almost unsteady on my feet for a second. Beth doesn't know it, but we're staring at the woodland behind my old house. The woodland where Elsie disappeared from.

We are standing at the edge of the trees – to call it the woods sounds a bit dramatic, but the trees are dense enough that the house they protect is barely visible, just the tip of the roof and a chimney. When you're a five-year-old, these woods feel like they stretch to the end of the world. I suppose my parents would be considered irresponsible for letting us play in them now, but this was the early nineties, everyone on the island knew each other by first name and the only harm anyone could imagine a child coming to was a scraped knee or a twisted ankle. Until Patrick, that was.

'Do you think the police will be in there?' I whisper.

'Nah,' Beth shakes her head. 'They'll have searched this bit a million times already. There's nothing to find here. There might be someone at the front of the house.'

As I stand and look into the darkness, that's when I hear it. Someone, a child, calling my name. I freeze. It must have been a trick of the wind – but there it is again. A light, tinkling laugh and my name.

'There's someone in there,' I say, and without the slightest of hesitation, I walk into the woods.

The trees don't whisper my name, or look any more familiar than any other tree in any other wooded area. There's a chill in the air and as I move through the trees what light was left of the evening recedes until we come to a clearing in the canopy overhead and some faint illumination breaks through. I hear Beth call my name and the sound of her following behind me.

I come to a clearing, leaves and twigs blanketing the ground. To the left is a large boulder that is the perfect shape for a seat, it even has a little dip in the middle as though decades of tiny bottoms have worn it into a groove. The sight of it is like a punch in the stomach. The woodland suddenly seems to narrow to the size of that boulder – and the *little blonde girl sitting on it*.

'There's no one in here,' Beth says, looking around. 'This bit has been searched loads. We shouldn't be in— Are you okay?' Beth asks when she realises I've stopped.

The little girl sitting on the rock cocks her head as if to say, *Yeah, Kitty Kat, you okay?*

'Uh-huh,' I whisper, unable to take my eyes from the spot. I know she's not there – I mean I know I'm seeing the image in my head rather than some kind of ghost or apparition, but for a second I had almost called out her name. For a second, the five-year-old Elsie Button is more real than Beth standing next to me.

As I walk closer to the boulder, the picture of Elsie fades and by the time I'm close enough to touch it she's gone completely. I run my hand across the cool stone and sit down. My bum no longer fits into the dip and it's uncomfortable.

'...much closer,' Beth says. She's obviously been saying something and I have no idea what.

'Sorry?'

She points over my shoulder and I turn to see what she's gesturing at. I've been so entranced by finding a place I recognised that I haven't realised that just through a gap in the trees is a house. *The* house... *my* house. The rickety old fence has been repaired – Mum would be pleased, as she was always annoyed about the way you had to sort of lift it as you opened or closed it – but the whitewashed walls are the same.

'I don't think we should go much closer,' Beth repeats. 'When you come out of this clearing, the woods basically open up onto the back garden. This is where Abigail was playing this morning. The same place Elsie and Kathryn were playing when Elsie was taken. We should get out of here.'

A shout comes from the house, a man's voice. I jump and stumble, but Beth doesn't seem to have heard anything. I'm about to ask her, but I realise the shout sounds strange somehow, like I'm hearing it with my head underwater. He's shouting my name, but it's not my name, not Kathryn Starling, but Katy, Katy Bowen. It's coming from the house, there's no doubt about that and my heart begins to race. I feel frightened – not now, not here, but somewhere locked in my memory. Deep down, Katy Bowen is panicking. Not because of the man shouting from the house, even though it's not my dad's voice I can hear, but because there's something behind me. *Someone* behind me? They're in the other direction to the voice, I can hear them, hear Elsie's muffled moans as if there's a hand over her mouth. My knees buckle and I fall back to the ground – *It was the monster in the woods, Katy*, I hear a voice – Elsie's voice say. *There was a monster in the woods, remember?*

'A monster,' I mumble, and I'm vaguely aware of Beth at my side. She's calling a name – Verity. Is Verity here? Why would this woman I've only just met be calling my sister-in-law's name? Then I realise, it's my name she's calling, Verity is supposed to be me.

'I'm okay,' I say, pulling myself to a sitting position and feeling very stupid.

Beth looks horrified, like I've just had a full-on mental breakdown. 'Is this about your sister? Are you okay?'

'Honestly, I'm fine.' I let her help me to my feet. 'I haven't had anything to eat and I felt a bit woozy, it's dark in here and a bit creepy.'

'Of course.' She nods and starts walking with me away from the clearing.

It has gone quiet now, the shouting subsided. As soon as the boulder and the house are behind me, I begin to feel better.

'I just need to get back to my B&B, get something to eat. Hopefully wake up to the news Abigail is home safe.'

'We're all hoping that,' Beth says, and although she seems to have accepted my explanation, she has a curious expression on her face. I'm starting to think that Dai was right – this island is a very dangerous place for me.

–

'Thanks for walking me back.' The embarrassment is still clear in my voice and Beth smiles and shrugs. She insisted on accompanying me to the B&B after my wobble in the woods, but it's been awkward and a bit intense. *This is why you don't make friends*, that cruel voice reminds me. *Sooner or later, you have to lie to them.* 'I'll be fine, honest. I'm sorry about back there. I'm not sure what came over me.'

'Is it because of your sister?' she asks.

We're standing outside the B&B and I swear I just saw the curtains twitch slightly. I'm tired, fed up and I'm not even sure anymore why I came here. Some sort of self-flagellation is my only reasonable explanation. Was I really hoping to prove that Patrick didn't murder Elsie? Who was I hoping did, then? Would it end this if I knew?

'Maybe,' I say, non-committally. 'I probably shouldn't have come here. Nothing good comes of bringing up the past.'

'Oh, I don't know,' Beth replies. 'Maybe you've got to face the past before you can escape the hold it has on you.'

We stand in an awkward silence until we both start laughing.

'That's £40 for the therapy session,' she says.

For a second, I almost say that's cheaper than my current therapist but manage to stop myself just in time. Instead I smile. 'Write me an invoice?'

'Will you be searching again tomorrow?' Beth asks. 'I've got work until 12, but I can meet you after that if you are?'

This sounds dangerously like *getting a friend* to me. And Anglesey is the last place on earth I want to do that. But for the first time in years, I find that I don't want to be alone either.

'I'm probably just going to see how I feel tomorrow,' I say, not wanting to commit to anything right now. It feels more like accepting a date than the offer of companion-ship. I'm so rubbish at this friendship thing.

Beth nods. 'Oh yeah, sure, of course. That's cool. Well, if I see you, I see you, and if I don't…' Her voice trails off.

Wow, this is really awkward. If this is what making friends is like, no wonder I don't do it very often.

'Thanks for keeping me company tonight,' I say. 'I should probably get inside though, I don't know what time I get locked out for missing curfew.'

'Ha,' Beth grins. 'Nora is fine really, even though I suppose she comes across a bit strange. She's a good person. Anyway, take care.'

Before the exchange gets us in any deeper, Beth turns and walks away.

As I enter the B&B, the curtain falls back into place.

Chapter Twenty-Two

She's here. She thinks I haven't seen her, or maybe that I don't know who she is after all these years, but I do. I've had a very good reason to keep an eye on that family, although they have done their best to forget what happened here. I knew one day one of them would come back and I should have guessed it would be her. She's the one who can't move on, she's the one whose life has been in free fall for years. And now she's here, sniffing around, looking for answers she doesn't really want, trying to dig up secrets no one else wants uncovered. Someone is going to have to stop her. She'll know soon enough how unwelcome she is here. The island has a long memory, and what that family did is written into every blade of grass, every grain of sand. It's in the wind. She can't escape it. She should never have come back here.

Chapter Twenty-Three

Kathryn

I pull the pillows into a pile on the bed, make myself comfortable and dial my brother's number. He answers on the first ring, as if the phone was already in his hand.

'Kat,' he says, sounding a little breathless. 'Are you okay? Where are you?'

'Where are *you*?' I ask. It sounds like he's outside, maybe even driving with the phone on hands-free.

'Tech emergency at work,' he answers. 'Did you get to Anglesey okay or did you change your mind?'

'No,' I say, 'I'm in Anglesey. I got here around six and joined the search for Abigail, I've just got in now. How's Mum?'

'Stable, no change. Have they found anything about the girl? Where are you staying? Did you see anyone you know yet?' His voice is a panicked flurry of questions and I feel a pang of guilt at the worry I'm putting him through, *again*. Just once it would be nice for me to be able to worry about him for a change.

'We found a tissue that looked like it has blood on it,' I tell him. 'But it could be from some random getting a nosebleed. The police took it. I'm staying at a B&B, The Swimming Unicorn. It was the only place I could find, there's journalists everywhere, the place is high-season busy. And how could I see someone I know? I don't know anyone. I don't remember anything about this place at all.' I decide not to tell him about seeing Elsie Button in the woods behind our old home. I'm guessing that isn't the kind of 'see anyone you know' he means.

'Well, it was a long time ago, you were really young. I didn't expect you to remember anything anyway.' Despite his words, he sounds relieved. I know how much my brother worries about me, he always has. Ever since Patrick… did what he did, Jordan has taken it on himself to become my protector. And a lot of the time I rebelled against him, the way you would against your father. 'So are you coming home?'

I resist the urge to throw out the old cliché *but I am home.* 'I don't know, maybe tomorrow. It was probably a mistake coming here, I don't know what I was thinking. Maybe that I would come down here, search the library archives, find a secret clue to who really murdered Elsie and get Patrick out of prison?' I try to fake a laugh, but Jordan sees through me.

'This isn't a joke,' he says, his voice strained. 'It's dangerous for you there. That's why we left, it's dangerous for our whole family. I think you should come home, first thing in the morning.'

'Yeah, okay, maybe you're right.' I think of what Dai might or might not have been insinuating in the pub. The problem is, I don't know what I'm going home to. I don't have any kind of real life back in Manchester, temporary jobs, temporary flat – my whole life is impermanent, my entire identity forged by a single act from twenty-five years ago, an act I didn't even commit. And if I'm honest, I'm a little afraid to go home and face the reality of my mum in a coma and whatever had pushed her to put herself there.

'Do you remember anyone called Beth?' I ask. 'About my age?'

There's silence for a minute while Jordan considers my question. 'I don't think so,' he says at last. 'Not from your friends. There was Scarlett Jones, remember? Tommy's sister. She sometimes came over.' Tommy was Jordan's best friend on the island. When I try to picture him, I just see a red cap with a New York logo on the front and messy brown hair poking out from underneath, nothing more. 'And you had a friend at school, Clare. Apart from that it was always just you and Elsie.'

Just you and Elsie. Me and my shadow, cute as a Button, Elsie.

Before I can reply, there's a sharp, violent bang on my door.

'Jesus, that scared the life out of me. Wait a second, Jord, there's someone at the door.'

'Find out who is before you open it. Better yet, don't open it at all. Pretend to be asleep.'

There he goes, being overprotective again. It's likely just crazy Nora with more towels.

I slide off the bed and place my hand against the door. 'Hello?' I call. 'Who is it?'

Nothing, just silence.

My hand is on the door handle, ready to open the door against my brother's orders, when the banging starts again, this time it's as if someone is hitting it with something heavy, making it rattle on its hinges, and I scream and jump back. The phone slides from my hand and hits the carpet. My chest is thumping, what should I do? Stupidly, I shout again, 'Who's there?'

I can hear a voice, but it's not coming from outside – it's coming from my phone on the floor. I pick it up to hear Jordan urging, 'Hang up, Kat, call the police.'

'And tell them what?' I shout, my voice betraying my panic. 'That someone is knocking on the door?' To whoever is banging, I yell, 'I'm calling the police.'

Why is no one else coming? Why isn't everyone out of their rooms, demanding to know what all the noise is?

'Stay where you are,' Jordan says, and I can tell he's searching for a solution that isn't going to present itself. He's not going to be able to come and help me, and he knows how ridiculous the idea of calling the North Wales police to the island to report someone banging on the door is, especially when they have a five-year-old girl to find.

As abruptly as it started, the banging stops.

I go back over to the door and listen, I can't hear voices or footsteps, just silence.

'They've gone,' I tell Jordan, my voice betraying my relief.

'Are you sure?'

I slide the chain and ease the door open just an inch. I've seen how easily these chains are kicked in on TV, I'm not taking any chances. The corridor beyond is empty.

'Yeah, there's no one there.'

'Come home now,' Jordan urges. 'You don't have to wait until morning. Just get in the car and drive back. You can wake up tomorrow in your own bed like none of this happened. As soon as Mum is well enough we'll go on holiday, get away for a while. Figure out—' He stops. Because what is it that I need to figure out? There's no magic wand I can wave and put my life back into place – no book I can read or podcast I can binge.

'I'm tired,' I sigh. 'And I can't face driving anywhere, I just want to sleep. It was probably someone drunk banging for his wife to let him in the wrong door. I'll come home tomorrow.'

Jordan hesitates. 'Fine. Pack your stuff tonight and call me when you're on your way in the morning.'

'I will,' I promise. 'Oh, before you go...'

'Yeah?'

I hesitate to bring it up, but I can't help myself. 'Do you remember me ever talking about a monster, in the woods behind our house?'

Jordan laughs. 'Oh yeah, I *do* remember that. I think you called him Bobbly or something like that, said he lived in the woods.'

'But we still went to play there?'

'Well yeah. You weren't scared of him. Bobbly was your friend.'

'What, and our parents never thought that was weird? That we had a friend who lived in the woods?'

'No one lived in the woods, Kat. It was barely even a "woods" anyway. I think Mum and Dad would have noticed if a big hairy monster with a bobbly head lived there. It was just yours and Elsie's version of an imaginary friend.'

I think about the feeling I had in the woods this evening, of my little legs pumping and the blood pounding through my veins as I ran in terror. Jordan might have thought the monster was in our heads, but to us it was very real, and I had been terrified of something in those woods again today.

—

It takes me a few minutes when I open my eyes the next morning to remember where I am. My packed bag sits on the plum-coloured chair next to my bed – I'm in Anglesey and I've got to drive home this morning, tail between my legs to admit that Miriam and Jordan were right – this was a stupid idea. Out of habit, I pick up my phone from the bedside table before my eyes have even fully adjusted to the fact that it's daytime and begin flicking away notifications. A new YouTube video by someone I subscribe to has been added, the weather is 23 degrees, I have one new message from Miriam. Short and sweet as ever it just reads: ?????

There are no social media notifications because I don't have Facebook or Instagram or whatever the cool thing to have right now is. I deleted all my accounts years ago thanks to an unhealthy relationship with the internet. The only time I regret that decision is when I need information faster than the news can provide it. Whenever anything is happening in real time, you can guarantee Tracy on Facebook has more info than the local constabulary, and she's much more willing to share too.

There is still one place I can rely on though. I'm less of a regular there than I used to be, but I've kept my hand in enough that everyone still knows my username – I'm one of the handful of people that have been around long enough to be labelled an 'old faithful'. I open my internet browser and log on to ArmchairPoirot.com.

As I expected, there's already a board for Abigail Warner. A quick look at the thread headers tell me that a) Abigail hasn't yet been found and there are no real leads, and b) the armchair detectives are heavily debating the significance of Abigail being snatched on the twenty-fifth anniversary of Elsie's disappearance. Knowing these guys, I would expect nothing less, and as expected too, the consensus is that it definitely means something. They just can't agree on what.

> **M4RPL31970** I definitely think it's a copycat. If the original killer wasn't Bowen why wait 25 years to take another child?

> **UNT1LDawn25** Would this be enough to secure a new trial for Bowen? Maybe he's orchestrated it to prove 1st murder couldn't be him?

> **ReDrUmReDrUm1981** I suspected the dad all along. They forced Bowen to confess and now Rowley Button has come back and done it again. The police have that little girl's blood on their hands.

> **Mustangsally590332** They never found Elsie's body. I've always said she was stolen to order and the traffickers just wanted another one. Date is coincidence?

There's a thread named NEW INFORMATION which I navigate to and type:

> **QueenAggie67845** Lazy I know but hit me with the latest.

Newbies to the site wouldn't get away with pulling this kind of shit. The other Armchair Poirots do not exist to shell out information to people too lazy to watch the news or read the threads, and they have a deep-seated dislike for outsiders who think they are a gossip hive. As far as they are concerned, they are serious researchers. That's one of the benefits of being chat-room royalty. I've offered enough input over the years to warrant mining the collective on the odd occasion. Sometimes I'd love to see their reactions if they knew who I really was.

> **Shakespeareisafraud** NOTHING. NADA. ZIP. No one is talking on any of the local gossip channels.

Now this is unusual. Shakes has his or her finger in local community pies across the country – they make it their life's mission to be able to find information within hours of any major investigation being launched, and usually they succeed. They (I've never confirmed whether Shakes is a male or female but I suspect it's a guy) have multiple Facebook accounts and a huge portfolio of Buy and Sell pages, You Know You're From *insert place name here* When, or Community Support groups to mine information that would usually be unavailable in mainstream media.

> **QueenAggie67845** Impossible. Small town on an island, someone must know something.
>
> **Shakespeareisafraud** If they do they aint talking. The silence is frankly suspicious. Places like that usually can't stop talking when something big kicks off. Press conference last night please bring our little girl home blah blah. Parents didn't even look suspicious.

I close down the page with a sigh. It's nearly nine a.m. – breakfast is only until ten, so if I want to eat before I leave, I need to jump in the shower now and get going.

I'm just sliding out of bed when what I see pins me to the spot, freezing me in fear. I don't scream, the danger isn't immediate, but bile rises in my throat all the same.

I sit back down on the bed hard enough to jar my backside. I can't believe what I'm looking at, it's so out of place, yet it's so obscenely *there*. On the inside of my bedroom door, where yesterday had been smooth brown polished wood, are the words:

GO HOME

Carved crudely in capital letters. The wood shavings are still on the carpet behind the door. Someone was in my room with a knife, carving this into the grain while I slept soundly a few feet away. Someone knows Kathryn Bowen is back on the island and they are not pleased about it.

Chapter Twenty-Four

Maggie

Maggie rubbed a hand over her face and blinked rapidly, trying to clear her eyes and her mind. She'd come back to the station to run yet another briefing, but where she really wanted to be was out at Memorial Hall, in the thick of the search. It's what she missed most about being less senior, the feeling that you were working the case on the ground. She knew that for most PCs the legwork, knocking on doors, interviewing people on the street, felt like grunt work, but to her she'd always felt like she was making more of a difference than she did now, rehashing facts endlessly, of which there were so very few. Even on door-to-doors, she'd always had the sense that the next door could be it, could be the one that yielded the clue they were looking for. Last night's search had given them nothing more than a tissue that might not even have anything to do with the case. More than likely dropped by some dog walker when they were pulling out their poo bags, but you never knew until you knew.

She leaned her forehead against the cool glass of the bathroom mirror and closed her eyes for a second, willing herself not to fall asleep. She'd managed to sleep for an hour in the cleaning cupboard of the Memorial Hall, locking it from the inside so she wouldn't get caught and ordered home by DS Bailey. He'd kept up an impressive vigil as well, only reluctantly going home at four a.m. to have a power nap and get changed for this morning's briefing. They were lucky, really, that it was nearly summer and both the weather and the light had been generous to them. Trying to search in the rain and freezing cold would have just added another layer of shit on for everyone.

Maggie started as her mobile phone began to buzz in her pocket. Shit, she'd been drifting off even as she promised herself not to. She stood upright, trying not to notice how absolutely terrible her reflection looking back at her was.

'Bailey, what is it?'

'Sorry to bother you, ma'am, I was just picking up coffee from Barbara's cafe and wondered if I could get you anything to eat. I don't suppose you've eaten this morning.'

It was more a statement than a question.

Maggie smiled in spite of her exhaustion. She knew DS Bailey didn't like her, she knew most of the team didn't like her actually, but she also knew he wasn't brown-nosing calling her like this. She'd seen, somewhere around two-thirty a.m., when she had taken over on the tip line so one of the volunteers could go home to sleep, a grudging respect enter his eyes. Maggie knew that plenty of DIs used their position as an excuse to lock themselves away in their office and 'lead from the top', but in cases like this she knew the only place for her was on the ground. She'd deal with budget issues and the media during the day. At two a.m. pretty much the only place she could be was with her team.

'Thanks, Bailey, I'll take an extra-strong coffee and a packet of cheese and onion crisps,' she said. Then, not wanting to disappoint, she added, 'And don't be late for the briefing.'

–

The team that faced Maggie looked like an entirely different group of people than the one she'd left the day before. Gone were the enthusiastic, hopeful, energetic looks, replaced by masks of exhaustion and despair. She knew what they were thinking – the crucial first twenty-four hours without anything at all. It was looking increasingly unlikely that Abby would be found alive with every minute that passed. Still, for the family's sake they couldn't let that show.

Her eyes scanned the room for Rob as they always did when their paths crossed at work. He was with the officers standing around the edge of the room; there were too many now to seat them all. She saw him catch her looking and looked quickly down at her notes.

'Morning, everyone,' she said, realising that her own voice had a despondent note that hadn't been there before last night's soul-destroying search. Hours and hours, hundreds of people, only to find not one single trace of the five-year-old. 'I know this is tough on you all. Some of you were here until late last night, others came in early hours of the morning. The Warner family is grateful to every single one of you and so am I. We know what the ticking clock means. They don't have to. I want us to remain as upbeat as possible when dealing with members of the public and the press. If you need five minutes out, take it in the back courtyard where you can't be seen.

I don't expect this to be just another day at the office for any of you and I know plenty of you have families to think about. Please talk to me if you are feeling the strain. This is now officially the biggest search operation Wales has ever seen. The helicopters are preparing for another day of searching, the volunteers are arriving at Memorial Hall in droves – some never left. Unlike previous searches, we don't have one single viable suspect.' She took a breath. 'Mel, do you want to tell everyone what you found out about the car?'

Mel, the girl she'd berated yesterday afternoon – had it really only been yesterday afternoon? – about the CCTV looked flustered now. Maggie guessed she wasn't used to speaking in front of a group this big. Another twenty officers had been added to the core investigation team, which meant they had a total of forty officers of varying ranks just following up tips and leads.

'Um, yes, of course.' Mel cleared her throat. She fixed her gaze at a spot just above the group's head. Bless her. 'The CCTV at the laundrette showed only one car going in and out of the street. The car seen on these photos,' she handed around a couple of glossy black-and-white A4 stills, 'meets the description of the one Mrs Warner saw in her street yesterday morning. The CCTV shows the car entering the street at nine oh seven and leaving at nine fourteen. The car has been confirmed to be owned by Doctor Will Roberts. Ted went to speak to Doctor Roberts and he confirmed that he was in Sidney Betts Close yesterday. He planned to drop in on one of his regulars at the surgery, pulled into the street but received a call from the surgery to say he was needed earlier than expected, so he left.'

Maggie noted the use of DS Rollins' first name by a junior PC. Was it possible Ted's pecker was only out of use by his wife? That was none of her business – as long as the job got done and nothing was compromised, Maggie had fucks to give about who was shagging whom. Not that she could really talk, after her dalliances with DC Murray. She tried not to look in Rob's direction again as she thought of how she'd left him yesterday morning.

'Thank you,' Maggie sighed, watching another lead slipping from her grasp. 'Follow up with the surgery when you get the chance, but I'm guessing it will all line up. Who was working on Mr Warner's whereabouts?'

'I'm waiting on a call back from the stationmaster at National Rail,' a voice Maggie didn't recognise piped up. The alibi work had obviously been fenced off to one of the lower-ranked officers. 'He was off shift when I called yesterday. Back any time now.'

'Right, thanks. Anything on the bracelet found in Abby's room?'

'Generic make, sold at Claire's accessories across the country and online. It's gone for fingerprints with the five-pound note.'

Maggie sighed. Another dead end. John Warner had denied knowing anything about either the money or the bracelet, but in reality the trinket could have come from school or anywhere and the money could have been from a birthday or a relative. All they could do is hope that the forensic team came up with something useful.

'What's the deal with what Warner said yesterday at the press conference, boss? About anyone who has a grudge against them?'

'I asked the same thing after the press conference,' Maggie replied. 'He said it was all he could think of, that no one would have anything against Abby, so it must be against him or Caroline. I'm not sure I believe him, but right now it would be unwise to accuse him of withholding information. We're looking into his background, why they left the last place they lived and their jobs, aren't we?'

Someone shoved a hand in the air and Maggie nodded. 'We might need to start looking into finances. She's a gambler and it sounds like she has a problem. Do they owe money to someone they can't pay? Is this a warning?'

At the back of the room, a door opened and closed, but Maggie didn't see who had gone out or come in.

'Right, that's great, everyone. Keep up the good work. I've got meetings half the morning with those upstairs who want to know what we're doing to find this missing girl – their words not mine – as if they couldn't just take a bloody look around them, but still. I really appreciate all your work. If anything comes up, just interrupt me – I'll probably buy you a bacon sandwich if you can get me out of any of these meetings.'

'Ma'am?' The door opened again and the officer following up on Warner's alibi was waving his phone in the air. 'Warner's boss. He wasn't at work yesterday.'

Chapter Twenty-Five

Kathryn

Nora is behind the front desk and looks up in surprise when I approach.

'You okay, love? You look a bit shook.'

'I need to show you something in my room.'

'What is it? If it's the hot water, there's—'

'It's not the hot water,' I cut her off with an impatient wave. 'Can you just come with me? Please?'

She must see how desperate I look because – somewhat reluctantly – she puts down her pen and follows me up to my room. I'm walking fast, but she keeps pace well.

When we get to my room, I unlock the door and usher her inside. She stands by the bed and looks expectantly at me, one hand on her hip. I motion for her to turn around.

When she sees the words carved into the wood, her face whitens. She moves towards the door and touches its ruined flesh with the tip of her fingers, tentatively at first, as though the words might burn.

'When did this happen?' she says, her voice hushed.

'At some point in the night. Someone came in and did that while I was lying there asleep in bed. Who could have done it? Who can get into the rooms?'

Nora shakes her head. 'Only me and my husband – but I hope you're not accusing us?'

'Of course not,' I say quickly – I don't want to insult Nora and I hardly think she's going to give me a room, then deface her own property to try to get me to go home. If she hadn't wanted me here, she could have just told me the rooms were full. 'I'm just a bit shaken, that's all. Should we call the police?'

Nora looks just as scared as I felt when I first saw the message. She shakes her head. 'No. I think you should go.'

I blink, stupidly. 'Sorry?'

'I think you need to leave. I think you should leave the island altogether, but I can't make you do that of course. I'm not sure you'll find anywhere else to stay anyway. Best you go.'

'Wait – are you blaming me for this? How is this my fault? Someone breaks into my room while I was asleep, that's not my—'

'I won't expect you to pay for the room,' she says. 'Have a safe journey back to Manchester.'

And before I can even think about what I'm going to say next, she leaves the room, and I'm left standing with my mouth agape at her retreating back.

My hands shaking slightly – more from the abrupt way I've been unceremoniously evicted from my room than the fact that someone had been standing over me as I slept, someone who clearly wished me harm and had been holding a sharp implement – I throw my PJs from last night (very glad I'd decided to actually wear some) and my washbag into my suitcase and give the room a once-over before dragging my things downstairs.

Nora is nowhere to be seen, clearly I'm not getting my promised breakfast.

I don't know why, but my body is shivering from the humiliation I've just suffered. How dare she treat me that

137

way? I picture the fuss I'd be kicking up if I were a normal person, not the daughter of a killer who is trying to avoid confrontation and drawing attention to herself. If my life was regular, there's no way I could just be kicked out onto the streets and told to 'go back to Manchester'. Then again, if my life was regular I'd at least be questioning why someone might be leaving me messages to 'go home' in the first place. It's hardly the most normal of circumstances where that can happen and you don't even ask why.

But then again… why? I mean, I know why the message would be left for me in particular, but what difference does it make that I'm here? I didn't hurt anyone all those years ago, and your average person in the street won't know who I am. Obviously someone has recognised me quicker than I expected – I'm sure that's what Dai was telling me in the pub, but I've as much right to be here as any of the other volunteers that have arrived to help with the search for Abigail. At least we know my dad's definitely not guilty this time.

I stash my case in the boot of my car. I'll get something to eat before I decide what to do next. My stomach is used to my 'never skip breakfast' promise and it's gurgling like mad. I remember seeing a cafe on the way in and it doesn't take me long to find it again. It looks busier than it will probably be all summer, crammed with people in searching gear, some of them clearly exhausted and despondent, others fresh-faced and hopeful. The night shift stopping in before going home to bed, the day shift fuelling before they begin. I've never seen anything like it.

'Holiday or searcher?' the woman behind the counter asks, as if she's enquiring if I want white toast or brown. She has a friendly face and no trace of a Welsh accent. My first thought is relief – she probably wasn't here when my family lived here.

'Searcher,' I say.

The woman grimaces. 'Terrible business, isn't it? Poor thing'll be starving now. They want to be checking under everyone's boat tarps, didn't I say that to you, Dom?'

'The police have been saying that already all morning.' Dom, a huge bear of a man with a thick mane of grey hair, a white beard and a navy angora jumper that looks incredibly itchy gives an exaggerated eye roll. 'They should make you head of the search, Barb – they could put you in charge of the "state the bleeding obvious" division.'

Barb doesn't look in the least bit stung by Dom's solid burn. 'Yes, well I only hope they find her soon. Poor love will need her mam and a hot meal inside her. What can I get you, love?'

'Beans on toast please.'

'Anything to drink?'

'Black coffee please.'

'Three fifty, love. That table over there'll be free in a minute, those kids've had a Diet Coke between them for half an hour and I can't spare the seats for arsing around at the moment. Just wait off to that side while I tell 'em to sod off to school.'

She bustles off to evict the teenagers, who put up only the tiniest of good-natured protest. Barb grins, threatening each one of them by name, and in a few minutes the table is free and she gestures for me to sit down quickly. Beggars can't be choosers in here this morning, but I'm glad it's facing the door. What happened last night and Nora's reaction this morning have lifted my paranoia levels above their usually already sky-high levels. But here's the thing: it hasn't made me want to leave. If anything, it makes me want to find out who wants me to leave badly enough to risk being caught breaking into my room.

'Thank you.' Barb sets down my coffee with a small smile and leaves me to my thoughts. It's like I have a million of them rushing through my head, clattering into one another and none of them making any sense. How can Abigail's disappearance have anything to do with a man who has been in prison for twenty-five years? Can it really be a coincidence that two girls who look so similar, who are the same age, disappear from the exact same place on the same date? Of course, the answer to that must be no. Either Abigail's abduction is a copycat or my dad wasn't responsible for Elsie's death. Both possibilities are unsettling.

I'm still watching the door, torn between writing down some of the questions buzzing in my head and not wanting to do anything that might draw attention to myself in public, when the chime above the door rings and Beth walks in. She sees me and waves.

'Penny for 'em?'

I smile at the irony of her words – journalists have been offering me more than a penny for my thoughts on Elsie's murder for years.

'I thought you had work this morning?' I motion for her to join me, which she does without going to the counter to order.

'Dai gave me the morning off to help with the search. Just means he can't be arsed and he wants one of us to show our face – you know the rest of the island is out looking?'

'I saw the searchers heading out on the way here,' I reply.

'I went to the B&B to see if you'd decided to stay, but Nora said you'd gone home. You change your mind?' She looks hopeful. I wonder if she's not a bit lonely herself, or maybe she's at the age where if you haven't escaped the island by now you know you're stuck here, waiting for middle age to kick in. I don't know anything about her at all, really.

'I wanted some breakfast,' I say non-committally. I promised Jordan I'd be home by this afternoon, and if he knew about what had happened at the B&B he'd probably drive here just to escort me back himself – and he'd bring Miriam. Not to mention that I don't have anywhere to stay – Nora all but kicked me to the kerb when she saw what had happened. I wish I could tell Beth about that to check if she thinks it's as weird as I do. Someone breaks into your room and instead of apologising and offering to call the police the owner tells you to get out? I get that she was probably annoyed about her door, but that wasn't my fault, was it?

'She said you checked out though. So you're going?'

'Yeah, the, um, the heating made a noise all night, didn't sleep a wink,' I lie.

Beth nods.

Barb approaches the table with two plates, despite the fact that Beth hasn't ordered anything. 'Beans on toast and a bacon sandwich with egg yolk on white,' she says, placing them down in front of us. 'Anything to drink, Beth?'

'Diet Coke'll do, Barb, thanks.'

'You come here a lot then.'

Beth grins. 'Not many places else to go around here.' She picks up her bacon sandwich and seems to wrap her entire jaw around it.

We sit in silence while we both eat our breakfast, but considering we've only known one another less than twenty-four hours, it's a companionable silence.

'You like it here?' I ask eventually.

'I guess,' she says, picking up a napkin and wiping brown sauce from the corner of her mouth. She takes a swig of her Coke. 'I don't really know any different. My parents adopted me when I was five, and I've been here ever since. Suppose I'll be here forever now, unless some millionaire holidaymaker sweeps me off my feet and takes me far away.'

'Do you want to leave then?'

She shrugs. 'The good thing about an island like this is that everyone looks after their own. Then something like this happens and it makes you question if that safety ever existed, or if we were just being naive all along. My mum and dad were here when Elsie Button went missing, they said it was the same then, everyone looking suspiciously at their neighbours – not wanting to believe it could be an islander.'

'But it was then,' I murmur. 'Do you think it is now?'

'I think the past has a funny way of repeating itself if we aren't brave enough to confront it the first time,' she says, finishing her bacon sandwich. My plate of beans sits half eaten – I'm not one of those people who eat their emotions, the slightest bit of stress can put me off food for days. Then again, maybe that's because you don't need food when your body is fuelled by vodka.

'I just can't see what this has to do with the past,' I say. 'Elsie's murderer was caught.'

'Unless he wasn't the only one.' Beth stands up. 'It's been good to meet you, I'm sorry you're not sticking around. I'd better go and join the search.'

'Wait – what do you mean "unless he wasn't the only one"?'

Beth shrugs. 'Just that there was an awful lot that went unsaid about Elsie Button's murder. I don't think we can rule out the theory that more than one person was involved. And if that's the case, then there's been an unchecked evil on the island for twenty-five years – perhaps this time someone can stop it for good.'

I almost choke on my tepid coffee.

Beth's eyes widen. 'Are you okay? Sorry, I realise I sounded like the tagline for a bad horror movie then.'

'No it's fine,' I say. 'I'd just better be going.'

'I'll walk you to your car,' she says, 'then I'm going to go and join the search. Gutted you're going though, I'll have no one to help me wind Aled up.' She grins as we head out of the cafe and I can't help smiling back – her playfulness is infectious. I wish it was as simple as just deciding to stick around for another day because I don't have to be back at work, like all the other people who have shown up to help. But the island remembers.

'Here she is,' I shrug as my car comes into sight. 'Wait, does it look a bit weird to you?'

'Shiiiit,' Beth whistles through her teeth. 'Doesn't look like you're going anywhere.'

The car is tilted oddly to one side and it doesn't take a genius to see why. The two tyres closest to the kerb have been slashed straight through and are completely flat. Given that they weren't like that this morning when I went to throw my overnight bag in the boot, someone must have walked up to my car in broad daylight, while I ate breakfast in the cafe a few doors down, and stuck a knife in both of my tyres.

I glance at the other cars on the street for signs of vandalism – nothing jumps out at me. Although the side of a lipstick red Peugeot looks like it's been hammered with a baseball bat, I think it's more a shitty parking habit than vandalism. None of the other cars have flat tyres or wing mirrors hanging off or anything to suggest a drunken teenage crime spree. After last night, this feels targeted – although if it's the same person, they have seriously got to get their messages on brand. You can't tell someone to get the hell out of Dodge in a creepy carving, then slash their tyres so they can't go anywhere, it's counterintuitive.

So two different people then. And while I don't appreciate the first person's delivery, I understand their message. They know who I am and they want me to leave the island, presumably because my family is still as hated here today as we were twenty-five years ago. And if the Buttons still live here, then I'm not surprised I'm not welcome. But the tyre slashing? An act of violence and hatred, yes, but hardly something you'd do to someone you wanted to get in their car and leave. It feels like someone younger, someone who hasn't really thought it through and to whom slashing someone's tyres is the obvious way of telling them you don't like them without considering the consequences.

'Bastard kids probably,' I hear Beth mutter. She has no reason to think otherwise.

Maybe it's down to the fact that I've been without a real father figure my whole life, or that I've never liked looking like I need anyone's help, but I don't instinctively feel the need to solicit someone else's opinion about what I should do. Maybe most women in this situation would call a boyfriend or their dad – or maybe I'm dramatically old-fashioned and just assume the white knight is still actually a thing. Either way, I don't possess a white knight, but I do possess a mobile phone and Google. AA informs me they could have someone out to me in forty minutes – had my road cover not expired two years ago. As the voice on the phone is saying it, I can remember cancelling the cover – who needs the AA when your licence has been taken off you? – and I completely forgot to set it up again when I got my licence back. They can still come, she says, but it will cost twice the amount of my yearly cover and they can't guarantee to get to me until late afternoon. I doubt a local garage will be much quicker and I can't be bothered to ring around so I just agree.

It seems impossible that this could have happened without anyone noticing. On a normal day perhaps, but in the middle of such a massive search effort? Police are up and down people's paths knocking on doors, locals are standing in their front gardens shaking their heads and looking worriedly up and down the streets as though Abigail Warner might come wandering down them any moment. Someone must have seen the assholes who did this.

Resisting the urge to scream unacceptable words into the air, I take a few deep breaths, in through the nose, out through the mouth, centring myself like Veronica taught me in our earlier sessions. This is something I can't change, so I'm going to let it go. I've got hours until the repair people get here. 'I may as well come with you then.'

Beth punches the air. She makes me smile despite the general crappiness of the situation.

–

Memorial Hall is as busy as it was yesterday, if not busier. The field next door is now filled with cars and there are people standing around like they're waiting for a donkey ride at a fete.

I remember to sign in as Verity at the volunteer table and the search coordinator points to an area on the huge map of the island spread out across the table. The map has been divided into squares in black Sharpie and the coordinator has a clipboard with each square numbered on a list.

'We're widening the area,' he says to us, barely glancing up. 'There's a Land Rover with a group leaving for this area in five minutes – are you happy to join them?'

My answer is cut out by a scream that rips the air in two. Every single person in the field swings towards the source of the anguish, perhaps expecting to see the body of a small child being carried across the grass. Instead, there is a woman on her knees, despite the dirt that has been churned up by the constant stream of boots that have passed through here in the last day. She isn't dressed for a search, with a swollen cardigan at least two sizes too big wrapped around her and a faded, ankle-length, navy-blue skirt with small flowers that perhaps used to be white but are now grey. She isn't wearing a coat and those might even be slippers on her feet. Is this Abigail's grandmother?

'Helen!' A man's deep voice cuts through the horrified silence of the hundreds of onlookers. He is running towards the woman, a sense of urgency on his face. He looks to be in his mid-fifties, but looks well for it, his short hair is almost completely grey, but it suits his distinguished face, chiselled features. He's wearing a navy cashmere jumper with a red gilet over the top of it, blue jeans and expensive-looking walking boots. His face looks so familiar I feel like I've been punched in the face. 'Helen, what are you doing here? Come on, you must be freezing – let's get you home.'

Helen. No… Helen Button? My own legs start to feel shaky as I realise that the woman on her knees in the dirt only twenty feet away from me is my best friend's mother. Does that mean the man now helping her back to her feet, snaking his arm gently around her waist… is that Elsie's dad? No, I'm almost certain it can't be. For a start, the thought of these two people in front of me, this handsome, distinguished man and this pale slip of a woman so fragile she looks like she might break if you hugged her too tightly, the thought of them being married is just ridiculous. She looks old enough to be his mother, although I know she's only the same age as my mum, fifty-nine this year.

I squeeze my eyes shut tightly at the thought of my mum lying in her hospital bed, willing myself to believe that she will be fine. When I open them, Helen Button is being walked straight past me. She's too distraught to notice me – would she recognise me if she did? – but the man at her side does. He looks straight at me and the stab of recognition seems to hit both of us at the exact same moment. His eyes widen and he drops Helen's hand. He looks as though he's about to speak to me, but Helen lets out a sob and the spell is broken. He turns to tend to her and doesn't look back at me.

'Bringing it all back, I suppose.'

Beth's voice comes from behind me.

I'm not supposed to know who the woman is, having allegedly never set foot on Anglesey before, and I remember just in time to ask, 'Who is she?'

'Elsie's mum.'

'That's Helen Button?' I say. 'She doesn't look anything like the photos in the papers.'

'Those are from twenty-five years ago,' Beth replies. 'I'm just surprised she's still here at all. Elsie was her only child, she didn't have anything else to live for. She's never managed to recover from what happened. Then again, you wouldn't, would you? Jill Bowen was her best friend, apparently, the two families did everything together. Which might have been the problem.'

I frown at her. 'What's that supposed to mean?'

'Well,' Beth looks around, even though everyone has stopped staring at where Helen has been led away and gone back to their roles in the search. When she's satisfied no one can hear us, she says, her voice lowered anyway, 'There were rumours that Helen Button and Patrick Bowen were having an affair. Some people thought Elsie might have been his daughter.'

A cold sensation washes over me, like I've been dumped into ice water. I struggle to find the right words to reply without giving myself away. How do you remain disinterested and casual in the face of the revelation that the girl your father murdered might have been your half-sister?

'I've never heard anything like that,' I manage to say, when my silence has stretched to snapping.

It's not strictly true though, when I think about it. With any murder case that gets as much attention as Elsie's did, so many wild theories were bandied around that at one point I had a spreadsheet to keep track of them all. According to Armchair Poirot, Reddit and countless other Facebook pages and true crime blogs, there have been a million reasons Patrick killed Elsie, one of them being that my mother and Rowley Button had been sleeping together and Patrick killed his daughter out of a twisted revenge plot, or Patrick and Helen had been sleeping together and he killed Elsie because Rowley had demanded a DNA test. Another one was that Elsie walked in on something she shouldn't have – I think one theory had my mum being the real killer because Elsie found out she was sexually abusing my brother. As if the murder of a five-year-old girl isn't juicy enough for them, there has to be sex and rape and incest thrown into the mix for it to get a sniff. Satanism too – if that can be hinted at, then that guarantees you another five pages of comments to scroll through in the dead of the night.

No, what I mean when I say I've never heard that theory is that I've never heard it from a credible source – let alone someone who lives on the island. Come to think of it, I've never heard a credible theory for why Patrick killed Elsie from anyone using their real name.

'That's because we don't talk to outsiders about our business,' Beth says. 'You're unlikely to find a single interview with anyone on Anglesey about what happened to Elsie. It's a very private place.'

'You want to be careful then, talking to me,' I try to make it sound like a joke, but actually I'm serious – I don't want Beth getting into any trouble – she has to live here once I'm gone and after what happened in my room last night and my car today, she could get herself into trouble by befriending me and she doesn't even know it. It doesn't seem fair.

'I know, I wouldn't usually just start up conversations with a complete stranger, but you seem different. It's like you belong here, like I've known you ages.'

'I've never been here before,' I lie quickly and it's unconvincing. Better cross international espionage off the list of potential new careers.

Beth looks at me a little oddly but carries on unperturbed. 'Maybe because of what happened to your sister? Like you understand all this.' She sweeps her hand around at the hordes of people poring over maps and crossing off huge areas of land, others handing out cups of tea and coffee, a group of Search and Rescue in full gear, teenagers standing around, none of them laughing and joking but listening to instructions and handing out fliers. 'But the last time anything like this happened here was twenty-five years ago. The community is stunned, and they're scared.'

Delayed slightly by the appearance of Helen, the driver of the Land Rover whose group I had been allocated to approaches.

'Only room for one,' he says in an accent so thick it takes my brain a moment to untangle his words.

Beth holds up her hands. 'Don't worry,' she says, 'I'll go and do a shift on the tea stand, get in Dai's good books.'

'I'll stay and help too,' I offer quickly, giving the man an apologetic look.

He shrugs as if I didn't look like I'd be much help anyway and heads off to round up the others in his group.

'You didn't have to,' Beth says, but she looks pleased I did.

'It's okay, I'd like to.'

I've realised, since being here, that it doesn't matter how many theories you read on the internet, or how many chat groups you join, it's all going to be supposition and speculation unless you talk to the people who are actually close to what's going on. And yes, Beth might only be my age and she probably remembers as little as I do about Elsie's disappearance, but she stuck around afterwards. She grew up with the aftermath and it's unlikely the island has ever been able to forget and move on, the way the rest of the world has – well, until Abigail disappeared, anyway.

We start walking over to where a long white table has been set up full of mugs that look like they came from a village hall, two huge silver water containers and a stack of boxes of tea, coffee and sugar.

'Who was that guy with Mrs Button, then?' I say quickly, before we get too close and have to stop talking. 'Was that her husband?'

'Oh no,' Beth says in a bit of a laughing tone. 'That was Doctor Roberts, he's the local GP. He's very fond of Helen, looks after her a lot. She's had these episodes before, where she just starts shouting at people in the street.' Beth pulls a sympathetic face. 'You can hardly blame her, I guess. We know to call Doctor Roberts if it happens – he just comes and gets her.'

I think of the look he gave me and wonder if Dr Roberts had taken care of me as a child. Did he recognise me just then? Or am I getting more paranoid by the minute?

A harassed-looking woman behind the drinks table looks up as we arrive. Her eyes seem to widen slightly and she is practically staring at me, even while she's speaking to Beth.

'Oh Beth – are you here to help? Dai said he'd send you over – bless you. And…?' The question doesn't need asking. I'm not from here, that much is clear.

'This is Verity,' Beth offers.

The woman is still staring at me as though I'm a strange species of butterfly. 'Verity,' she repeats. 'Okay. Hi Verity, it's nice to see you. I'm Pamela. I used to teach at the primary school here. For a long time.'

'Nice to meet you too,' I offer, trying not to show how weird it is that she's *still* staring at me, and being very strange indeed.

'Nasty business, this,' Pamela finally turns to address Beth directly. 'How's the investigation going?'

'Dad's not in the force anymore, Pam, remember?' I wonder if it's early-onset dementia because Beth is speaking to her like she's a small child.

Pamela looks pulled up short. 'Oh yes, of course. I'm all over the place. It's got me shook, you know. I only saw the little one the other day playing on the green and now she's...' She takes a deep breath in as though to stop herself saying the words. *Now she's gone.* 'And her poor parents must be wondering why they ever bought that blasted house.' Her eyes widen again, as though she's shocked at herself. 'Goodness, I'm so sorry. Maybe I should just go.' Her hand jerks forward and I think for a second she's going to grasp my hand until she thinks better of it and snatches her hand back. 'It was nice to see you, Verity, but don't stay here too long, will you? This place, it's not safe for you.'

And before I or Beth can reply, she grabs her handbag and practically runs away from the pair of us.

Chapter Twenty-Six

Kathryn

This place, it's not safe for you.

What's that supposed to mean? Me in particular, or not safe in general? And if she meant me in particular, then which me? Verity me? Or Kathryn Starling me? Or Katy Bowen me?

'She means because you're an outsider,' Beth says, as if she's read my thoughts. Or maybe my panic-stricken face. 'Sorry about her. The older islanders can be a bit stuck in their ways. I suppose no one wants to believe a local might be responsible for...' She stops, not wanting to say, 'for kidnapping a child', but that's what hangs in the air anyway.

'It's fine,' I wave a hand and try to sound breezy. 'It's a difficult time for everyone. Bringing up all those old memories. And thinking of where that poor girl might be. Her parents must be going crazy.'

Before Beth can reply, my phone pings a message and a group of four searchers approach the table for hot drinks. Even in June, people turn to a cup of tea when things look bleak.

Beth has got it under control so I pull out my phone to check the message. It's Shakes. That's weird – they never usually DM me out of the blue. Sometimes we've carried on a conversation privately but always when we've both already been online shooting the shit.

I open the message.

> Still interested in the Bowen case?

This is what Shakes is always like. Can't just get straight to the point. They like to tease a bit, whet my appetite.

I type a casual reply back, wouldn't do to sound too keen.

> You mean Abigail Warner case? Bowen case is SOLVED.

'Have you got any more sugar, love?' one of the searchers asks, holding up the empty sugar jug.

'Under there,' Beth points to underneath the table where all the supplies donated by the pub and the cafe are piled up. Everyone pulls together in a time like this, all wanting to do their part. Come lunchtime, batches of bacon and egg sandwiches will begin to be delivered, the food donated by the corner shop and cooked by the cafe, distributed by volunteers.

I pull out the sugar and fill the bowl for the guy. My phone buzzes again.

> We've been through this a million times. ACP want to relook at Bowen in light of Abigail's abduction. We've missed you. Want to play?

It's nice to be missed – even if it is by a group of people who don't even know my real name. At one point in my life, the Armchair Poirots were all I had, or so it felt. I'd comment on plenty of cases, but they all knew that Elsie Button was my pet project case. We all had them; GrislyP was obsessed with Dahmer, HellHathNoFury was a Wuornos enthusiast. Me and Shakes, we were Bowen experts. Of course, none of them knew just how close I was to the case.

I send back my response.

> You flatter. What you got?

Shakes has been sitting on this message a while, it comes back immediately.

> Witness tip.

How is that even possible? If there had been a witness to Elsie's murder I'm pretty sure I would have heard about it by now.

> Stop teasing. Witness to what?

I leave my phone face-up on the table and start replacing used coffee cups with fresh ones, one eye on the screen the whole time. When it lights up, I almost knock the stack of cups clean off the table. Beth gives me a sideways glance and I mouth 'sorry'.

The message is a link to a news article from 1994, but it's not an online article, it's a scan of an actual newspaper. It's behind a paywall, except the headline: LOCAL PSYCHIC CLAIMS SHE SAW BOWEN ON MORNING OF ELSIE'S MURDER.

I must have been staring at the headline for longer than I realise because the first I know of Beth being right beside me is when she places a hand on my arm.

'Are you okay?' she asks, her voice quiet. 'You look like you've had some bad news.'

'I'm fine,' I mutter, denial my default setting. She smiles and nods and I realise in that instant that I want to talk to someone, I need to tell someone. 'Actually...'

She'll run, the voice says. *She'll run as far from you as she can and she'll tell everyone. It'll be in all the papers. You have no car, you can't get away.*

'Yes?'

I shake my head. 'I'm really sorry, but I have to go. Is there anywhere nearby I can use the Wi-Fi?'

'It's free at the library,' she replies. 'Or the cafe we had breakfast in. Are you sure you're okay?'

'I just need to do something I completely forgot about. Are you okay here without me?'

Beth nods. 'Of course, they're pouring their own tea anyway. I'm just replacing cups. But, oh wait, I get it...'

I frown. 'Get what?'

'I get it. Now I know. I know who you really are.'

Chapter Twenty-Seven

Maggie

Maggie walked into the Warners' house without knocking on the door. Caroline's sister had arrived at eight a.m., along with her husband and adult daughter. John's brother, mum and stepdad had been there since the previous evening, and the house was beginning to groan under the pressure. The TV was still on, showing the search for Abigail, but the sound had been muted.

'Is there news?' Caroline asked the minute she saw Maggie enter the room.

'Nothing yet, I'm afraid.' Maggie gestured for Caroline to follow her into the hall, which she did. 'I need to talk to John, where is he?'

Caroline's face darkened. 'Why do you need to talk to him? What's happened? What can he tell you that I can't?'

'I really have to discuss it with him, Mrs Warner,' Maggie said, trying for an apologetic tone. She was never quite sure she hit the mark when going for a softer touch. In her ears, she could always hear only the impatience in her words.

'He's sat on the bench in the back garden, just staring at the woods,' she said, and Maggie thought she could detect bitterness. 'It's all he's done all morning and half of last night. Is this about what he said at the press conference?

Because if he knows why Abby's been taken, if it's because of him that she's missing, I swear I'll kill him.' She clamped a hand over her mouth as if realising she'd just threatened to kill someone to a police officer.

'It's okay,' Maggie replied, rubbing a hand up and down her arm. 'If he knows where Abby is and he hasn't told us, I think you'll have to get in line.'

The idea that John Warner might have something to do with Abby's disappearance wasn't exactly 'out there', but Maggie also hoped it wasn't true. She was a DC when nine-year-old Shannon Matthews went missing from a housing estate in West Yorkshire and could remember the horror at realising that her mother had known where she was all along, and had hidden her under the bed at an uncle's house. Maggie didn't get the sense that the same thing was happening here, but John's outburst at the press conference, coupled with lying about his whereabouts on the morning Abby went missing, weren't filling her with confidence.

Abigail, Maggie reminded herself to get it right in front of her father. She noticed how Caroline called her Abby when he wasn't around and wondered how controlling he was.

As Caroline had said, John was sitting on a peeling, flaky old bench in the garden. The Warners had only been in Anglesey a couple of years and it didn't look like they'd spent any of that time on their back garden. The lawn was unmown and a border of bushes around the edge were overgrown in some places, patchy and dying in others. There was a pink bike abandoned against the side of the house and several colourful plastic plates on the grass, a Barbie with no clothes on and three stuffed toys. At the bottom of the garden was the gate that led into the patch of trees so often referred to as a 'woodland area' on the news over the years. Maggie thought it was as much of a woodland area as a puddle was an aquatic area, but it sounded dark and ominous which was what the papers wanted, of course.

'She knew not to go out of that gate,' John said, without looking up at her. 'I'd told her a million times.'

'Did she listen?' Maggie asked.

John shook his head. 'She never listens. If she wants to do something, she just does it and says sorry she forgot afterwards.' He smiled. 'I don't know if she was turning six or sixteen. And she always gets away with it because she's so beautiful.'

He turned his head, but not before Maggie saw that he was crying. It was the first time she'd actually seen any emotion other than anger from him.

'Mr Warner, you weren't at work yesterday,' Maggie said. She kept her voice low and soft, had to make a real effort not to sound accusing. 'Where were you when your wife called to say Abigail was missing?'

He didn't reply, just went back to staring at the gate at the end of the garden.

'I should have put a proper lock on it,' he said at last. 'I said I would loads of times. I said a lot of things, I suppose.'

'Mr—'

'Yes, I know,' he said. 'Answer the question or you'll have to take me to the station. I suppose you probably already think you know what I was doing? You've already guessed I was shagging around when my daughter was being taken. That I took the day off work to have sex with my married colleague. There, I said it. I'm a piece of shit. What do you think of me now?'

Given that she was having sex with her married colleague when Abigail went missing, Maggie didn't think she had much wriggle room to judge, but she wasn't about to tell John Warner that. Somehow she didn't think it would be of much comfort anyway.

'I'm going to need her name and contact details, and any evidence you have that can back up your new whereabouts,' Maggie said, with emphasis on the 'new'. She may not care about his philandering, but she had absolutely fucking had enough of being lied to by these two. Somehow she didn't think he was lying this time, but she was sure as hell going to make sure he backed up this story. John nodded. 'Why did you tell us you were at work when it was so easy for us to find out you weren't?' Maggie asked. 'You must have known you were going to get caught.'

'I thought she'd be back,' he said. 'I thought she'd wandered off, she'd be found and no one would ever have to look at where I'd been. I did not ever for one second think I'd need an alibi.'

'And what you said at the press conference last night? About someone having something against you?'

He shrugged. 'I can't help thinking we've brought this on ourselves. That there's something about us, some reason this has happened to us. Like a punishment for my affair, or for Caroline putting those fucking online bingo sites before our beautiful girl. Do you know how many times Abigail has asked one of us to play with her and I've said "not now" because I'm texting Debbie, or Caroline has said "after I finish work" when we know full well she hasn't brought in any new clients in months. She's just glued to those bouncing balls, hoping her numbers come up. Probably so she can leave me. I wouldn't blame her.

And all that time, Abigail just wanted someone to play with.' He turned to properly look at Maggie for the first time since she had gone outside. 'Bring her back to me, DI Grant. Bring her back to me and I'll play with her whenever she wants. I'll be better, I promise. Just please bring back my little girl.'

Chapter Twenty-Eight

Kathryn

'I get it. I know who you really are.'

I hear Beth say the words and my head spins. Heat spreads up my chest and face and I think I might pass out. What did I do to give it away? Has she known all along?

'What?' I stall for time, maybe I could just run for it. But my car still hasn't been fixed, where would I go?

'You're a journalist.'

I'm just about to apologise and beg her not to tell anyone when my brain registers her words. *Oh thank God, she just thinks I'm looking for a story.* I try to let out my breath slowly so she doesn't see how terrified I was at being caught out.

'I'm not a journalist, I promise. Look, you can call my work if you want. I've just got a lot of personal stuff going on at the moment and I probably shouldn't have come here, I just wanted to try to help, but I don't feel like I've helped at all.'

'Well, you filled the sugar,' Beth smiles weakly. 'Look, here's my number.' She pulls out a pen and scrawls a number on the side of a white plastic cup. 'If you want to talk about anything or just get a drink or whatever, just give me a call.'

'Thanks,' I give her a smile and try not to look too relieved that she's dropped the questions. It's a shame that we can't be friends – it's not often I meet someone I want to spend any amount of time with. 'I'm probably just going to go as soon as my tyres are fixed, but it was really nice to meet you, I appreciate you hanging out with me, keeping me company and all that.'

She shrugs. 'Sure, no problem. It was nice to have some fresh—' she laughs. 'God, fresh blood isn't exactly appropriate considering the circumstances, is it?'

I laugh back, pleased to have found someone as inappropriate as I am who isn't related to me. 'No, it's not, but I won't tell.'

'And I won't tell anyone you're a journalist.' She grins to let me know she's joking. 'You don't have to worry, I know how to keep a secret.'

The way she says it makes it sound like Beth knows all too well that I have secrets to keep.

–

My phone rings just as I'm leaving the village hall – for one stupid second, I think it's Shakes, but that's ridiculous, they would never call me, would they?

'Hello?'

'I've come about your car, I'm at the B&B you mentioned, but the woman says you checked out this morning.'

Well, at least she's not telling people I was thrown out, I reason. 'Yeah, I'm just down the road, you're earlier than I expected. I'll come back now, be about five minutes?'

'No worries, love, I'll wait in the van.'

He's still in the van riffling through paperwork as I approach and knock on the window. I point towards my car a few metres away, although I'm fairly certain he could have figured it out himself and made a start by now – it's the only one with two flat tyres.

When he gets out and sees them, he whistles through his teeth.

'Someone's done a job on them,' he says. 'Did you report it to the police?'

'Yes,' I lie, not wanting to get into a discussion about it. 'They said they probably wouldn't catch who did it, there's been a few cases in the area lately. Kids,' I add, because people will accept that kids are responsible for just about anything.

To prove my point, he nods knowingly.

'Bored, not enough to keep them occupied. Anyway, this'll take me about an hour. You got anywhere to go?'

'As a matter of fact, I do,' I say, pulling out my wallet. 'Shall I pay you now, then you can just go when it's done?'

'You need to pay the office over the phone,' he replies, pulling out a business card. 'Then you can just leave me to it, I don't need the keys.'

The bored-sounding woman on the other end of the phone takes my payment and gives me a number to pass back to the mechanic. He types it into some sort of device and sticks a thumb up to me.

'Excellent,' he says. 'You'll be on the road in an hour or so.'

I don't think I will, I ponder, my mind going to the woman who claims to have given Patrick an alibi for the day Elsie was murdered. *I think I'll probably be sticking around.*

–

After a quick phone call to Jordan to check on Mum's condition – stable – and to tell him I've decided to stay on the island for a little while longer – cue anger, exasperation, disappointment – I google the local library. I'm not sure about Wales, but in the libraries in Manchester, we can access a lot of archives for free, as well as Ancestry.com and other genealogy websites, that might get me past the pesky paywall on the newspaper archive site Shakes has linked to.

Like everything else here, the library is a short walk, past the cafe, but away from Memorial Hall rather than towards it. I pass groups of people on the way, some nod, others try to shove missing posters into my hands as though I might not have heard about the only thing anyone is talking about in the whole village. The signal is so bad here that I'm not surprised to find that the library is relatively busy with what looks to be press, probably taking advantage of the Wi-Fi to send soundbites and copy back to their editors.

'Computer access?' the man behind the counter says, without looking up. He's a perfect librarian, with a shiny bald top, brown hair around the sides and a pair of wire-rimmed glasses. I'm disappointed he's not wearing a burgundy tank top or a tweed jacket, but his faded blue sweater does the trick anyway.

'Yes please,' I say. 'I'd like to—'

'You'll have to wait,' he interrupts, clearly not caring what I'd like to do with my computer access. Serve him right if I spent the afternoon looking at porn now, I think. 'I don't know how long these lot are going to be.'

He says 'these lot' in a tone usually reserved for paedophiles and serial killers. I know how he feels. When you're the news of the hour – especially from the side I've been on, which is to say the side of the bad guys – journalism can seem like the lowest way to make a living. Unfair really, because I guess if your father never killed anyone, they are probably perfectly nice and respectful towards you. Case in point, the lovely young man who smiles up at me and says, 'I'm done here, you can have this one.'

I give him the most winning smile I've got and am about to sit down when the librarian says, 'Hold on, you can't just take the computer, I've got a system!'

I look around to see if there's anyone else waiting – there isn't. 'Sorry,' I say, taking a slow step backwards despite seeing no one.

'Here,' he thrusts a pen and a pad at me. 'Put your name there. Do you have a library card?'

I weigh up the situation. My library card, if he looks it up himself, will say Kathryn Starling. I'm not sure the press have ever printed my new name, and although I've been using Verity's just in case, I doubt this guy is going to know who I am – unless he's an armchair detective, of course, those people know everything.

In the end, when he gives me a funny look, I pull it out of my bulging wallet and pass it over. I needn't have worried, he doesn't even beep it, just copies down the number next to the ID of my computer terminal on his fancy paper-and-pad 'system'.

'Okay, you can use it now.' He dismisses me with a wave of his hand.

As I sit down, the person on the PC next to me gives me a grin – clearly he had to endure the librarian's fussy disinterest too.

For once, I don't feel self-conscious pulling up articles about Patrick Bowen in public. After all, everyone around me is researching links between the abduction of Elsie

Button with the disappearance of Abigail Warner. I type in the link Shakes sent me and the article pops up. On a full screen, it is slightly more legible.

LOCAL PSYCHIC CLAIMS SHE SAW BOWEN ON MORNING OF ELSIE'S MURDER

A local woman, Harriet Tremayne, whose occupation is listed as Psychic in the Yellow Pages, claims that Patrick Bowen must be innocent of the murder of Elsie Button, because he was with her at the time Elsie disappeared.

'Patrick and I are old friends,' she says. 'He'd come to help me with some DIY on the morning Elsie disappeared. That's how I know it can't be him who's responsible.'

DI George Fisher, in charge of the case, commented that Ms Tremayne's statement had been looked into, however the timeline did not completely exonerate Bowen.

'They didn't want to know,' Mrs Tremayne said in response. 'They were just desperate to pin it on Patrick so they don't want to hear anything to the contrary.'

Bowen remains in police custody and will be seen before a bail magistrate on Wednesday.

'Excuse me?' I wave towards the librarian, who ignores me for long enough to make the point that he is Very Busy. 'Do you know if Harriet Tremayne still lives here?'

He scoffs, not bothering to hide his contempt. I do not like this little man. 'The psychic? Are you looking to have your fortune read?'

'Something like that,' I say. 'Is she, then?'

'Rabbit's Forge – up the bank and off to the left, then keep going about a mile,' he says. 'But I shouldn't bother if I were you, she's never managed to predict so much as a leap year.'

'Thanks,' I say, already preferring Harriet Tremayne to the snotty librarian. 'I'm finished here.'

I pick up my handbag and scoot around the table.

'But you haven't signed out!' he shouts after me.

It makes me childishly delighted to think that I've got in the way of his system again.

–

'About a mile' turns out to be nearly two, and 'up the bank' feels more like a mountain, but I can't miss Rabbit's Forge when I arrive. It's a slate and render cottage, covered in sprawling ivy, almost completely hidden by bushes and wild grass flowers. Spidery cracks run over the face of the house, some of them so large that weeds have begun to snake their way out. A cracked, weathered stone sundial presides over the front lawn, the grass grown up around it so high that it looks as though it sprouted up one April morning with the tulips and daffodils. Wonky, badly cobbled-together birdboxes and feeders have been dotted about sporadically – I'm half expecting Snow White and half of the forest animals to pop out and do a number.

Someone steps out from the shadow of a thick oak tree and I take a quick step back. It's a woman, tall, with a mass of curly brown and grey streaked hair. She looks solid

– the kind of woman you expect to be holding a spear, only what she's actually holding is a pair of secateurs in one gloved hand and a bin bag in the other. She'd clearly been leaning against the tree, silently watching my approach in the shadows. There are smudges of mud on her face and her clothes are garden dirty. This must be Harriet Tremayne.

I go to call out a greeting, but she speaks first.

'You took your time.'

Her voice is sharp and she turns just as sharply and walks inside the cottage, leaving the door open as though she expects me to follow. Maybe she thinks I'm the gas woman or the Avon Lady or something. *Or the human sacrifice for her Pagan ritual.*

This is the bit in the horror films where everyone yells at the dumb big-breasted chick not to go into the creepy house with the crazy lady. I'm wishing I'd confided in Beth and begged her to come with me, but I'd kind of been expecting a placid old lady knitting in her wheelchair over Xena Warrior Princess's scarier-looking older sister.

I came here for a reason, though, so I suppose I'm going to have to dig in, but still, I wish I'd mentioned to someone that I was coming here. Maybe after my disappearance, Shakes will go to the police and tell them about the article they sent me, and eventually they will put two and two together and they can return my remains to my family for burial.

Like your dad refused to do for Elsie's family? the voice mutters.

Jesus, I can't even have an internal sense of humour without my brain going dark on me these days.

Inside the cottage is as chaotic as it is outside. The entrance hall is dark and gloomy, but I can make out bookshelves against two of the walls, jammed full of tatty books that look older than me. A pot of ivy sits on top of one of the shelves and has crept down the side and begun to spread across the front, pawing tentatively at the books.

Harriet has already disappeared and I take a guess that she's gone straight ahead into what looks like the kitchen and I follow quickly, irrationally afraid that the front door will slam behind me and the ivy will begin to reach out its tentacles towards my ankles.

In the kitchen, it almost looks like the outside and the inside are one, plants growing wildly on shelves, surfaces and windowsills, blocking out most of the natural light. Pots and pans – clean by the looks of it – are stacked up next to piles of cookbooks and pots of herbs. The air is thick with the smell of damp soil and leaves. The overall effect isn't unpleasant – there isn't a surface that is clear or uncluttered, but it isn't a dirty house, rather one that looks as though it has been cultivated, grown from the ground itself and is fighting to stay as close to nature as it can manage.

Harriet is at a Belfast sink in the corner of the room – not the ones that people pay thousands of pounds for in their fake country-style kitchens, but an original, scuffed by pans – filling a kettle, which she places on an ancient Aga. She takes two mugs from a wooden mug tree and spoons tea leaves into a strainer.

'Ginger and turmeric,' she explains, motioning towards the tea. 'And some star anise. I make 'em myself. Never know how much plastic there is in the shop-bought teabags.'

'Thanks,' I say. I clear my throat, but it still feels like there's something lodged in it. 'Um, I should probably introduce myself.'

Harriet lets out a bark that I think is probably a laugh. She lifts the kettle from the stove, pours the water between the cups and hands one to me. 'Let it brew a few minutes. I leave mine ten, but might be a bit strong for you. I know who you are.'

I take the tea. 'Thanks,' I say, then I realise what she's said. 'Wait – what do you mean you know who I am?'

'You don't remember me, I guess?' She smiles and I see that despite the scary, wild woman vibe, she's actually quite beautiful. I try to imagine her twenty-five years younger but my mind fails me. Nothing from twenty-five years ago comes willingly anymore. 'Well, I'm not offended, I suppose, although I always thought you enjoyed coming up here. I was in love with your father, Katy. I suppose that's why no one believed me when I said I'd seen him that morning. They all thought I'd say anything to keep him out of prison – even when his own wife wouldn't.'

Her words plough into me like a truck. 'You were having an affair with my father?'

Harriet smiles again, only this time it looks sad and mournful. She shakes her head. 'Never. I loved Patrick my whole life – no one else ever even compared to him as far as I was concerned. Unfortunately for me, he felt the same way about your mother. He was a devoted husband, Katy – don't let anyone tell you differently.'

'Is that supposed to make up for him being a murderer?' I ask, my chin jutting out defiantly. 'Because it doesn't.'

She looks at me with undisguised pity. 'I'm so sorry for what you've been through,' she says quietly.

'If my father loved my mother so much, why would he have brought me here to see you? If you weren't sleeping together?'

'Patrick was my brother Phillip's best friend growing up. When Phillip was killed in Iraq, Patch used to come up to check on me, do jobs for me sometimes. He felt sorry for me.' She says it as if it's so simple, but I can see it breaks her heart. The man she loved coming by to do odd jobs, taking pity on the lonely spinster, and her not wanting to tell him to stop, her need to see him stronger than her pride. 'I think he brought you with him so that your mother would know there was nothing going on. There's no way we could have been up to anything nefarious with such an inquisitive five-year-old bounding around the place. You brought Elsie with you sometimes, too,' she says, with a meaningful look.

'What was she like?' I ask, not sure I want to hear the answer.

'She was a pretty little thing, that's for certain,' Harriet says, but she's not smiling. 'Too pretty, if you ask me. She got away with far too much because of it. Those blonde ringlets and big blue eyes – she could wrap the adults around her little finger, but I had her number. You, on the other hand, with your messy hair and always mud on your face, poking around in the stones…'

As she speaks, an image tries to worm its way to the front of my mind, a pile of stones – no, a ring of stones, like a portal to another dimension. 'The fairy door,' I murmur.

Harriet beams. 'You do remember! That's what you used to call the empty well out the back. You said it looked like a doorway to a fairy dimension. I had to watch you like a hawk when you were here – you were always poking around in the most dangerous places.'

I don't like it, buried memories pushing themselves to the surface – even the nice ones, like the smell of Harriet's garden, a mix of every type of herb you could imagine, or the tiny translucent wings I always swore I could see peeking over the rim of the well. The garden had been so full of magic, I remember. The tinkle of the wind chimes in the shapes and colours of the chakras. She taught me that word, Harriet. She always knew when my chakras were out of balance, she said.

But if those memories can push through, then so can the bad ones. Memories of how it felt to find out my father had killed my best friend, that neither of them were ever coming back. That he was evil and probably my mum too, because how could she not know what he was like? And if they were evil, then I might be too, and even Jordan, who, after Dad, was the best man I ever knew.

'I'm sorry,' I reach down and grab my handbag from the floor, knocking into a fruit stand and causing it to wobble precariously. 'I shouldn't have come here, I don't know why I did…'

I turn to escape from the kitchen as quickly as I can, but Harriet puts down her tea and moves lightning fast in front of the doorway, blocking my exit.

'You're here because you want to know about your father's alibi,' she says, reaching out to put a hand on my shoulder. 'You're here because I'm the only person on this island who knows for sure that your father didn't kill Elsie Button.'

Chapter Twenty-Nine

Maggie

Abigail just wanted someone to play with.

The words had been turning around in Maggie's head ever since John Warner had uttered them a couple of hours ago. Had Abby needed a friend? Lonely little girls would talk to anyone. Had she wanted her mother to play, then wandered off in search of someone to play with?

The problem with that idea, of course, was that if little Abby had wandered off in Pentraeth, the most likely outcome was that she would be found by someone walking to school, or going to work, and returned to her mum before Caroline Warner had even realised she was missing. That's the way it was here. The chances of a random paedophile happening upon a lost five-year-old in Anglesey were practically none. And if no one had picked her up, the search teams would have found some trace of her by now. Which still left them with two equally horrific options. One: that the parents had harmed Abby and were covering it up. Maggie still knew that this was statistically the most likely outcome, and yet somehow she just didn't think that was what had happened here. Which left option two: Abby had been taken by someone who had known exactly where to find her. A local.

For the first time in days, Maggie was alone in Investigation Room One. Every single officer she had available was following up leads pulled in from the tip line, or checking CCTV footage, or combing the beaches. The room was silent, save for the ringing of the phones in the offices beyond. She looked up at the board, at the picture of Abigail Warner, and not for the first time she felt a stab of unease at just how similar she was to little Elsie Button. How she fit a 'type' so perfectly, with her blonde hair and blue eyes. Was something more sinister at play here? Was there a sex trafficking ring operating on the island? Had Abby been stolen to order?

The idea was ridiculous, she knew that. But however much she wanted to deny that there was a connection to whatever happened to Elsie, the parallels were just too eerie. Was there something significant about the date? She made a note to check the satanic calendars herself – God knows she didn't need anyone else getting wind that she'd even thought as much. Any mention of significant dates and you'd have headlines screaming of ritual sacrifice sooner than you could say Beelzebub.

'Maggie?'

She didn't need to turn around. She knew the voice straight away, and besides, barely anyone at work called her Maggie. It was either 'ma'am' or 'DI Grant'. She sighed.

'Hey.'

'How are you doing?' DS Rob Murray's voice was full of genuine concern. No one ever asked how *she* was doing. It made her want to cry.

'I'm okay,' she said, turning to face him and resolving not to let him see her cry. 'Well, I guess I've been better.'

'You want me to come round when you get off shift?'

Maggie laughed. 'I won't be "getting off shift" until she's found – or at least until there's no chance of bringing her in alive. Unless by "my place" you mean the Pit.'

Rob smiled and reached out to touch her but thought better of it and glanced at the frosted windows to check no one was peering in. 'I wish I could just pull you in my arms right here,' he said. 'And hold you.'

Maggie shrugged. 'We don't get to do those normal things. We're the bad guys, remember? The liars, the cheaters. We get the stolen hour for sex, then it's back to pretending we barely know one another.'

It was how it had been for the last seven months, and she was used to it by now. She'd thought he was too.

'What if it wasn't? What if…' he looked over to the door and lowered his voice. 'What if I left her? What if we could be together permanently, like normal people?'

Of all the things that had happened the last few days, this was perhaps the most surprising. Where had it come from? Rob had never so much as hinted that he wanted them to be anything more than they were – a decent shag in a lunch break.

'Don't be ridiculous,' she said. 'Why would you do that?'

Rob looked confused. 'Because I want to be with you. Haven't you realised that by now? I've been falling for you ever since I met you.'

Oh Jesus. This was not what she needed right now.

'No you haven't,' she countered, taking a step back. 'You've been enjoying the excitement of it all. It's not me you like, it's the forbidden nature of it. You don't want to leave Su— Angelica.' She'd almost said 'Superintendent Murray'.

'It's not that. It's you,' he insisted. 'You make me smile. You're honest, and clever, and... well, obviously, you're hot as all hell, but it's not—'

'Rob,' Maggie held up her hand. 'Just stop. Listen. You are not leaving your wife for me. You love her. And even if you don't... well, look. I think you're great. And if I was the type of woman to take a husband—'

Rob snorted. 'Take a husband?'

Maggie stuck up her middle finger and carried on. 'Then you would be top of my list.' Maybe second after Scott Marshall, she thought, but decided against saying it out loud. 'But I'm not looking for a relationship – and certainly not one that will end my career.'

Rob stared at her as though he didn't quite understand. She wasn't sure how he had expected his grand gesture to go, but not like this, she guessed. 'So what are you saying – you're dumping me? Is this because you're stressed about the case? We can talk about it again afterwards...'

'Woah,' Maggie put up her hand. 'I never said I was dumping you. I have a great time with you. I'm just respectfully asking you not to leave your wife.'

'And if I do it anyway?' he asks, his tone defiant.

'Well then, we're over,' Maggie said, making a move towards the door. 'I'm not going to take the blame for your marriage falling apart, Rob. As much as I like our arrangement, I'm not going to lose my job over it. So let's just keep things as they are, okay?'

She chose not to give him time to argue, leaving him staring after her, dumbstruck.

Chapter Thirty

Kathryn

The day is still relatively warm, so Harriet suggests we take our tea outside. I jump at the idea, because quite frankly this place gives me the creeps. It's as if the whole house is caught between the worlds of living and dead, past and present.

After her bombshell announcement, Harriet refuses to say any more until we have a fresh mug – peppermint this time – but once out in the back garden, she can't avoid me or my questions.

The back garden is as wild and unruly as the front. It's long and thin, overhanging trees forming a luscious green archway above our heads. Weeds and wildflowers co-exist in the beds and a jumble of flowerpots in assorted sizes and colours. There's a bench that I assume we're supposed to sit on, but the ivy and the weeds that have wound their way through its split and peeling wooden slats look about ready to pull it to the ground underneath, like killer plants in an eighties horror movie.

Harriet doesn't seem concerned about this as she carries her tea and an armful of blankets to the bench and sits down, looking at me expectantly. When I gingerly perch myself on the edge of the bench, she looks like she's suppressing a smile and hands me a blanket. I'm about to say I'm not cold, but I do love a blanket.

'I remember how much you love a blanket,' she says, making me think for a second that I said the words out loud.

'What else do you know about me?' I ask, a little sharply. 'And my family? What makes you so sure my father is innocent?'

'Patrick was here the morning Elsie went missing,' she says, staring straight ahead at a bush clad with berries. 'He had been trying to find the source of a leak in my kitchen ceiling. He was here all morning. Then he got a phone call and said he had to go. An hour later, the entire island was looking for Elsie.'

'How do you know he didn't...' I can't bring myself to say the words.

'Kill her in that hour? Do you think your father such a monster that he had to run off in the middle of pulling up floorboards to satisfy his bloodlust?'

I don't much like her tone. 'That's the point – isn't it? I don't actually know. I don't know anything about him. I was five years old when he went to prison. I grew up believing he was exactly the kind of monster who would do that. As much as I'd love to believe that one half of my DNA wasn't provided by a monstrous paedophile, I don't have much evidence to the contrary, given that *he confessed*.'

Harriet looks at me in silence – the kind of look that makes you believe in ESP because it feels as though she's reaching into my mind with her eyes, probing around to gauge how much to tell me – how much I will believe. 'There was just no way he had the time to get home, kill Elsie, clean up the evidence and hide her body well enough to never be found before raising the alarm. His house – *your house* – is about ten minutes in the car from here – less on Google Maps, but that doesn't account for parking up. So that's about fifty minutes. That's not a lot of time to kill a child and get rid of all the evidence.'

There's an idea forming in my mind – one that still makes my father a bad person, sure, but less of the monster than I've believed for most of my life. It feels strange and almost exciting, to know that I can begin to believe he might not have killed Elsie through true evil. 'What if he was rushing home, because of this phone call saying there's an emergency or whatever, and Elsie steps out in front of him, into the road? He hits her with his car—'

'Van,' Harriet corrects. 'He had a little pickup.'

'Fine, hits her with his van. He gets out to check her, but she's dead. In a panic, he gets something out of the boot to wrap her in and drives her somewhere to hide the body. Then he gets back home and calls the police to report her missing. That could be done in an hour, for sure.'

Harriet nods. 'It could,' she agrees. 'And I could even believe that Patrick could have killed Elsie by accident – anyone can have a momentary lapse in concentration, anyone can make a mistake. But even if I believed that he panicked and instead of calling the police he hid her body, there are still some gaping holes in your theory. For a start, your father confessed to killing Elsie. Why would he go to all the trouble of hiding her body then confess?'

'Because of the evidence against him. The blood, her underwear…' A thought occurs to me. 'If it was an accident, why would he have her underwear?'

Harriet grimaces, as if even hearing me say the words causes her physical pain. 'The million-dollar question,' she says. 'Not to mention, once he confessed to Elsie's murder, there was no reason for him not to tell the police where her body was. The police always suggested he refused to tell them because he didn't want it to come out what he'd...' Another grimace. 'What he'd done to her. But that doesn't sit well with me either. After all, surely it couldn't be worse than what everyone assumes? Another theory was that it was a way of keeping control over the situation.'

'Maybe that's what it is,' I sniff, thinking of the question I've asked Patrick every month for two years. *Where is she?* 'How are we supposed to second-guess what goes through the mind of someone like that?'

Harriet looks disappointed. Obviously she wants me to be so desperate for Patrick to be innocent – like she clearly is – that she thinks I'll blindly accept any theory she wants to throw at me. The problem with that is that I've had twenty-five years to come to terms with what Patrick did. I've done the denial thing – that's when I joined all the true-crime boards – and eventually came to the same conclusion as William of Ockham – the simplest solution is usually the truth. And in this situation, the simplest situation is that Patrick killed Elsie Button and refuses to tell us where her body is because, once we find her, he becomes a nobody. No use to anyone for anything.

'And what if he won't tell because he can't? What if he doesn't know where she is? Or what if she's not dead at all?'

I let out a sigh. I'd been hopeful that Harriet had something concrete for me, hard proof rather than the 'what ifs' I've lived with for my whole life.

'So what, you think my mum called him because she was looking after Elsie and she lost her? Then why did he confess to killing her?'

Harriet frowns. 'It wasn't Jill that called your dad that morning. It was Kevin.'

'Wait, Kevin as in *Kevin Wilson*?'

Harriet nods.

Neither of us need to ask the question, because we know the other won't have the answer. Why did my father's solicitor call him an hour before Elsie even went missing?

'Do you know who these people are?' I ask, suddenly remembering the photograph shoved into the bottom of my bag. I pull it out and smooth it on my jeans.

Harriet takes it from my outstretched hand and a smile plays across her face. 'Of course I do. Thick as thieves, they all were. That's why I couldn't understand why George didn't try harder to find the person who really took Elsie. He loved your dad so much. And your mum.'

'Wait,' I say, remembering the article that had led me here. 'Are you saying one of those men is George Fisher? DI George Fisher?'

'Well, he's retired now,' she says. 'But yes, this one here.' She points to the man on the end, the one beaming at whoever is taking the photo and gesturing for them to hurry up. 'And that's Rowley Button, of course – you'll recognise him from the news. He was a farmer, him and Helen ran the farm until Elsie disappeared. And here is Kevin Wilson, your dad's lawyer, and Will, he was the local doctor. Well, still is as a matter of fact.' She looks sad and wistful. 'They were always together, the five of them, and your mum, Helen and Linda. Kevin and Will weren't married then, Will never got married at all, I think

182

Kevin did, but by then it was different around here. None of them were drinking together in the pub anymore, or taking you kids fishing or to the park. Helen and your mum used to organise most of the village events, so they stopped for a long while. Of course, new blood came in, new children to replace the sounds of you lot and new families to organise the school fete. George and his wife adopted. Helen and Rowley retreated into themselves and eventually they split up, sold the farmland and the livestock, all the machinery. Rowley moved away and Helen refused to leave the farmhouse. He couldn't stay and she couldn't leave. Then life moved on, just differently, like everyone was moving underwater for a while, quieter and slower. Then when we think it's all forgotten and done with, here we are again.'

'Did Patrick owe any of them anything?' I ask. 'A debt of some kind?' *A reason he would take the blame for them murdering Elsie?*

Harriet looks surprised. 'Not that he'd ever have told me,' she says. 'Although actually, if anything, it would be the other way around with George and Linda.'

'What do you mean?'

'Linda was attacked,' Harriet says. 'Before you girls were born. It was a violent assault, and your father stopped it, scared the attackers away. Linda was beaten up pretty badly – there was talk of a sexual assault, but if that's true, George kept it out of the papers. I suppose that's what happens if you're the local police.'

'So Patrick saved her?'

Harriet nods. 'Not soon enough though – he always seemed guilty about that. And Linda found out later she couldn't have children; Patrick told me he thought it might be linked to the attack.'

I sit and contemplate the new information in silence. Did Patrick feel so guilty about Linda's attack that he took the blame for something terrible one of them did? It sounds so unlikely.

'Do you think it's connected, what happened then and what's happening now?' I ask, but I know what her answer will be.

'Of course it's connected,' she says. 'It's all connected, like the butterfly effect. Elsie's death all those years ago caused a rift in this island that will only be closed when we find out where she is and lay her to rest. And I don't think we will find out where Abigail is unless we uncover who really killed Elsie.'

Chapter Thirty-One

Maggie

If her head hadn't been a complete mess before, it certainly was now. Maggie didn't do relationships. That wasn't to say she'd never had one – of course she'd had boyfriends as a teenager, and even a fiancé when she was twenty-six, but that felt like a lifetime ago now, a different her. She didn't know if she had the time or the headspace for a boyfriend – God, could you even call it that in your forties? – but what she did know was that it wasn't going to be her boss's *boss's* husband, even if she did. And to want to talk about it right now, in the middle of the biggest investigation she would probably ever handle in her career? North Wales wasn't well known for its career-making cases, and she wasn't about to screw this one up because she was doodling hearts in the back of her notebook with Rob Murray's name on.

She headed out of the station as fast as she could so she could be sure Rob wasn't following her. Although she was fairly certain even he wouldn't be that stupid. She was almost at her car when she heard a voice call out her name – one that was almost as unwelcome as Rob's right now.

'DI Grant!'

Maggie sighed. Without turning around, she said, 'What do you want, Jim? I don't have any new information at this time.'

'I know, I was just wondering if you were able to clear up some facts on the Elsie Button case.'

This time, she did spin around. Jim's eyes widened in fear. 'I've already told you that we're not making any connection whatsoever between this case and the tragic murder of Elsie Button. Isn't that enough facts?'

'Well,' Jim looked down at his feet and scuffed the ground with the toe of his trainer. 'My bosses want me to do a comparison thing. They want to run the "Bowen House Curse" angle. We know Elsie talked about a man who played with them in the woods behind the Bowen house.' He checked his notes as Maggie's heart began to race.

A Bowen house curse? That was a new one on her. And so was this man Jim alluded to. She realised she knew embarrassingly little about the case that for twenty-five years had defined the island she had moved to.

'The Boggly,' Jim confirmed. 'Have Abigail's parents mentioned anything about someone in the woods?'

'Don't be fucking ridiculous, Jim,' Maggie snapped. 'Are you seriously expecting a comment from the senior investigating officer about whether we are looking for a man called "Boggly" who has been cursing the woods for twenty-five years? I may be sleep-deprived, Jim, but I've not completely lost it yet.'

Jim, to his credit, looked abashed. 'Okay, point taken. But can I just—'

'No you can not.'

Maggie pulled open the door to her car. She had been planning on going to check on the search efforts again before this afternoon's briefing, but now there was someone else she needed to talk to. Someone who might know about the Bowen house curse, and what the hell a Boggly was. She was damned if she was going to know less about her job than Jim bloody Taylor.

Chapter Thirty-Two

Kathryn

Through the miracle of Google, I have Kevin Wilson's work address and phone number. I don't want to go there. I don't want to see him, or speak to him – I'm a coward, I know, shoot me, but he's a grown man and right now I feel like a tiny little girl. And all of a sudden I'm angry: at my brother for not caring enough to come here, to help me find the truth; angry at my mom for being so cowardly; at myself for being drunk when she called for help. Angry at Patrick for starting this in the first place. Even angry at poor Abigail Warner for dragging it all up now. It suddenly just seems so, so shit. I am thirty years old and my entire life has been lived under the shadow of this one event, and now the shadow is a huge black mass bearing down on me. I'm not ashamed to say that I sit down on the gravel a quarter of a mile from Harriet's house and start to cry. Angry, frustrated, self-pitying tears. I sit like that for ten minutes, maybe more, my backside getting cold and numb until my phone starts to ring. I pluck it from my pocket, the name on the screen says 'Mim'.

'Miriam, is everything okay? Is it Mum?' I try not to sniff audibly and I'm forced to wipe a disgusting trail of snot onto my sleeve.

'No change,' she replies quick as a flash. 'I was just calling to see if you'd cracked the case yet. What are you crying about?'

How the hell does she know everything? 'Am not,' I lie churlishly. 'The little girl, Abigail I mean, she's still missing. There are people everywhere searching for her. It's a total circus.'

'And that's why you went there, is it? To find this missing girl?'

I sigh. There's no point in beating around the bush with Miriam – as she once told me, she's allergic to bullshit.

'Okay, fine. If you must know, I've found nothing to suggest that Patrick lied in his confession. Nothing to suggest that anyone else killed Elsie and I still have no idea why Mum did what she did. I'm just going to come home, I think. Forget all this.'

As I speak, I see something move in my peripheral vision, ducking into the trees on the other side of the field. An animal? Harriet come to watch where I go next? Or someone else?

'Good idea. That's definitely what I would do. Just drop it. Probably spend the next fifty years wondering – you I mean, I clearly don't have fifty more years. But the easy way out, that's the way to go. I mean—'

'All right, fine, I get the point,' I interrupt, still looking out to where I'm sure now that someone has been standing watching me. I get to my feet and brush the dirt from my bum. 'I guess there are a couple of leads I could follow up before I call it quits.'

'Well, that sounds a bit more like the Kathryn who left here two days ago,' Miriam says cheerfully. 'Get it all out of your system, ask all your questions and then, when you come back here, you can move on with your life.'

I know she means well, but she says it as if she's suggesting a spa weekend and a tub of Ben and Jerry's to get over a bad break-up. Even so, she's right about one thing – I can't go home until I've exhausted all of my options here. I don't want to leave with regrets, because I know damn well I won't ever be coming back. Which means I'm going to have to visit Kevin Wilson.

'I'm right, aren't I?' Miriam gloats when I still haven't spoken.

'I can neither confirm, nor deny,' I say. I can feel her wicked grin from here and I wish she were with me now.

'Be careful young lady,' she says, her voice suddenly gentle. 'People don't always like it when you drag up the past.'

–

Kevin Wilson's secretary sounds dog-tired as she informs me that Mr Wilson is working from home today. Wilson didn't defend Patrick in court – he is a family lawyer, not a criminal one – but he was widely known to be *our* family lawyer and so I can imagine he's nearly as besieged by the press as I am on the anniversary of Elsie's disappearance. Given what's happened here, I'm not surprised he's taking the day off to go into hiding. I'm also not surprised that she immediately follows up by telling me that she can't give me his home address. As if that's a problem. A place like this, I could stop anyone on the street and ask them where Kevin Wilson lives and I'd probably have his home address, a full account of his marital problems and his irritable bowel in minutes. Luckily, I don't have to stop someone randomly on the street – I have Beth.

'Why hello,' she says on answering and her jolly tone makes me smile. 'Still here?'

'Just can't seem to get away,' I remark dryly. 'Look, I was wondering if you knew where Kevin Wilson lives?'

It occurs to me and – yes I know, far too late – that she's going to ask why I want to know. Shit, shit, shit. I'm not supposed to know anyone here, let alone be making house calls. Luckily she doesn't ask any questions.

'The lawyer? I don't think he even lives on this side of the island anymore. Oh wait…' I hear someone saying something in the background. 'He's staying here at the moment apparently. At your old digs funnily enough.'

'The Swimming Unicorn?' I ask, groaning internally. So my father's lawyer and I practically collided, but that B&B is the last place I want to go back to. 'Great, thanks.' But bringing up The Swimming Unicorn has reminded me that if I am planning on staying in Anglesey I'll need somewhere to sleep. 'Wait – I don't suppose you know of anywhere I could get a room, do you? I might stay another night.'

Surprisingly, Beth doesn't ask why I suddenly want to stay, or why I even more suddenly want to see a lawyer. She just pauses a minute, as though deciding something, and then says, 'You can stay with me if you want to?'

'Oh, I wasn't asking… I mean I wouldn't ask that of you, it wasn't a hint,' I babble ridiculously.

Beth laughs, cutting me off. 'I know you weren't asking, I offered,' she says. 'It's fine, you totally don't look like a killer. I'll text you the address, let me know when you're on your way and I'll pop down and let you in.'

I'm not sure what to say. It should occur to me how dangerous it is for me to accept board from someone I don't know, but for this moment I'm just genuinely touched. 'Thank you,' I say. 'That's really kind. Any news on Abigail?'

'There's going to be another press conference at six,' Beth says. 'Karen – the one giving out bacon sandwiches earlier – says the theory has changed from lost to definitely abducted now. They've searched that far that if she'd wandered off somewhere we probably would have found her by now.'

'Don't give up hope,' I say, feeling like a complete hypocrite. I had no doubt this was an abduction from the moment I saw Abigail Warner's face.

–

I'm a ten-minute walk from The Swimming Unicorn according to Google Maps, but I've walked further this morning than I have in the last six months and I'm wishing I'd taken my newly fixed car. Still, it's not like I have the option to just crash in my bed with Netflix and my weighted blanket, I just don't ever remember Nancy Drew or Columbo walking this much.

Nora is behind the desk when I walk in and when she sees me, her eyes do a kind of cartoon widen and she attempts to take a step back. Before she can run away – although I'm still flummoxed by why she would want to – I hold up my hands in a 'don't shoot' kind of gesture.

'I'm not here to cause trouble,' I say, despite the fact that I didn't cause any trouble this morning either. 'I was told that Kevin Wilson was staying here and I just wanted to speak to him.'

'I can't give out the names of my guests,' Nora says, her voice defensive. 'Data protection.'

'So he *is* a guest?' I ask quickly.

Nora frowns, caught in a catch-22.

'It's fine, Nora.' A weary voice comes from behind her and a man steps out of the office. He has thick grey hair and a lined, kindly face. He is instantly familiar: this is one of the men from my dream. 'Hello, Katy,' he says, and Nora doesn't react to my name, making me wonder if she's known all along who I am. 'Long time no see.'

Chapter Thirty-Three

Maggie

Maggie drove out towards the coast, the built-up housing area giving way to green grass and blue sky, and eventually sparkling turquoise sea. Sunlight winked off the glassy surface of the water, broken by foamy white streaks left behind a jet ski, or the dark outline of a swimmer. Outside of the village, looking towards the horizon, you could almost imagine that Abigail Warner wasn't missing, that everything was still right with the world. Then you would catch sight of another search group, or a poster on a lamp post fluttering in the breeze, and realise that this tragedy wasn't just affecting Pentraeth, it was touching the whole island, probably the whole of Wales.

'Maggie.' Linda Fisher opened the door and wiped her hands on the front of her apron, looking every bit the Welsh country housewife. She was about five foot three, and her brown hair fell in natural waves to her shoulders when it was left down. Maggie couldn't imagine it being cut short like a lot of women her age were prone to do. Today though, Linda had been baking and her waves were tied back into a ponytail, only the odd wisp flying free. She pulled the door open wider and stepped back to allow Maggie in. 'You'll be wanting George, I suppose? Only he's gone shopping.'

Maggie could hear the disapproval in her voice, but she didn't care. The rest of the island was helping to search for Abigail Warner – why should George Fisher be exempt? Because he failed to find a missing girl twenty-five years ago? All the more reason to do everything he could now, as far as Maggie was concerned. 'I won't take too much of his time, Linda. I understand what an effect Elsie's disappearance had on him.'

'I don't think you do, actually. Although if you don't find Abigail Warner, you'll have a small idea, I suppose, but you still won't truly know. Not unless you have to arrest your best friend for murdering a five-year-old girl. Not unless you have to tell another best friend that you have no idea where their little girl's body is, that they can never lay her to rest. Even after Jill and Katy and Jordan left, and people started to move on, it was like Elsie hung over all the families that were close to the Buttons and the Bowens. Like there was a little corner of the community that would never be the same again. People moved on and new people moved in, but as long as she's still out there, the island can't forget. And now Abigail...' Linda tailed off, her voice choking up. She looked at Maggie. 'I used to do sewing club with Jill Bowen and Helen Button. They ate cottage pie at this very table, and drank wine in that sitting room. They weren't some story you read in the paper. Beth didn't even know Elsie, but she used to dream about finding her alive and just trapped somewhere and letting her out.'

Maggie looked at the woman's face, drawn and pale, and realised she'd never seen her looking so old. The toll this must be taking. But still, she had a job to do, and she wasn't going to apologise for doing it.

Before she could say the words out loud though, Linda sighed. 'I know that none of what I've said will make a difference. You're here because it's your job, and you're good at it. But so was George. And he still couldn't bring Elsie Button back alive. You just remember that. Just in case.'

—

Linda paced the stone flagged floor in the kitchen, wiping her hands on the tea towel she'd been clutching for the past ten minutes while she continuously pressed redial on the phone. She'd agreed to call George, but he wasn't picking up and Linda had no idea where he was — he was only supposed to be popping to Hardy's for some dog food and wine, but Linda had phoned the shop and the man who ran it, Geoff Landsdowne — there hadn't been a Hardy in Hardy's for ten years or more — said he hadn't see George all morning and he was run off his feet with people searching for the little girl and had been besieged with reporters for the last two days. He was on his last nerve, he told Linda, and he knew he shouldn't say that because it was a terrible business and it was good that all these people had come so far to help — he met one woman who had driven from Derby, if you could believe it, and—

'Yes, Geoff, it's lovely, really good of them, and I hope they find her soon too, but I need to go for now,' Linda interrupted. 'But tell Gina I'll need some of that raspberry filling in the week for a pie and I'll be down to see her for it myself. Love to.' And with an exasperated huff, she hung up the phone. 'Well, the long and short of that is that he's not been to the shop. So Lord knows where he is, but it isn't exactly unusual — George could spend seven hours being stopped by people for a quick chat and never come back with what he went out for.'

'Why isn't he out searching for Abigail, Linda?' It had been bugging her ever since the first time she'd gone to see her old DI. She knew he was retired, but everyone else on the island was out looking. Why wasn't he offering his time? Did he know that the search was pointless? What information did he have that she didn't?

'I don't know if you know this,' Linda said, 'I don't suppose you would. But George and I, well we never completely lost touch with Jill Bowen after she took the kids away. It wasn't her fault, what happened to poor Elsie, and her life was completely ruined. I'd call every few weeks just to see how she was coping, then later on it became every few months, but she'd tell me about what Jordan and Katy were up to.'

'I guessed you were still in touch when you said that Jordan had called you to tell you about Jill's suicide attempt. It's a strange coincidence, don't you think? That she tries to commit suicide on the day Abigail goes missing.'

'No more than this girl going missing on the anniversary of Elsie's disappearance,' Linda said, clicking the kettle on to boil even though she'd already boiled it once while she was on the phone to the shop. She busied herself taking mismatched cups and saucers out of the cupboard. Maggie couldn't help but notice that she hadn't said Abigail's name once, and yet she didn't have a problem saying Elsie's name.

'Kathryn is here,' Maggie said. She probably shouldn't have, but she had wanted to see Linda's reaction.

Linda froze, the spoon of sugar suspended just above her cup.

'On the island. She came when she heard about Abigail Warner. Your Beth has been keeping an eye on her.'

'She didn't mention it to me,' Linda remarked, her voice barely above a whisper. 'I don't understand why Kathryn would think she needed to come here. I mean, the more the merrier when it comes to searchers, but didn't she see that it might be a bad idea?' Before Maggie could answer, the back door slammed. 'That'll be George,' Linda said, getting to her feet. 'Oh hell, Maggie, I don't suppose there's any way you could leave this alone, could you?' She was speaking quickly, hoping to get it all out before George could hear. 'It's just that it was such a horrible time for everyone, but especially George, and there's really no point in dragging it all up again now, is there?'

'Does George know something, Linda? Do you? Why would Katy Bowen come back to the place where her dad murdered a child? Unless she thinks he didn't, for some reason? Unless she's got some idea about clearing his name now another girl is missing?'

'Hush now, *please*.'

George appeared in the doorway, a frown on his face. 'Maggie, I saw your car. Is there news about the girl?'

Maggie shook her head. 'No news. I came because I need your help. I'm running out of ideas, George. No one else knows what this is like, no one but you. And now I've got Jim Taylor asking about the bloody Bowen house curse and a Boggly. What the hell is a Boggly?'

To Maggie's surprise, George gestured to the sitting room off the kitchen, his face etched with despondency. 'If we're going to talk about this the least we can do is make ourselves comfy,' he said, going over to the glasses cabinet and taking out a tumbler. 'And I'm going to need something stronger than a cup of tea.' Maggie followed him, but not without catching a glimpse of Linda's face, almost pleading her to leave George out of all this.

–

'The curse was just one of those stupid schoolyard things. *Don't go to the Bowen house or Patrick Bowen will get you.* Never mind that Patrick Bowen was alive and behind bars… kids don't care much for common sense and fact. But the Boggly… he first came up during one of the interviews with Child Services.'

George blew down the blow-poke into the fire and it seemed to magically spring into life. Maggie had always wondered at how people could do that, sending flames dancing up the chimney like a mystic shaman charming a snake. Now he placed the blow-poke back into its holder and sat back on his heels, rubbing his hands together and warming them against the heat of the fire.

'She was asked about where she and Elsie had been that morning, and if they had seen anyone she knew there. "Yes," she said, "we saw the Boggly. He was hiding in the trees. Elsie screamed and wanted to run away, but I wasn't scared and I made her come with me to find him." "And did you find him?" the psychiatrist asked and Katy waited a few seconds, maybe thirty or so, and said, "Yes. We found him and he got Elsie but not me. Maybe I'm his favourite."'

Maggie's jaw dropped open. 'She literally said "he got Elsie?" Could she ID this guy?'

George shook his head sadly, threw another handful of kindling onto the fire and retreated back to his favourite chair. Linda came in and sat opposite him silently. 'She couldn't ID him because he didn't exist,' he said, his voice sounding sad. 'The psychiatrist said Katy had probably seen her father hurting Elsie, or maybe just taking her off somewhere, and the memory of it was so terrifying that she ascribed this kind of bogeyman creature to block out the fact that the person who hurt her best friend was someone she loved and trusted.'

'So you think Katy saw what happened that day?' Maggie asked. She stood up and gestured towards the whisky bottle with her tea mug. 'You mind if I get in on that?'

George nodded. 'Help yourself. We don't see know how much she saw, not really. We know she went into the woods with Elsie that day and we know that she wandered out and told her mum she was hungry. When her mum asked if Elsie had gone home, which she sometimes did, Katy said she had been playing with the Boggly and she hadn't seen her since. Jill called Helen – she said she wasn't concerned, but she'd been meaning to call her that day for something anyway so she just phoned to check Elsie had made it home okay. Helen said she hadn't been back all morning and got her shoes on and went straight to the Bowens' house, where Jill – and Patrick – were already searching the woods. Helen later said they both seemed panicked, Jill looked as though she might have been crying, but she couldn't be sure. After knocking on all the houses between the wooded area and the Buttons' house, half the village was out searching and the police had been called. We searched the entire area, but there was no evidence of either Elsie or anyone else having been there. No one had seen anyone unusual or suspicious, so Katy's story about the Boggly was put down to kids' games, until her father was arrested.'

He looked as though it had cost him his entire week's energy to get that story out after all these years.

Maggie slugged back her whisky and stared into the empty mug.

'Do you think that now?' she asked quietly. 'Now that another girl is missing?' She saw Linda shudder.

George looked up at her sharply. 'Abigail Warner's disappearance has nothing whatsoever to do with Elsie,' he said, his voice sharper than Maggie had ever heard it before. 'If I know anything, I know that is true. The person who killed Elsie has been far away for twenty-five years and digging into the past isn't going to help us find that poor child.'

'And the fact that she was taken from the same house? And that you never found the Boggly?' Maggie knew deep down that what she had told Jim Taylor was true – there had been no monster living in the woods for twenty-five years, waiting to snatch another young girl.

'Coincidence and kiddies' stories,' he said, shaking his head. He stood up, conversation apparently over. 'And I don't see how any of it is going to help you find this girl. That should be your focus, what's happenin' today, not twenty-five years ago. That and getting Katy Bowen off this island. She should never have come back here. She has no idea how dangerous it is for her here.'

Chapter Thirty-Four

Kathryn

'What do you want from me, Katy?' Kevin asks when Nora eventually leaves us alone. We're in the corner of the empty 'restaurant' – the one I didn't get to use this morning thanks to my unceremonious removal – and Nora has busied herself making a fire, bringing us tea, and doing everything she can to overhear something. We sit in weird uncomfortable silence until she can't find any more reasons to hang around, which is when he poses his rather blunt question.

'Is that anyway to greet an old family friend?' I snap, feeling suddenly very tired and defensive.

'You do know what's going on here, don't you?' he asks slowly, as if speaking to a small child. 'You can see, perhaps, why this might not be the best place for you to be right at this very moment?'

'I don't know why,' I say, holding up my hands in an 'I'm innocent, guv' gesture. 'After all, Patrick is about the only person who can't have done this, am I right? This time the Bowens are innocent. Unless you think maybe I came here to carry on the old man's legacy? Twenty-five years later, the prodigal daughter returns to finish what her child-killer father started?'

Kevin flinches, as though every word is a dart thrown at his face. 'I know life has been difficult for you, but I don't think there's any need for you to talk like that.'

I'm certain he has no idea how difficult life is when the person you hero-worship turns out not to be human – after all, it's hard enough to find out that your parents aren't infallible and as liable to fuck up as anyone – but to find out that no, your father isn't human but an inhuman monster, evil, paedo, the devil, vile, wicked – the list went on – no, I don't think Kevin quite knows how that feels. Years of expensive therapy means there is no emotional outburst from me though. I give my best abashed look and apologise.

'I just guess I have so many questions still,' I say, trying my best to sound like the sad little girl everyone thinks I should be. 'With Patrick, I mean... my dad...' the words almost choke me, 'pleading guilty and refusing to tell anyone why he did what he did or how Elsie died or even where she is...' I look up at him through my lashes. 'I don't suppose he ever gave you any answers, did he?'

Kevin takes in a deep breath. 'I wasn't his defence attorney, you probably know that already.'

'But you were his friend,' I interject. 'He told you something, didn't he? That's why he called you the morning Elsie went missing.'

Kevin's eyebrows almost disappear into his hairline. 'Who told you that?'

'It's in the police report,' I lie quickly, then, before he can ask how I've seen the police files, I say, 'or maybe my mum told me, I don't know, so much has been said. But it's true though? You called him that morning, before Elsie was reported missing? What did you call him for?'

'I don't remember,' Kevin says too quickly. He's lying. 'I spoke to your father a lot around that time, I might have called him that day.'

'Oh come on,' I say. 'You expect me to believe that you can't remember what you said to the infamous Patrick Bowen on the day a five-year-old girl was killed, and he said he did it? Was it just a "Hey Pat, how's it hanging? Did you see the game last night like?" or more of a "Hey Patrick, someone just killed a kid and I could really use you taking the blame for it y'know"?'

Kevin blanches. 'Did you come here to accuse me of setting your father up? On the basis of a single phone call?'

I was being blasé, of course, it's what I do when I'm tense or angry, I get flippant and offensive. I sigh. 'No, not really, Mr Wilson. I'm not suggesting that. But something is wrong here, and I think you know what I mean. I think if there was anyone who knows more about what happened to Elsie Button than they have made public, it's you.'

Kevin stands up, he's going to leave. Before he does, he looks at me, deep into my eyes like he's trying to decide something. 'We all make choices in life, Katy. And we all have to live with them afterwards, for however long that may be. I was sorry to hear about your mother, I hope she comes around soon.'

I don't know why I lie, when he can so easily check, but I guess I just want to see his face, to gauge his reaction. 'Oh, don't you know?' I say quickly, before he can walk away. 'My mother came out of her coma. She should be able to speak to someone later today. She should be able to tell us why she tried to kill herself.'

He doesn't turn away fast enough to mask the way his face completely drains of colour. 'That's excellent news,' he says, his voice strained. 'Please send her my love. I have to go now.' He turns back for the most fleeting of moments. 'It was good to see you Katy, but I think it's best you go home now. We have enough to deal with on the island right now. Take care of yourself.'

As he walks away, I see him slide his mobile phone from his pocket. I'd give anything to be able to hear the call he's about to make.

Outside, I check my phone and, true to her word, Beth has sent me a text with her address. She's not going to be home for an hour – will I be okay until then? I text back that of course I will, I have my laptop to keep me busy and I'll see her back at hers in an hour. After a quick text to Miriam, who informs me that my mum's condition hasn't changed and she's glad the lawyer didn't have me killed, I decide to head to the pub to avail myself of their free Wi-Fi. Perhaps that's where Beth is anyway. I can give her a lift home.

The pub is fuller than it was when I came in here with Beth last night, more with outsiders than locals by the looks of it. It makes me wonder for a minute what the holidaymakers who were here when Abigail went missing are doing. Have they joined the search? Is the beach still full of children running in and out of the surf, screaming delightedly as the waves catch their feet, or is everyone too scared that an abductor is on the loose? I remember what happened to Praia da Luz after Madeleine McCann disappeared – people either went there to see the scene of horror or didn't go there at all. This place probably suffered the same after Elsie, and unless Abigail is found safe, the islanders have a tough time ahead. Even if she is found, with the news coverage Abigail's disappearance is getting, the name Pentraeth will probably once again become synonymous with missing children.

Dai is behind the bar again, a seemingly permanent fixture like Ted Danson in *Cheers*. At the pubs in Manchester, I don't think I've ever been served by the same waiflike teenager more than once.

He nods his head slightly to indicate that he remembers me, but he doesn't smile or speak. Sitting with Beth doesn't get me a free insider's pass then. I remember his words of warning last night and wonder if I should have chosen somewhere else to wait, but what is he going to do to me in front of a pub full of people? I clear my throat to make sure my words don't come out as a croak and order a vodka and tonic. Well, at least it's not on the rocks. 'Beth not here?' I ask as Dai places the glass in front of me.

He looks around in what I assume is supposed to be sarcasm, but he actually just manages to look like he can't really remember. 'Can't see her,' he says, and turns back to the till. Charming.

I take my drink and sit down at the nearest table. If Beth isn't at work, I'll just stay for one and then I'll go and wait in the car. Google Maps assures me it's only a short drive to her apartment, but I don't really want to draw attention to myself with a drink driving arrest today.

I'm reaching down to pull my laptop out of my bag when a shadow falls across the table. A man, probably late fifties, casually dressed, with a backpack slung over one shoulder, is standing next to my table.

'Mind if I sit here?' he asks.

I look around, not caring about being obvious. I actually can't see any other seats and he's already got a drink in his hand. Letting out a very obvious sigh, I gesture at the spare seat at my table. 'Be my guest,' I say.

'Thanks.' He sits down and an awkward silence hangs between us.

I need to get my laptop out quickly before he feels he has to start a conversation, but it's jammed in my bag and… Fuck, too late.

'You here helping with the search?' he asks.

'Yes,' I reply, hoping the shortness of my answer indicates that I don't want to make friends.

'Horrible, isn't it?' he says, clearly not one to take a hint. 'Do you think they'll find her?'

'I d—' My eyes narrow in suspicion. He said 'they', not 'we'. 'What are you here for?'

The man scrunches up his face in a 'you got me' kind of gesture. 'You'd think after nearly thirty years I'd be better at hiding it. I'm working on a story about the disappearance.'

'Reporter,' I say, my heart sinking.

He nods and leans in close.

'Thing is, Kathryn,' he says. Hearing him say my real name makes me feel sick. How had I been so stupid to think I could come here in the middle of a suspected abduction case and no one know who I am? 'If I got a quote from you – that would pretty much make the last thirty years worth it.'

All of a sudden, I'm aware that more than one person in the pub is sneaking surreptitious glances our way. Shit. Shit, shit, shit.

'Piss off,' I say, glad that I haven't managed to take my laptop out after all. It makes it easier to grab my bag and stand up to leave.

'That's what your mother said, twenty-five years ago,' he says, quiet enough that only I can hear. 'But we printed the story anyway. You can't stop the news, Kathryn, but

207

you can work with it. How do you think tomorrow's papers are going to look? Word that you were here got out earlier this afternoon when you were spotted in the library – plenty of time for you to make the front pages. I can't stop that now, but I can put your side across. I can tell your story from your point of view, rather than the one they give you.'

I hate myself that I'm even considering his words. I know how journalists work – nothing he does is for my good. But that doesn't mean he's wrong. On a slow news day, me being here might warrant a local scoop. On the day after a child goes missing on Elsie's anniversary, that's front page, baby.

'Wait,' I say, lowering myself back into the seat slowly. I don't know if there's some journalist's code that has stopped the rest of the pub descending on me like a pack of wolves, but I almost feel the collective sigh as I sit back down. 'What do you mean, "what my mother said"? What she said to *you*? Did you cover Els— the murder here before?'

He smiles confidently and I curse myself for not realising he was press the moment I saw him. I can only argue that he caught me off guard.

'I did,' he says. 'I was on the scene within hours of Elsie's disappearance.'

'Who do you work for?'

'*The Guardian*.' He fumbles in his back pocket for ID. He's not lying this time.

'I'll talk to you,' I say, without thinking it through any further. He's right, after all, the story is going to be out by morning, there's no chance of me staying here now, so I might as well see what information I can get from him. 'But not here.'

He nods eagerly; his face looks like I've just asked him to come back to mine and told him I'm not wearing underwear. 'We can go to my car?'

'As tempting as that sounds…' I wince. 'This is my friend's address. Meet me there in forty minutes.'

I'm going to have to admit to Beth who I am before the morning papers. Hopefully she'll either be cool about it or too stunned-slash-intrigued to refuse to let us in. If not, we'll have to find somewhere else for our little chat. Forty minutes gives me time to decide what to say to him and what I want to ask.

He takes the piece of paper I hold out to him. 'This the police officer?' he asks.

The question throws me off guard. 'Huh?'

'The girl you've been hanging around with? PC Fisher, I believe. This her place? Are you sure she's going to be okay with me turning up there? They don't usually like us, the police.'

Warmth floods my cheeks, his words ringing in my ears. I've never felt so stupid in my entire life. A police officer. She knew who I was from the moment she ran over to me on the search field. And I walked straight into it.

'I've got to go,' I say. 'Meet me outside that address. Make it an hour. PC Fisher and I need a chat first.'

–

Outside, I scurry down a side alley and lean out of sight against the back wall of the pub, breathing in as deeply as I can manage. The smell round here is rank, this is where they keep the bins and anyone who's been in a pub the morning after the night before knows the smell of stale alcohol. Add to that the stench of urine and what smells like a rotting animal and you've got some idea what the alley behind the Old Lion and Tap smells like. I try holding my breath as I dial Beth – sorry, *PC Fisher's* – number, but it rings out, no answer. Fisher? Haven't I heard that name before?

I can't think straight. Everything is thumping around in my head, every word I said to her, everything she said to me. I'm mentally scanning every conversation to see if I've said anything that she can use against me. Does she think I kidnapped Abigail? Is that why she's been sticking to me like glue? Maybe she thinks I'll lead her to where Abigail is being kept. Well, she's wasting police time on that one.

I put my hands over my face and resist screaming. I dial again; the loud ringing in my ear means I don't hear the footsteps behind me, I don't even know anyone is there until something goes over my head and I'm being dragged to the floor.

Chapter Thirty-Five

Maggie

Maggie sighed when she saw Beth Fisher's name flash up on the screen of her mobile. She'd only given her number to the girl in case of emergency, and the only emergency Beth should be concerned about right now was one concerning Kathryn Bowen.

'DI Grant,' she said, hoping the tone of her voice would make Beth reconsider the phone call and hang up.

'DI Grant, I'm so sorry to bother you,' Beth sounded like she'd rather be calling anyone but Maggie right now.

Still, Maggie struggled to quite manage a conciliatory tone.

'Then don't.'

'I… um…'

Maggie sighed. 'Just spit it out. What's she done?'

'What's who done?'

'Kathryn Bowen. That is who you're calling about, isn't it? So what's she done?'

Beth paused. 'She's not answering my calls, ma'am. She was going to see Kevin Wilson at The Swimming Unicorn earlier, then she was supposed to meet me fifteen minutes ago, but I missed a call from her and now I can't get hold of her.'

Maggie waited for the emergency, but Beth had stopped talking – that was obviously the only information she had to impart.

'PC Fisher,' she said slowly, trying not to sound as angry as she felt. 'Every available officer – in fact every available person – in a hundred-mile radius is searching for Abigail Warner. I have been awake for what feels like four years. Are you seriously calling to ask me to pull resources from a missing child case to follow up on the Case of the Late Grown Woman?'

'No, ma'am, of course not. I just thought I should let you know sooner rather than later.' Maggie heard a doorbell ring in the background of the call. 'Wait a sec…'

Wait a sec? Had she just been put on hold by a bloody PC? A new one, at that? 'No comment,' she heard Beth say in the background. A male voice cut over her.

'Kathryn Bowen told me to meet her here,' it said. 'She was going to give me an interview.'

Oh brilliant, Maggie thought. Now they had the Bowen girl giving out interviews. Any minute now Paul Gascoigne was going to show up with a chicken leg and a fishing rod. She strained to hear PC Fisher's reply.

'Why would she talk to you?'

A pause.

'Because I told her the papers were going to run the story of her being on the island whether she spoke to me or not. And I told her I could give her some information about the original Elsie Button case.'

'What information?'

'Nothing the police don't already know,' he said. 'Although I got the distinct impression she didn't know that she was mates with a police officer. Been doing some undercover, have you?'

Maggie's heart sank.

'And you filled her in, I suppose?' she heard Beth say.

'Only fair. Not right to lie to the poor girl, she's been through enough. She's not here then, I take it?'

'No she's not,' Maggie heard Beth snap. 'And she's not bloody likely to be now either. Where did you see her?'

'The Old Lion and Tap. No point in going there though, she left before me. Her car is still by the B&B.'

'Right, well thanks a bunch.' Maggie heard the door slam closed. 'Wanker.' Then... 'God, sorry, ma'am, I forgot you were on the line.'

'Yeah, I thought as much,' Maggie replied. 'Did I hear all that right? Kathryn Bowen knows you're an undercover and she's talking to reporters?'

Beth sighed on the other end of the phone. 'That was about the gist of it, yes, ma'am.'

'You'd better get back here then,' Maggie said, glancing at her watch. George Fisher's words rang in her ears and she was torn between getting back to the search ground and finding Kathryn Bowen. She did not have time for this. She sighed. 'We need to find her before she says – or does – something stupid.'

–

While she waited for PC Fisher to arrive, Maggie googled the number for The Swimming Unicorn and dialled.

'Nora, it's Maggie Grant. Is there a woman staying there by the name of Verity something? Might have been talking to Kevin Wilson.'

'Sorry, love, I don't know who you're talking about. We haven't had anyone by that name staying here and Mr Wilson has been out all day.'

Maggie gaped at the phone. Her bedside manner was really being tested today. 'Did I forget to identify myself properly, Nora? It's DI Maggie Grant, as in really-important-police-person–Grant, so stop pissing me around and tell me where the girl is.'

'I'm sorry, Dee Eye Grant,' Nora said the letters slowly and clearly. 'But I don't have a clue who you're talking about. If I see anyone called Verity wandering around here, I'll let you know, will I? But I doubt I'll see anyone of that name.'

So Nora knew who Kathryn really was. Hardly surprising. She looked the spitting image of Patrick, all that red hair and those blue eyes.

'Put Wilson on,' Maggie snapped.

'You just missed him, love. I'll tell him you called.' And just like that the infernal woman hung up. *Hung up.* She was lucky they were in the middle of the biggest case to have hit Anglesey since Elsie Button, otherwise Maggie would have sent someone to arrest the insolent old bag.

When Beth arrived, she hung sheepishly around the doorway. Maggie called her in with an impatient wave. 'Come on,' she said. 'I've got about forty places I need to show my face in this afternoon. We need to get this situation under control, and quickly. Is there any chance she's just gone back to Manchester, knowing that everyone knows who she is here?'

'Her car is still at the B&B. Shall I call Nora?'

Maggie grimaced. 'Don't bother, she's pulling the innocent old woman act.'

Beth's phone began to ring and they both stared at it.

'Are you going to answer that?' Maggie asked.

'Oh god, yes, sorry.' Beth answered the call on loud-speaker. 'Verity?'

'Verity?' The voice at the other end snapped. 'Why would Verity be call— Oh bugger. Is this Beth?'

Looking totally confused now, Beth nodded her head. 'Yes, this is Beth. Who am I speaking to?'

The woman sighed as if coming to a difficult conclusion. 'You are speaking to Miriam Walker and that's because Miriam Walker isn't speaking to Kathryn Starling, née Bowen, the girl I'm assuming has been calling herself Verity. I can't get hold of her, I've been calling for hours. She gave me your number and said she was staying the night with you.'

'She was supposed to be,' Beth replied. 'She never showed up. She's not answering the phone to me either.'

'Have you called the police?'

'She's only been out of contact two hours. I—'

'Long enough, given the circumstances. Look, I'm on my way, but I'll be a couple of hours even breaking every speed limit. You need to go to the police and I'll meet you there. Just as long as I don't end up the main suspect. I've seen those bloody Poirot films. I just hope they take you seriously.'

'I have a feeling that won't be a problem.' Maggie saw Beth grimace. 'I'm with DI Maggie Grant now. I'm a police officer, Miriam. I was assigned to get close to Kathryn the minute we found out she was back on Anglesey.'

After a few choice cuss words and a promise from Miriam that she was obviously only joking about breaking the speed limit, Beth managed to convince her to meet them at the police station, even if the old lady sounded angry as hell that she'd been deceiving Kathryn for the last two days.

'If something is wrong, I'm the best hope Kathryn has. You'll do better to work with me. Then you can cuss me and flip me off as much as you like. When she's found. Safe.'

A grunt of concession came from Miriam and Beth raised her eyebrows at Maggie.

'She sounds delightful,' Maggie commented. She pointed a pen at Beth. 'Make a list of all the places she might want to visit and I'll send someone to check them out. When this friend of hers gets here, ask her for the number of anyone Kathryn might have contacted to say where she was going. Then get out the Elsie Button case file and make a list of all known acquaintances of the Bowen family mentioned in there. If she's still on the island, I want her found without a fuss. Does this journalist know she's missing?'

'No, just that she didn't turn up at mine. I think he assumes she's just annoyed at me.'

'Good,' Maggie said. 'Let's keep it that way. We don't need anyone else finding her before we do. I'll go and speak to Dai.'

–

The pub was considerably less busy than it had been the last time Maggie had popped in there to pick up some sandwiches. Dai had been good to the police, sorting them out with food and drinks in takeaway cups whenever they popped in. Now, the pub looked almost deserted. Maybe Ken, the reporter, had told the rest of his lot that that Kathryn had gone home, taking their Bowen angle on the missing chid story with them. Everyone else was back at the search ground. Maggie wondered how long that would last. How many nights would people give? As many as it took? No, people would start to drift back to their lives, they had families to go to and livings to be made. The only lives that wouldn't go back to normal were the people who lived on the island.

'Dai in?' Maggie asked the girl behind the bar. Sally, she thought her name was. Sloppy Sally, Dai called her behind her back, on account of how many times he had to empty the slops tray when she was working.

'In back.' Sally motioned her head and Maggie took that as a sign to go through.

Dai was indeed in the back, in the cubbyhole that constituted an office, his feet on the desk, reading one of the red tops – or looking at the pictures more likely. When he saw her, he gave her the once-over like he did every time. She was used to it by now, but she still recognised how gross it was.

'Maggie,' he said with a nod. ''Ow can I help you?'

'I'm looking for a girl who was here recently with Beth Fisher. Do you know who I mean?'

'Reckons I do, yeah. Where's she gone then? Run out of kids to snatch?'

'Give over, Dai. She can't help who her dad is.'

'She can stay the fuck away from here though, can't she? Rubbing our noses in it, pretending we won't know who she is. On the anniversary as well, of all days. I'm just glad Helen hardly leaves the farmhouse these days – if she'd seen her, it would have tipped her over the edge. Maybe she's gone back to Manchester where no one knows what blood she's got.'

'Her car's still here,' Maggie said. 'And she was last seen in your pub. I'll have to go and speak to Helen, obviously, but seeing as you're making no secret of how much you disliked the Bowen family, maybe I should pull you into the station for questioning first.'

Dai stood up, towering over Maggie. 'You won't do that,' he said, his whole demeanour exuding confidence. 'Practically the whole of Anglesey dislikes the Bowens. You going to arrest us all?'

'Ever heard the words "last to see the victim"?'

'Ever heard the words "watertight alibi"?' Dai retorted. 'I saw her walk out of this bar and I stayed right where I was, serving pints for the next hour. Dozens of witnesses, journalists, film crews. There's no way I could'a done anything to her.'

'And you didn't see which way she went after she left?'

'Nope.'

'Can I see your CCTV?'

Dai sucked through his teeth. 'Broke. Sorry,' he added, not sounding at all sorry.

'And you didn't call anyone to say she'd been in here, like you did the first time?'

'Don't know what you're talking about.'

'So if I pulled your phone records there won't be any outgoing calls at all?'

'Not made by me. Sometimes punters ask to use the phone and I just tell 'em to put a quid in the tip jar.'

'Convenient in a time where everyone has a mobile.'

Dai grinned. 'Some calls you don't want traced back to you though, eh?'

'And might one of these mystery punters have used the phone at the time in question?'

Dai shrugged. 'Always possible. Look, if there's nothing else I'll have to get back to the bar before half my stock ends up in the slops tray. But when you find Beth's new friend, you can tell her from us that she's not welcome here. But I'll reckon she already knows that by now.'

Chapter Thirty-Six

Kathryn

s Images swirl in and out of my head. I try to focus on one, but it's like an old showreel playing over and over and I can't find a pause button. There are men – how many, I can't see, four, five? Or is it just the same man on a loop, over and over? One of them looks like Patrick, only he's young, like when I was a child, and he's in sepia tones like in an old photograph. He's angry, and sad... and scared. He's yelling, and there's a boy – is that Jordan? He looks more frightened than Patrick. Another image fades in and I'm there this time, like I'm watching a grainy home movie from the eighties. I'm grasping a teddy bear and being pushed out of the house – there's yelling and screaming, this man he wants us out desperately, but I'm not afraid of him – he's helping us.

My head hurts so badly – am I in hospital? It doesn't smell like a hospital, but it hurts to open my eyes, so I won't for now. I'll just sink back into the pictures, the man whose name is Doc and the little bear I clutch so tightly because it reminds me of Elsie, except now it's being taken away and Elsie is lying dead in the woods— Wait, no, she's dead on a table and she's looking at me like it's all myfault and I try to scream at her to run, but the words won't come out and anyway she's not running – why isn't she running? Doesn't she know how dangerous the monster is?

Chapter Thirty-Seven

Maggie

The mysterious disappearance of Kathryn Bowen was one saga Maggie didn't need right now. She was under pressure from every side, making hourly phone calls to the Warner family, who were falling to pieces – the FLO had proved her worth more than once over the last two days – and constant updates to the DCI, who was spending all of his time doing press conferences and asking her what to say in them. What no one wanted to be discussing right now was Patrick Bowen and his family. For a start, it distracted from the fact that a small child was missing, but most of all it raised suggestions that something had been done wrong the first time around. She needed to get her mind back on the case she was supposed to be focusing on and let PC Fisher deal with Kathryn Bowen.

The door to The Pit shook with the sound of someone knocking.

'Yes,' Maggie called. Jesus, you escape for two minutes…

'DI Grant, there's a woman at the front desk to see you.' The duty officer barely poked his head around the door. 'She's got a little girl with her, says it's about Abigail.'

'The little girl wouldn't happen to *be* Abigail, by any chance?' Maggie muttered, knowing there was not a universe, this one or parallel, in which she was that lucky.

'Afraid not. Same age though. Maybe our guy tried to strike again.'

Maggie could have sent one of the team to speak to the woman, but if she stood in one place too long, the powers that be could sense it and would inevitably ring to tell her they really needed this wrapped up, as if Abby's disappearance was a drill she could bring an end to at any time. No, if she was locked in an interview room with a neighbour who saw someone without a waxed jacket on the island in 2006 and it's been on her mind ever since, at least no one else could get to her. She made her way to the front of the station.

'DI Grant,' Maggie held out her hand to the only woman in the reception area clutching a small girl like she thought the abductor might jump out and grab her any second. 'You asked to see me?'

'DI Grant!' A voice came from the other side of the reception and Maggie looked over to see Jim Taylor waving a pen in the air. 'Can I have a quick word?'

'Sure you don't want two?' Maggie called back, a smile on her face to soften the blow of her insult.

Jim grinned. 'I've been waiting all morning.'

'Half an hour more won't kill you then.' She turned to the woman, who looked startled by the exchange. 'Sorry about that,' Maggie said. 'Gets a bit busy in here at the moment, as I'm sure you can appreciate. Do you want to come through where we can chat somewhere quieter?'

The woman gave one glance back at Jim and nodded quickly. Dragging the girl alongside her, she followed Maggie to the interview room they used when children were involved. It wasn't much different to the others, except the chairs were a bit comfier and there were a few pretty paintings on the walls. A bucket of toys lay discarded in the corner – thankfully they didn't have to use this room often.

Maggie showed them both in, expecting the girl to be shy and intimidated. Instead, she looked at her mum and said loudly but politely, 'Can I play with those please?'

Her mum looked at Maggie, who nodded. 'Sure you can. We're going to have a little chat, okay? About what you said to me earlier.'

'I didn't mean it,' the girl's eyes widened and the mother's face fell.

'What do you mean you didn't mean it?'

'I don't really think Jessica smells, she just said it to me first.'

Her eyes began to water and Maggie's heart sank. Whatever the woman was here for had come from the kid. Evidence from children was notoriously unreliable and most of the time barely understandable.

'My name is Fran Harding,' the woman said. 'Josie goes to school with Abby Warner, they were best friends.'

'Were?' Maggie raised her eyebrows, but the woman didn't blush at her mistake.

'Well, I thought they still were, until this morning. We were supposed to have a play date with Abby this half-term, but Josie had seemed reluctant to go. When I asked her why, she just shrugged. This morning, she asked me if they'd found Abigail yet. I said not yet, she must be hiding really well. Josie said she was glad, because it meant she didn't have to go to play at her house.' Fran took a breath and made a face that said 'What can you do?' in reference to her daughter's insensitivity. Obviously Josie had no idea how serious Abby's disappearance was, all it meant to her was a dodged play date she'd been dreading anyway. 'I asked her why – I thought Abby was her best friend. She

224

replied by saying that Abby didn't want to be her friend anymore.'

'She doesn't,' Josie chipped in from the corner. 'She's got a new friend.'

'At school?' Maggie asked.

Fran shook her head slowly and widened her eyes.

'Not at school,' Josie said. 'At her home. Her new friend lives in the woods, I think. Behind her house. They play together after school sometimes, but Abby isn't allowed to tell her mummy.'

'Why isn't Abby allowed to tell her mummy?' Maggie asked, her heart thumping. She needed to get a trained child psychologist in here now, do this properly, but she didn't want to interrupt Josie while she was opening up.

Josie swung one of the bears into the air. 'Mums don't like it when you get grown-up friends,' Josie said. 'They get jealous and yell at the friend. Abby didn't want her mummy to yell at her friend.'

'Did she give her friend a name?'

Josie shook her head. 'Nope. Don't know.'

'What else did Abby say about her friend, Josie?'

Josie shrugged. She chucked the bear back into the box and started riffling through the other broken old tat in there. 'Um, she said that her friend was funny. They said monsters lived in Abby's house.'

Maggie looked at Fran, who made an 'I don't know' gesture.

'Monsters?'

'Yeah.'

'Wasn't Abby scared?' Maggie asked.

Josie laughed. 'They didn't still live there, silly. The monsters lived there years ago. Maybe hundreds. I don't know. Before Abby was born though.'

'Okay, I see.' Maggie smiled at her, trying to make sense of what she was hearing. Jesus, was someone living in that patch of wasteland at the back of the Warners' home? Hadn't it been searched countless times already? If someone was living in there, Maggie had no idea where or how, but she needed to find out before the press did and she lost her job.

She saw the girl and her mother out and walked straight into a commotion at the front desk. Miriam had arrived.

Miriam Pike wasn't at all what Maggie had been expecting. For a start, she was at least five foot seven or eight – Maggie had been imagining a small woman, a stereotypical feisty spitfire, but this woman looked like she'd eat Maggie's stereotype for breakfast and spit her out for being too chewy. She had a sharp grey graduated bob with a lighter streak running through the roots. She looked as though she'd stopped on the way to the police station for a cut and blow-dry. She was wearing black winged glasses and bright red lipstick. Perfectly manicured eyebrows were currently furrowed at the officer at the desk and her voice was so loud, sharp and Mancunian that Maggie was sure that Kathryn would hear it from wherever she was and come running.

'You must be Miriam,' Maggie called out, reluctant to draw the furious onslaught towards herself, but it had to be done sooner or later. The front desk clerk looked like he would cry with relief. 'Come on, you'd better follow me.' She looked around at the attention Maggie was already drawing. Luckily Jim Taylor seemed to have disappeared. 'Quickly.'

Without turning back to see if Miriam was indeed following her, Maggie headed off down the corridor towards the room she'd given Beth for her assignment.

She didn't want a lot of attention drawn to the fact that Patrick Bowen's daughter was even here, let alone missing.

Beth jumped up when she saw them coming.

'Ma'am, I asked front desk to notify me when Ms Pike arrived—'

Maggie held up a hand. 'Stand down, PC Fisher, I was seeing out a witness and just happened to be there when I heard Ms Pike's dulcet Manchester tones.'

'I'd like to just join the search party as quickly as possible,' Miriam said, slamming her bag down on the desk without responding to Maggie's jab. Clearly introductions and small talk weren't on the cards.

Maggie frowned. 'Search party?' she said, confused. 'I thought you were here about Kathryn?'

It was Miriam's turn to frown. 'I am. Don't tell me you've bloody found her already? I've been calling her phone this whole way, two hours of pressing redial and hearing the BT answerphone has driven me crazy.' She held up her hands. 'All hands free of course, officer.'

'No, we've heard nothing from her. It's just… well, the search parties are all for Abigail Warner. Surely you've heard about the missing girl?'

Miriam gave an exasperated sigh. 'Do you think I'm blind, deaf and stupid? Of course I know about the girl – that's why Kathryn was here in the first place, wasn't it? But are you telling me that not one of those search parties is looking for Kathryn? Then who is?'

Oh God. Maggie looked at Beth, who clearly didn't relish having to say, 'Well, just me at the moment. And you now,' she added hastily, as if this would make all the difference.

Miriam's eyes widened in horror behind her glasses. 'Just you? No offence, love, but you're the one who lost her in the first place, isn't there anyone more...' Maggie thought she was going to say 'competent', but Miriam chose tact and went for, 'more senior searching for her?' She looked at Maggie. 'You're the one in charge. Why aren't there more people looking?'

'Because I have a vulnerable five-year-old child whose parents are out of their heads with worry. And if Kathryn wasn't Patrick Bowen's daughter, we probably wouldn't be looking for her at all, not yet at least. She's an adult, she's not vulnerable and she's not from here. She could have just gone home for all we know.'

'Except her car is still here, so unless you're suggesting she fancied a very long walk to clear her head, she's somewhere on this island. And the fact that she hasn't turned up at your place and she isn't answering her phone suggests she's in danger.'

'I'm worried that if the press get hold of her being missing they'll go in a slightly different direction,' Maggie admitted.

'Which is?' demanded Miriam.

'A girl goes missing on the same day Patrick Bowen's daughter turns up on the island after twenty-five years? Some might say that's a hell of a coincidence. Some might even say that Kathryn is picking up where her dad left off, like father like daughter.'

Miriam looked like she would be prepared to fight anyone who dared suggest it. 'Ridiculous,' she snapped. 'Kathryn was miles away when she found out about the missing girl.'

'And that would come out, eventually,' Maggie said. 'The press already know she's on the island. If they find out she's missing, she might get the blame for Abigail's disappearance and she doesn't deserve that. If we can find her as quietly as possible without any fuss, that would be best all round. Because once the papers get wind that Patrick Bowen's daughter has absconded from the island on the same day a girl is kidnapped, on the anniversary of Elsie's disappearance – well, let's just say there's still a lot of bad feeling for the Bowens around here, and if she's not in danger now, she will be soon.'

Before Miriam could respond, Maggie turned to Beth.

'I managed to get hold of Kevin Wilson. He says he had no idea Kathryn was back on the island.'

'Probably lying,' Miriam said.

'Have you ever thought about joining the force?' Maggie muttered. 'Observation skills like those.'

'Oh no, love,' Miriam said without missing a beat, 'I can't stand the senior ranking officers, all sarcasm and coffee breaks,' she looked pointedly at the coffee in Maggie's hand. 'Who did you say you were again?'

'DI Maggie Grant,' Maggie replied, her voice stony. She saw PC Fisher trying to stifle a smile. 'And I'm the reason you – a civilian – has been allowed anywhere near this office to assist with our enquiries.' She took a deep breath and counted to three. 'What Kevin Wilson did tell us is that from his memory of the Bowen family's time on the island, there are very few people Kathryn would either remember or get the time of day from. Of course, we know that the Buttons were the closest family to the Bowens, but it's unlikely Kathryn would be stupid enough to show up there. Perhaps if we knew what she was trying to achieve coming back here?'

She raised her eyebrows at Miriam, who seemed not to have heard her.

'Ms Pike, we're just trying to help.'

'Kathryn's mother made an attempt to take her own life,' Miriam said, her voice reluctant. 'But before she did, she left Kathryn a voicemail that led her to believe that Patrick had been lying when he said he killed Elsie. That she wanted to tell Kathryn the truth before she took her life.'

'Is it a leap to assume that Kathryn's mother's message and subsequent attempt on her own life was some kind of confession? That Patrick took the blame for something his wife did?' Maggie asked Beth.

Beth shook her head. 'I don't think it's a leap to assume that – given that if she was guilty enough about something to try to kill herself, then it's entirely possible she was involved, but there's no proof of it anywhere. And even if it's true and Jill Bowen did kill Elsie – how does that help us with either Abigail's or Kathryn's disappearance? We know it would be highly unlikely Jill could be responsible for Abigail, she was in Manchester taking a lot of pills. So here's the question – did Jill see the news about Abigail's disappearance and try to kill herself because she was afraid the person she and Patrick covered for had struck again?'

'That would presumably explain the guilt, and the message to Kathryn,' Maggie mused. 'But as you say – it gets us no closer to explaining where Kathryn actually is, or who took Abigail.'

'Of course it does,' Miriam snapped. 'Because if PC Fisher here is correct and Patrick Bowen is innocent then the most likely person to try to get Kathryn out of the way is the one who doesn't want her sniffing around digging up the past. The person who really killed your Elsie Button. You solve that mystery and you find Kathryn and probably Abigail. Hopefully alive.'

Chapter Thirty-Eight

Kathryn

There are times I think I'm dreaming and times I know I must be awake. It feels like that moment just before you wake, where you're not sure if the beeping noise you can hear is in your dream or in real life, only it feels like that all the time – noises, smells. I try to open my eyes, but there's something tied tightly around my face, it feels itchy like wool. The smell of fresh paint is strong in my nostrils. Cramps shoot up my arms that have been pulled so tightly behind my back that I can't even wiggle my fingers. This can't be the dream, pain doesn't feel that real in dreams.

Underneath me is soft carpet and I push my head against it repeatedly, desperately trying to dislodge whatever is wrapped around my eyes. A crackling, staticky sound comes from my left, then a voice shouts, 'Stop it!' It happens so quickly and is so unexpected that I don't have chance to take in the voice itself, only the words.

I continue furiously rubbing my face against the floor, I can feel it slipping down now. As the edge of the blindfold slips down, bright light hits my eyes. Everything around me is pink: the carpet, so fluffy it could have been laid yesterday, the walls, the bed. I have only a few seconds to catch a glimpse of the figure on the bed, propped up against the headboard like a living doll. Her head is slumped to one side and she looks like she might be wearing make-up on her cheeks and lips. I can't see her breathing... She's not breathing. Oh shit.

I try to take in as much as I can, but my head is still pounding, my eyes swim in and out of focus. There's a picture on one of the walls, but I can't make out what it is of. I lurch forward, but the sound of a door opening behind me makes me jerk in the direction of the noise, trying to get a look at my captor. They are too fast, I'm grabbed by the hair and the blindfold is pulled up over my face, everywhere is dark again. I feel a sharp pain in my neck and just have time to register the pain before, nothing.

Chapter Thirty-Nine

Maggie

It was gone ten p.m. when PC Mel Stagg came to Maggie to tell her that there was something she wanted her to see. Time seemed to have lost all meaning to the members of the team, half of them had brought spare clothes into the office and were taking turns to sleep for an hour or two in the break room. The canteen staff had worked out a shift system that meant there was someone on hand to provide hot food most hours of the day, and Maggie was certain most of her officers had been in the building for so long they had no idea what day it was.

Maggie and a team of her most trusted searchers had been going over the woodland and the back of the Bowen house for two hours in the failing light. Maggie's hands were cut and bleeding, there was soil under her nails and in her hair and still they had found no trace of anyone living there. All they had found was a miniature grey bow tie from a stuffed animal, which could well have been Abigail's, but given that it was found at the back of her house meant absolutely jack shit.

'It's probably nothing,' PC Stagg prefaced her story with, the Get Out of Jail Free card for if it was a load of time-wasting nonsense, but Maggie could tell she thought it was something. 'And I'd have taken it to DS Bailey, but someone said he's back at Memorial Hall so…'

'It's fine,' Maggie said, despite the fact that on returning from the search, bloodied and knackered, she'd been pulled into a meeting with the Chief Superintendent and her DI, who both wanted to know exactly how Kathryn Bowen's alleged disappearance from a place she neither lived nor was wanted was anything to do with their case. She wasn't sure it was, she'd said, but Kathryn had been reported missing so she still had a duty to follow it up, and had put one of her least senior officers on the case. That had seemed to placate them – they obviously didn't think that using too many resources on a Bowen was a good look given the circumstances. Maggie didn't entirely disagree. Kathryn was a grown woman and could go anywhere she wanted, especially if where she wanted to go was far away from Anglesey. If it hadn't been for the fact that her car had been left exactly where she'd parked it two days before, then Maggie wouldn't have so much as opened a case file until she'd been reported missing in her hometown. Still, her car might have broken down, sure it looked fine, but if the engine didn't turn over, then perhaps she'd just got a taxi out of there and was on the train home. Fingers crossed. Now Maggie just wanted to be left alone for a minute to wash her hands and have a coffee. Still, such was the job. 'Show me what you have.'

She followed PC Stagg over to the desk space she was sharing with three other PCs. Given how fast the investigation had grown, they were having to make do and mend with a lot of things – space and technology being two of them. Still, PC Stagg had managed to get hold of a laptop and turned it now to face Maggie.

'I've been asked to go through the social media related to the case,' she said.

Maggie resisted groaning on behalf of the poor girl. First CCTV, now social media duty? If she still wanted into CID after this, she deserved it.

'There are a lot of trolls, obviously,' she was saying. 'The usual nasty comments about the mum not looking after Abigail properly, et cetera. There are some really horrible ones about what might have happened to her, I've already taken screenshots and reported those ones, but I don't think they are related, just a lot of sick fucks out there.' PC Stagg reddened and clapped a hand to her mouth, then over her eyes. 'I'm so sorry.'

Maggie couldn't help laughing. 'Do you think that the F word is going to offend my sensibilities, PC Stagg?'

PC Stagg looked mortified nonetheless. 'No,' she mumbled. 'Somehow I think you've probably heard worse.'

'You'd be right,' Maggie said. 'So if I'm not here to see the sick fucks or the perfect parent brigade, what am I here for?'

PC Stagg pointed at a line on the screen, to a commenter called Shakespeareisafraud. 'This one,' she said. 'Looks different. See how they crop up pretty consistently on all these threads? And they're all saying a variation of the same thing, not that Mrs Warner was a bad mum or that Mrs Warner deserved Abigail to be taken – some of them actually say that you know – but that Abigail is better off where she is. Which is weird, don't you think? Because the point is that no one knows where she is, so how can they know that? And before you say that's not enough, here, look at this one.'

She flicked over to a different tab where Shakespeare-isafraud had commented they should stop looking for her if they knew what was best for the little girl.

'That's a little odd, right? Like even in the McCann case, I saw tons of people say that if Madeleine was found she should be taken into care or whatever, but I never saw anyone say it would be best if she wasn't found at all.'

'Hmm,' Maggie mused. She was a lot older than PC Stagg and had learned over her considerable years on the force that there was no underestimating the utter bullshit people could come out with, especially in the social media age. But, at the same time, it could be little things like this that helped you catch the bad guys. It wasn't a stretch to think that if someone had taken Abigail – which was the only plausible solution at this stage – then they might be reading the forums to see what had been written about the case. It wasn't unheard of for killers to reply to comments, integrate themselves into investigations and even send the police letters. Mitchell Quy sent the lead detective in his wife's missing person's case a bottle of hair dye. Either way, they couldn't afford not to follow up on even the smallest of leads.

'Find out what you can about this Shakespeareisafraud. Certain social media sites can be really shitty about giving up the data on their users. I don't think we'll be able to get a warrant, but if you find enough, we might be able to get an IP address. Look especially for anything that might constitute harassment or any kind of inciting behaviour – we might be able to get around the warrant issue that way.'

PC Stagg nodded, her face eager. Maggie had to admit she'd misjudged the young woman, based a lot on the fact that she looked more like an Instagram influencer for vegan health products than a police officer. She should have known better. 'Thanks, Mel. Let me know what you come up with.'

'Ma'am. Oh, and Beth Fisher called, asked me to show you this…' she clicked around on her computer and Maggie leaned over to look. It was a picture from the Elsie Button case file.

'Can you make that bigger?' she asked.

Mel zoomed in. It looked like a statement.

Maggie began to read out loud. 'Statement from Katy Bowen's babysitter: *Sometimes he would ruffle Elsie's hair and she would giggle all girlishly. One time I arrived and Elsie was sitting on Patrick's knee, he was reading her a story. Kathryn was playing with some toys on the floor, which I thought was a bit weird because Kathryn was his daughter and he was giving Elsie all the attention. I always felt a bit uncomfortable around him, but he never tried anything with me. I suppose I was too old for him. It makes me feel sick now, to think of what he might have been thinking and planning that whole time. I wish I could have stopped him, but even if I'd have said something, it was only a feeling and Jill would have stuck up for him. She would have done anything for him. I don't think she knew about what he did to Elsie, she loved her like she was one of her own children. Everything I have said is the truth to the best of my knowledge. Signed: Nora Bywater.*'

Maggie read it twice.

'Nora Bywater from The Swimming Unicorn?' she said at last. 'Nora Bywater was Katy's babysitter?'

She looked at Mel, who looked as confused as she felt. Only, Mel was confused about what a statement from Katy Bowen's old babysitter had to do with Abigail Warner's disappearance. Maggie was confused about why Nora had let Katy stay in her B&B knowing that she had given a statement that had helped put her father behind bars.

She was about to call PC Fisher for her interpretation of the statement when DS Bailey walked – or rather stormed – into the investigation room.

'Ma'am, good news,' he said, his voice terse.

They've found Abigail, was the first thought that ran through Maggie's head. The second was, *God I wish I'd had a shower*.

Bailey must have read her thoughts because his face fell. 'Oh no, we haven't found her, sorry, ma'am. Katy Bowen has been found though, and there's some DNA back from the tissue in the field. There were two matches – the blood matched Abigail's and a sample from a female, they are running more tests.'

'A female?'

'That's all they know at this time. Apparently it's not a great sample. The blood might have contaminated it, but there's a lab in London that might be able to get something more useful from it so they're having it couriered there this morning.'

'Right, okay,' Maggie rubbed her face. 'Wait, did you say Katy Bowen has been found?'

'I did, yeah. She's at the hospital; PC Fisher is going to call us as soon as she wakes up. Looks like she's been drugged. George Fisher found her trying to walk to his house half an hour ago.'

'Jesus,' Maggie breathed. She'd been inclined to think that Katy Bowen had run off to avoid the newspapers, but it sounded like she had been in trouble after all. 'Any indication of how she is?'

Bryn shook his head. 'She's alive, that's all that I know.'

'Well, I suppose that's something.'

Chapter Forty

Kathryn

I'm not really aware of the exact moment that my dream fades and I realise that I am awake. I think this is different to the last time I was awake, when I felt like I was there but not really there, not alive and not dead, just hung in some sort of hellish suspended animation. This time, I feel actually really here, my legs and arms feel heavy, as though they are pinned down, but they feel real, like they are skin and bone and tissue and muscle, not like they might float away at any moment. I try to open my eyes, but the light shoots a pain through my head, so I close them again.

'She's awake!' There's no mistaking Miriam's voice. It makes me want to smile automatically, but I don't seem to be able to communicate that to my face.

'Kathryn? Can you hear me?' A voice I only half recognise, I think it's Beth. I really want to open my eyes now, there's something I need to tell her I think... I'm sure before I went to sleep there was something I wanted to speak to her about, but everything just feels so hard to understand. 'I don't think she's awake.'

'I'm telling you I saw her eyes open. Fetch a nurse, will you.' Miriam's voice is so perfectly Miriam that I let out a laugh without thinking it through. It hurts my chest and I start to cough, which only hurts more. 'Kathryn, it's okay! You don't have to open your eyes, or talk, the nurse is on her way. You've had a nasty head injury and a ton of drugs.'

'Is this two thousand and nine?' I croak. It hurts, but I'm rewarded with a hearty cackle from Miriam. Prising my eyes open, I see her concerned face standing over my bed and hear a commotion at the door.

'Stand back then, give her some space.' A smiling woman appears in my eyeline. 'Kathryn, I'm Nurse Goodwin. You've had a nasty head injury and a lot of a sedatives called ketamine, but you're safe.'

Dammit, I wish I'd saved the two thousand and nine joke for her. Nothing seems funny though, when a thought occurs to me.

'Have I…?' I can't even say the words. 'Did they…?'

The nurse knows exactly what I'm asking.

'There's no sign of any sexual assault, love,' she says gently. I should feel relieved – I do feel relieved, but mainly numb. 'Your clothes were all properly intact when we found you, and you've been washed and examined.'

Even the thought of a professional undressing me, washing and examining my naked body while I had no awareness of it happening, feels like a kind of violation. But I don't say that to this woman who just wants me to be okay.

'Can I call my boss now?' Beth asks at last. 'She'll want to speak to her.'

'I think they can wait until she's managed to at least fully open her eyes.' The nurse almost sounds snappy. Good on her. 'I'll get you some water, Kathryn, and in a bit you can tell me if you want some toast. The doctor will want to see you before any police.'

The thought of a team of police officers swooping in is so horrific that I almost welcome being prodded and poked by the doctor. But there's something important I need them to know, I'm sure of it.

'Kathryn,' Beth's voice is urgent, as though she knows she's going to be kicked out for asking the question. 'Did you see Abigail?'

Abigail. That's what I needed to say. I think back to waning in and out of consciousness, the soft carpet, the bed... my mind conjures up a picture of a body on the bed, not moving. The blonde hair...

'I saw her,' I croak, and even the nurse doesn't dare interrupt. 'I think... I was dreaming a lot, but I'm certain I saw her. I think...' my throat lets out an involuntary sob and it scratches like hell. 'I think she was dead.'

Chapter Forty-One

Kathryn

The nurse agrees that, given the circumstances, Beth can call her boss and tell her to come to the hospital.

'But she can't come in here until the doctor has seen you,' she tells me. 'And even then, if you get tired, they're to stop straight away. It's terrible about that poor girl, but you are my patient and my main concern at the moment. We have to watch for the side effects of prolonged use of ketamine.'

While Beth goes to make the call, I look at Miriam.

'I didn't know she was police,' I say. My throat feels like I've spent the week in the Sahara.

I reach for the glass of water on the table in front of me and Miriam gets up to help. Bloody hell, I must look bad if she's fussing over me. Miriam can usually put a sergeant in the army to shame with her no-bullshit approach to life. She guides it to my lips and I take a sip. The cold water feels like a shock to my system, but it helps my throat.

'She pretended to be my friend.'

'I know, duck,' Miriam says. If there's anyone who knows how much this would have hurt me, it's her. My lack of friends and my apathy about the situation has been well versed between us. She knows I don't find it easy to trust people and what a punch in the gut Beth's betrayal

242

has come as. 'But here's the thing,' she continues. 'She's actually really quite a nice girl. And she was genuinely worried about you – we both were. Her boss said you'd probably just taken off because you found out the papers were onto you, but Beth wouldn't have it. She refused to stop looking for you. I think she's quite sorry about having to lie to you, but it was her job.'

'You're being suspiciously magnanimous,' I say, turning my mouth down at the corner. 'If I didn't know you better, I'd say you liked her.'

'She's not so bad,' Miriam replies.

I raise my eyebrows.

'She's not. And we're not schoolchildren, so I don't have to pretend to dislike her just because she's pissed you off.'

If I could manage it, I'd laugh. Miriam is one person you can absolutely count on to call you on your bullshit.

'Okay, fine. How long was I…?' What – missing? Kidnapped? Those words seem a bit dramatic considering I have been basically unaware of my situation the whole time. The word 'kidnapped' brings to mind visions of shackles and using pointy metal to try to scrape at damp bricks to escape. I just feel like I had a really weird acid trip.

'You were missing for hours. You were seen at the pub around three-ish and then no one had any idea where you were until you turned up here.'

Behind the pub. A memory of being in the pub, talking with a man, then going down the side alley, trying to avoid people…

'Journalists,' I conclude. 'I was avoiding the journalists coming out of the pub once I left. I made an appointment to meet one.'

243

'Yes, Jordan was less than pleased about that,' Miriam says.

'You've spoken to Jordan?' I try to sit up a bit, but everything just feels so heavy that I give up. 'Where is he?'

'He had to stay at the hospital with your mum. No, there's been no changes, but Verity apparently had to go into work and with me here he thought someone should stay there.'

'How did you find me?' I ask suddenly. 'If you don't know where I was, how did I get here?'

'There's going to be questions about that, that's for sure,' Miriam says, her lips pursed. 'George Fisher and Kevin Wilson brought you in. Said they'd been driving up to George's place and found you on the road, as if you'd been trying to get there and passed out.'

'Who's George Fisher?' I ask, but I think somewhere in my muddled mind I already know.

'He's Beth's dad. Retired police officer… he, um, he knew your mum and dad.'

'He arrested Patrick,' I say, remembering where I know the name from now – Reddit. 'But if he's Beth's dad and he was friends with my mum and Patrick, how don't I remember Beth? I don't even remember her name, and Jordan didn't recall her when we talked about my old friends.'

'George and his wife adopted her after… well, after you and your family left,' Miriam said. 'Fairly soon after, I think – apparently, they had been going through the process when Elsie went missing.'

'A bad time to be wrapped up in a scandal,' I say, without thinking. 'I wonder how close he and Patrick were?'

'Not close enough that he'd take the blame for murder, if that's what you're thinking.' Beth stands in the doorway, her voice stony.

'That wasn't what I said.'

'It's what you were implying. That my dad did something to Elsie and your dad took the blame so they could still adopt me. That's ridiculous. Your father wouldn't have ruined his whole family so my parents could have a child. Nobody would do that.'

'No, you're right,' I concede. 'I was just thinking out loud.'

'How are you feeling?' she says, stepping gingerly into the room.

'Like shit,' I say. 'And you're a police officer.'

She sags, as if she thought she might have got away with it. 'Yes. I'm sorry.'

'Miriam says you're all right.'

Beth looks at Miriam in surprise.

'Yeah, I was shocked too,' I say. The truth is, although I don't trust Beth any more, I don't have the energy to give her the roasting I would have done otherwise. She's got off lightly thanks to a nasty head injury and a ton of drugs.

'My DI is on her way,' Beth says. 'You think you're up to an interview?'

'I don't see that I've got much choice,' I say.

Chapter Forty-Two

Maggie

'Jesus Christ, don't let anyone around you hear you say that.' Maggie was practically having to yell herself over the noise from the search ground. The news she'd just heard from Beth Fisher was particularly hard to take, given that she was surrounded by people who had given up their time, losing pay at work or using their only day off to look for what they hoped would be a living, breathing five-year-old. Had it all been for nothing? Maggie knew how these types of investigations usually ended – she wasn't sure the people here were prepared for it. 'I'll be right there. Don't let her leave.'

'Right there' was in the hospital, back on the mainland. If she was lucky, word wouldn't have got out yet that Kathryn Bowen had been found on the island and taken to hospital by ambulance. Not that anyone had been able to miss the sirens that had pierced the air earlier that day, panic immediately spreading that the ominous wailing sounds had something to do with Abigail. Maggie had had to call the FLO to make sure Mr and Mrs Warner hadn't heard them and panicked too, but apparently he was upstairs in his office and hadn't come down, and she was lying on the sofa staring at the news, as if she thought she'd get more information from that than from the police.

Every time Abby's photograph came on the screen (which was every ten minutes or so), she'd break down into a fresh bout of tears. The FLO had tried to convince her to turn it off and she'd practically scratched her eyes out clawing for the remote.

Maggie let Bryn know where she was going and discreetly why. It was too soon and she had too little information to call off the search, but she still felt terrible seeing all those people setting off in Land Rovers and on foot, their faces still full of hope. She hoped to God that Kathryn was wrong.

–

The drive to the hospital was just long enough to put in a call to her mother, so Maggie took the opportunity. She felt bad she hadn't called yesterday. Since her dad passed last year, she'd tried to go and see her mum daily, but if she couldn't she always called. Her mum would know why, she'd be watching the news same as everyone else, but that wouldn't stop her fretting.

'Hello?'

'Mum, it's me.'

'Bella, is that you dear?'

Maggie tried not to sigh. Despite the fact that Bella barely called their mother once a fortnight and she herself called almost every day, she still asked if it was Belinda pretty much every time she picked up the phone. There was wishful thinking and there was her mother. She couldn't even blame it on age, she was only seventy-one this year.

'Maggie, Mum.'

'You didn't call yesterday, is everything okay? I almost called the police until I remembered that you are the police and probably wouldn't be very happy.'

'No, Mum, I'm fine, thanks. Just got a pretty big case on at the moment. There's a little girl gone missing in Pentraeth. She's only five.'

'Well of course, I've seen that on the news, it's awful. I saw you at the Memorial Hall doing the searches.'

And yet you were still worried enough to almost call the police, Maggie thought, but she didn't bother saying anything. There wasn't any point with her mum, she'd be picking at something else in a minute and forget about the last thing entirely. Maggie knew she was lonely and fed up, she missed her dad incredibly and was struggling to accept life on her own.

'It's been really busy.'

'Do you know who took her yet? I still haven't forgotten when the little Button girl went missing from the exact same place. There's something wrong with that house, I'm telling you.'

Maggie wasn't surprised to hear it said, but she was certainly surprised to hear it coming from her mum. Deidre Grant was about the least superstitious person Maggie had ever met in her life.

'Houses don't abduct little girls, Mum, people do.' Maggie held her badge up to the window at the officer still stopping and checking people at random on the bridge. She noticed they were stopping considerably fewer people than yesterday and resolved to radio in and tell them not to lose momentum. True, it was less likely that Abby would be moved now, under the glare of the country's media – and not likely at all if what Kathryn Bowen was saying was true – but that didn't mean they had to act like it.

'I know that, I'm not some Pagan or something,' Maggie rolled her eyes and wondered what her mum thought a Pagan actually was. 'I'm just saying, two girls missing from the same house – can't be a coincidence.'

'We're investigating all avenues,' Maggie intoned, using the voice she usually reserved for the press.

'So they are connected?'

'I didn't say that.'

'Why would you be investigating it if you don't think it's connected?'

This time, Maggie did sigh. 'We have to look at every avenue, Mum, whether we think they are connected or not. Anyway, I've not got long, how have you been?'

'I'm okay, love, you mustn't worry about me. Not when you've got such an important investigation on, finding that poor girl. I just worry if I don't hear from you, what with you having such a dangerous job. I'll never know—'

'Okay, Mum, as long as you're okay,' Maggie cut her off before she could launch into the 'I'll never know why such a pretty little girl wanted to go into such a manly job' speech. 'I'll try my best to call you tomorrow. Love you.'

'Right, okay, love you too.'

Maggie felt a twinge of guilt as she pressed the end call button on the centre console. It was true though, she was just pulling up at the hospital and the parking charges were far too extortionate to stop for a chat.

'Kathryn Bowen,' Maggie muttered to the woman on the check in desk, trying to keep her voice as low as possible. 'ICU.'

'Right to the end of the corridor, then left and straight on.' She barely acknowledged Maggie's existence and Maggie didn't even have to pull her badge. She wondered briefly if she should station some protection outside Kathryn's room. Was the girl in any danger?

PC Fisher was standing outside the room when Maggie approached. 'What's she said?' Maggie asked. 'Anything more than when you called me?'

'I didn't want to push her and wear her out before you got here,' Fisher replied, looking terrified that she might have made the wrong decision. 'The nurse said as soon as she gets tired we're out of here.'

'Okay, fine.' Maggie steeled herself to enter and pushed open the door.

The woman in the bed looked between her and PC Fisher and made four.

'DI Grant.'

'That's me. And I gather I have the pleasure of meeting Patrick Bowen's daughter?'

Kathryn snorted, then looked as though she regretted it.

'You okay?'

'My throat is a bit sore,' Kathryn replied, taking a sip of her water.

'Any other injuries?'

'Apparently just a gash on my head and a stomach full of sedatives. Just your standard hangover stuff.'

'The nurse said ketamine,' Maggie said. 'Party drug of choice for a long time. Not difficult to get hold of if you know the right people. Usually sniffed though, not injected.' Maggie moved further into the room and looked pointedly at Miriam. 'I'm going to have to ask you to leave.'

Miriam smiled. 'Ask away.'

Maggie sighed. 'This is official police business, Ms Pike. I've grown accustomed to your face, don't make me arrest you.'

Kathryn glanced between the two of them, a bemused look on her pretty face. Perhaps she could sense the blooming respect there. Maggie could hardly bear to admit it, but she liked Miriam Pike, and had it been her friend in the hospital bed, she'd want to stay as well.

'Is she entitled to counsel?' Miriam demanded. It didn't matter how much Maggie liked her, she was still a pain in the ass.

'Everyone is entitled to counsel, Miriam, you know that. Not everyone chooses to hold up an investigation of the whereabouts of a five-year-old girl while we find it. Only the guilty ones tend to do that.'

Miriam opened her mouth to speak, but Kathryn held up a hand.

'Firstly,' she said, and her voice sounded like she'd spent the last forty hours in the desert. 'I'd like it on record that I know that is bullshit. Innocent people need a lawyer the same as guilty ones – I've seen enough true-crime documentaries to know that. I'm not an idiot, and nor can I be taken in by the "innocent people do this or that" line.'

She stopped, as if speaking that much had finished her off. Maggie went to reply, but stopped when she saw Kathryn Bowen's glare.

'Secondly, I don't want to mess around wasting time. What I told Beth is true, I thought Abigail looked dead. But she might not be. I'm not sure how, but you seem to know each other, and despite Beth lying to me the entire time I've known her, actually she seems trustworthy. I'm going to tell you absolutely everything I can and just hope that you don't use it to pin this on me. But even if you do, I want you to know I went into this fully knowing that might happen.'

'Nice speech,' Maggie remarked drily. 'For the record, did all that waffle mean you are waiving your right to counsel?'

'For this interview.'

'Good. Thank you,' Maggie added as an afterthought, aware that somewhere in all that had been a compliment. She looked at Miriam, who held up her hands.

'Fine,' she said. 'I will wait right outside the door. Right outside.'

Maggie inclined her head to show she understood and took a seat next to Kathryn. Filling up the water glass for her, she placed it on the table and took a tape recorder out of her bag. She held it up as though seeking permission and Kathryn nodded. Maggie switched on the tape.

'Interview between Detective Inspector Margaret Grant and Kathryn Bowen.'

'Starling,' Kathryn corrected. 'My name is Kathryn Starling.'

'Noted,' Maggie said. 'Ms Starling is currently in hospital with a head injury. She has consented to this interview as a material witness. Ms Bowen, for the tape can you confirm that you have been offered legal representation for this interview and declined.'

'I can.'

'Right. I appreciate you speaking to me, and I know you are in some pain, so we will make this as quick as possible. You allege that you were kidnapped, yes? That someone else was responsible for your disappearance?'

'Well I didn't kidnap myself, if that's what you're asking.'

'We don't generally call running away "kidnapping yourself".'

'I didn't run away. Someone grabbed me.'

'The same person who abducted Abigail Warner?'

'I think so. I mean, they kept me pretty sedated, but as I told Beth, I'm certain I saw her. As certain as I can be.'

'Do you have any idea at all where you were taken?'

Kathryn shook her head. 'Not really where. A room, like a bedroom, but I suppose it could have been any room with a bed. It smelled of fresh paint and everything was pink, like a little girl's new bedroom. Everything was clean and crisp, like it had only just been bought.'

'What was the floor like?'

'Carpet.'

'How did you escape?'

Kathryn shrugged, then winced. 'I didn't escape. I passed out, woke up in a truck, passed out again. Woke up here. Apparently Kevin Wilson and George Fisher found me – I don't remember how I got to the road they found me on.'

Maggie sighed. None of this was particularly helpful. The place she described could easily be any room, anywhere. She wondered how viable it would be to get search warrants for every property on the island. Perhaps the fact that it was all new would be a lead – carpets and paint had to be bought from somewhere.

'You said to PC Fisher that you thought Abigail was dead? What made you think that?'

'She wasn't moving. My first impression – my *only* impression – was that she wasn't breathing. She was kind of slumped against the wall, like a doll. Part of me still wonders if I was dreaming, if the whole room was a hallucination.'

'Okay.' Maggie practically felt her blood pressure drop. It wasn't like Kathryn had seen the girl covered in blood or anything so concrete. She also didn't have anything that could help identify where Abigail was. 'Right. Let's try to see what we can figure out about what happened to you. Can you tell me what you remember from the nineteenth of June?'

'Would you like the whole day, or just the last part?'

'I think a quick rundown of what you'd done that day would be helpful.'

Kathryn took a weak breath. Maggie hoped she wasn't tiring her out already.

'When I woke that morning, I was in The Swimming Unicorn. I found that during the night someone had broken into my room and carved GO HOME on the inside of my door.'

Maggie nodded. She'd already heard about this from Beth and had her suspicions who might have been responsible.

'Why didn't you phone the police?'

'I didn't want the police to know I was here. I think it's obvious why.'

'Because of who your father is?'

'Yes.'

'Okay,' Maggie said, moving on. If Kathryn became a suspect, she would get a chance to ask her more about what she was doing on the island later. Right now, she had to treat her like a witness, not a suspect. 'But you didn't go home.'

'No, because after I'd had my breakfast, I went outside to find my tyres had been slashed.'

'Do you think that was coincidental?'

Kathryn raised her eyebrows. She took a sip of her water before she answered. 'Do you?'

Maggie didn't reply. She jotted the word 'Tyres?' on her pad and moved on.

'So you couldn't leave. Were you frightened?'

'I hadn't been threatened.'

'That's not an answer. Were you frightened?'

Kathryn shrugged. 'Not really. It was broad daylight and the most amount of police I'd ever seen were everywhere you looked. And, like I say, I hadn't been threatened. It didn't occur to me at that point that I might be in physical danger.'

Maggie looked at this woman, who had been through more than anyone Maggie knew of her age and yet she seemed remarkably calm. She supposed nothing was normal for the daughter of a child killer, and if there was no 'ordinary' then there could be no 'out of the ordinary'.

'What did you decide to do?'

'I called my breakdown service, then I went to join the search for Abigail. I figured if I couldn't leave I could at least be useful.'

'Which is where you saw Beth? For the benefit of the tape that is PC Fisher.'

'Yes. Although I didn't know she was also known as PC Fisher at the time of course.'

Maggie didn't react to the small dig. 'And then?'

'I, um…'

She may think she was streetwise, but she clearly hadn't got any kind of story straight, and Maggie could tell instantly that this was where the real story began.

'Beth said you left in a hurry. Where could you have to go? You'd been leaving the island less than an hour before, now you had important engagements?'

'There was someone I wanted to speak to about Patrick.' Maggie noted with some surprise that Kathryn didn't refer to Patrick Bowen as her dad. Actually, perhaps it wasn't so surprising – after all, Maggie often felt ready to disown her mum after a particularly annoying conversation. With a murder conviction between them, it was hardly going to be a normal father–daughter relationship.

'Who?'

Kathryn looked as though she was considering whether or not to answer. 'Harriet Tremayne.'

Maggie wrote down the name. It sounded familiar, but she didn't know everyone in Pentraeth and she hadn't been involved in the Elsie Button case. 'Should I know her?'

Kathryn shrugged. 'She was a friend of Patrick's. She claims he was at her house the morning Elsie disappeared. That he's innocent.'

'Oh God, the psychic.' Maggie rolled her eyes, knowing now exactly who Kathryn meant. 'Did you believe her?'

'I believe that she believes it,' Kathryn said, her voice level. 'And I believe he was at her house that morning. Whether that means he couldn't have killed Elsie… well, the police had her statement at the time and I trust that if it ruled him out, then he wouldn't be in prison.'

'That's very magnanimous of you,' Maggie commented, then realised the tape was still rolling and that taunting a witness wasn't entirely professional. 'Where did you go next?'

'I went back to The Swimming Unicorn to speak to Kevin Wilson, Patrick's lawyer.'

Maggie put down her pen and looked at Kathryn. She looked defiant, as if she was ready for any challenge Maggie put to her. She also suddenly looked very young, and very tired. 'It seems, Kathryn,' Maggie said, trying not to sound like she was being accusatory, 'like you were on some kind of investigation yourself.'

'I had some questions for Mr Wilson, yes. Being on the island for the first time in twenty-five years, it's hardly surprising I would want to speak to people who were close to my parents. Wouldn't you want to know, if your father did what mine did, why he did it? And why no one knew what kind of monster he was?'

'Of course,' Maggie agreed. 'I understand your wanting answers. What I don't understand, exactly is why you chose this week to come looking for them.'

'It suddenly became topical,' Kathryn returned. Maggie had to give it to her, she was a sharp one.

'Quite. Okay, so you spoke to Mr Wilson, then left the hotel. Where did you go next?'

'Beth, I mean PC Fisher, had told me I could stay at her place, but she wasn't free then. Thinking she might be at work – which I believed to be the local pub – I went there. She wasn't there.'

'And that's where you met Ken Langley?'

'Who?'

Maggie frowned. 'Ken Langley. The journalist you were seen talking to.'

'Oh, I didn't remember his name. But yes, that's where I met him.'

'And it wasn't a planned meeting?'

It was Kathryn's turn to frown. 'I'm certain it wasn't. But here's the thing, everything still feels a bit fuzzy. Like any of those things I just told you – if you said they didn't happen, I'd almost believe I'd dreamed them while I was drugged up. Harriet Tremayne, for one, seems a bit of a made-up character.'

'No, if I remember Harriet Tremayne, that description is perfectly accurate,' Maggie said, her voice dry. 'And what you've said so far matches up with what PC Fisher and your friend Ms Pike found out when they were looking for you. No one saw you after you left the pub. Your car stayed where it was and you didn't turn up for your meeting with Ken. PC Fisher thought it might be because you were mad at her for not telling you what her vocation was—'

'For lying to me, you mean.'

For the benefit of the tape, Maggie neither confirmed or denied. She still wasn't one hundred per cent sure of the ethics of sending Beth Fisher to 'keep an eye' on Kathryn Bowen, or Starling as she now wanted to be known. Although it could be successfully argued that if she hadn't, it would have taken much longer to register her as a missing person. And without Beth poking around, she might have stayed missing.

'What happened after you left the pub?'

'I had a feeling the other reporters might follow me out. They all knew who I was, that much was clear. So I slipped down the alley to the…' Kathryn looked up as though trying to picture the pub. 'Left, I think. I can't be sure of that though.' She paused. 'I don't remember anything after that. Just sort of drifting, like when you wake up from one dream in the night and fall back into another.'

'You didn't see or speak to anyone behind the pub?'

'No.'

'Smell anything? Hear a voice?'

'Nothing. Well, wait. Sometimes I got a feeling, just an impression of someone standing over me. They were big.'

'Big?' Maggie repeated.

'Large,' said Kathryn, 'bulky, imposing, colossal, vast… you want any more synonyms?'

'I understand the word "big", thank you,' Maggie said through clenched teeth. 'In what way were they big? Were they tall? Wide? Fat? Muscular?'

'I have no idea,' Kathryn replied. 'I told you, it was more a feeling. I was out of it. But I figure they would have to be strong to drag me away – even drugged I'm a lot bigger than a child. Lucky, as well, that no one saw them. Maybe one kept watch. Maybe there were two of them.'

'I'm not sure where you're going with this,' Maggie said, but that was a lie. She knew exactly where Kathryn was going with it, and she didn't much like it.

'Bit of a coincidence, don't you think? That the people who found me were Patrick's two best friends? Of all the people on the island?'

'You were dropped off outside George's house. Of course he was going to be the one to find you.'

'Was I though?' Kathryn said. 'If that's true, why don't I have any memory of being on the road? How do you know that whoever took me didn't just bring me straight to hospital?'

'Because if that were true, then that means the people who took you were a retired police chief inspector and a well-respected family lawyer,' Maggie replied. 'And if that's the case, the shit really hits the fan.'

Chapter Forty-Three

Maggie

Maggie had just sat down at her desk when her phone rang. The caller ID showed DS Bailey. On arrival at the station that morning she'd sent him straight out with a team to search Abigail's room again, and from the sound of his voice it wasn't going well.

'Do you have to do this again?' Maggie could hear John Warner demanding from the other end of the phone. She had instructed DS Bailey and his team to make another search of Abigail's room, and from the sounds of it, her father wasn't taking it well. 'Our daughter is missing, these things are all we have of her right now and you're trampling all over them.'

'Tell him I'm on my way,' Maggie sighed. She'd at least had a few hours' sleep last night and felt better equipped to deal with Mr Warner. She could hear Lesley, the FLO, in the background saying, '…number one priority now is to find Abigail, and if there's anything in this room that can help us, we need to find it.'

'Mrs Warner would like to speak to you,' Bailey said, and before Maggie could object, Caroline Warner's voice came at her, pleading.

'What are you looking for in her room? Is this to do with what you were asking about yesterday? About this new friend Abby— Abigail was supposed to have? Because I told you that's rubbish, she would have told me if she'd been playing with someone.'

'These people can be very sly about the way they choose their victims, Mrs Warner,' Lesley said before Maggie could reply. She cringed at the woman's and choice of words.

'Caroline, listen—' Maggie said, but it was too late. On hearing the word 'victim', Caroline had broken down into tears, violent sobs into the receiver.

DS Bailey must have removed the phone from her hand because the next thing she heard was him saying 'Fucksake. Sorry, boss.'

'Get her some medical attention,' Maggie said. If what Kathryn had seen was true, there was a whole lot more heartbreak coming Caroline Warner's way and having a doctor on standby wasn't going to be a bad thing. 'See if Doctor Roberts is available.' Maggie was still trying to process the information Kathryn had given her. How were George and Kevin related to this? Had one of them been Abigail's new 'friend'? If this all carried on in the direction it looked like it was going, this island was about to be blown to pieces, and Maggie wasn't sure it would ever recover. 'I'm in the car, on my way. What's going on?'

'We've got two forensic officers like you requested,' Bryn said. 'I've told them they're looking for anything that looks like it might be a gift, given to Abigail. That this new friend of hers is supposed to be a secret, so it's likely to be hidden or out of sight. Anything at all that might be relevant is being photographed and bagged.'

Maggie pictured the scene. Abigail's room was a typical five-year-old girl's room, she'd unfortunately seen a million like them when she'd worked in child services for six years prior to joining the police force. The colour pink might be a stereotype when it came to little girls, but it was a well-enforced one. Abigail also seemed to have a thing for owls; those kind of cartoony ones in pastel colours adorned one wall, while the other three were painted a light bubble-gum pink colour. Her wardrobes were cream and there was a handwritten sign in a beautiful childish scrawl that said KEEP OWT. ABBY'S ROOM. She pictured it being pulled apart by the men in white paper suits; the image was heartbreaking.

'Right, well I'll be with you in less than—'

'Bailey,' a sharp voice said in the background.

'What?' Maggie demanded. 'What is it?'

There was a few beats of silence, then…

'Get here now, boss,' Bailey said. 'You need to see this.'

Chapter Forty-Four

Kathryn

'Oh sweet Jesus.'

Nora turns to leave her own B&B as Beth and I enter. I was discharged from the hospital this morning and thanks to a night of fluid replacements and a decent night's sleep I actually feel human again.

'I don't particularly want to be back here either,' I say, injecting as much venom as possible into my words. The sage smells stronger today and I wonder if it's my energy she's been trying to get rid of.

'I've got nothing to say to you,' Nora says, but she decides not to leave. Instead, she points at the door. 'Get out.'

'Not… welcome home then?' I say. '"Good to see you Kathryn? How've you been, Kathryn? Sorry I pretended not to know who you were Kathryn?"'

'You lied to me,' Nora points out. 'You gave me a fake name. So don't come here acting all innocent, because you're not.'

'I am, actually,' I say. 'The rest of my family were as much victims of what Patrick did as the Buttons were.'

Nora juts out her chin defiantly. 'I don't want to talk to you.'

I lay both palms flat on the desk. 'You don't really have a whacking great choice,' I say. 'You owe me, Nora Bywater. You threw my dad under the bus the minute the police came knocking. Why did you say those things about him?'

For a minute, I expect her to say, 'Because they were true.' Instead, her face crumples.

'Do you think I wanted to say those things?' she snaps. 'I thought your father was wonderful, like everyone else around here. I never believed for a second that he was a paedophile or a murderer. I didn't believe Patrick Bowen so much as stole a penny chew from the corner shop! And yes he loved Elsie, but only in the same way you love a niece or a nephew. He would never have hurt her.'

Of all the things I was braced to hear when I came here – this wasn't it.

'So why did you make that statement?' I ask, looking at Beth. I'm still looking at Beth when Nora replies, which is why I see her face whiten.

'Because George Fisher told me to.'

–

'He is not a dirty cop,' Beth repeats over and over as we leave Nora shaking inside the B&B. She refused to say any more and threatened to call the police if we didn't leave, which wouldn't have been a good look, for Beth especially. I'm not sure there's much more she could have told us anyway; from what she said George Fisher basically wrote her statement and she signed it. She was twenty-three and had some previous minor drug convictions so she did what she was told so they didn't get any worse. And she has hated herself every day since.

'I know he's not,' I say, although I'm lying. If Patrick had an accomplice, or if he wasn't to blame for Elsie's disappearance, then George Fisher forcing people to sign statements that make spurious, untrue claims sounds like a dirty cop to me. But as a wise woman once said, we are not responsible for our father's fuck-ups. It was Beth – Beth said that.

Another sign that Miriam trusts PC Fisher is that she stayed at Beth's house last night, and is still there now. Beth came down to the hospital to fetch me. I'm still pretty furious that Beth lied to me about who she was, but Miriam's trust in her is going a long way to helping me forget. Also her guilty conscience meant that when I suggested dropping in on my former babysitter on the way home she didn't argue. I kind of wish she had now. This is awkward.

'There is clearly a lot you need to catch me up with,' I change the subject as smoothly as I can. 'Shall we grab some snacks before we go back to yours?'

'Bacon sandwich from Barb's?'

'That sounds amazing.'

Barbara's cafe is the kind you can smell before you see, and even though there aren't as many people as when I came the first morning I was here – just after I'd found the warning I should have heeded – Barbara stops us at the door.

'We're full,' she says, not even looking at me. Gone is the smiling, kindly face, replaced by thin lips drawn in a line.

Beth frowns, confusion lining her face. 'No you're not,' she says, making to move past Barb. 'There's loads of space. Besides, we just want a takeaway.'

'We're full,' Barbara insists. She throws a pointed look in my direction and looks back at Beth. 'There's room for one.'

'And suppose I said I'd send Kathryn in instead of me?' Beth asks.

I flinch at the use of my real name, but it's clear by this little performance that everyone here knows who I am and it would be embarrassing to keep up the pretence any longer. Besides – it's not me who has done anything wrong. I'm fed up of being tarred with the same brush as Patrick.

'Then we're full,' Barb replies. A for effort, she's standing by her guns.

'I haven't done anything wrong,' I say, loud enough for the people inside who are clearly listening to every word to hear. I can't see Ken Langley in there, he'll be gutted. 'I haven't ever hurt anyone.'

'Maybe not,' Barbara says, and it might be my imagination, but I feel like her voice has softened somewhat. 'But it was wrong of you to come here at this time. Insensitive. This island suffered for years because of what your father did, now isn't the time to come here pleading your innocence.'

'Barbara Tompkins—' Beth starts, but I grab her arm. The cafe owner is right, it is wrong of me to be here, when the island is in the midst of another tragedy, reminding everyone of Patrick Bowen's existence. I shouldn't be here. I don't want to be here.

'Come on,' I say. 'Let's just go.'

'That was ridiculous.' Beth is absolutely fuming.

'It's fine,' I say, but she shakes her head, furious.

'It's not. I'm sorry, Kathryn.'

'It's not your fault,' I say. I don't add, *it's Patrick's*. Because I'm not sure it is anymore. I'm not sure of anything anymore.

We drop in at the SPAR for snacks instead and Beth promises to make me a bacon sandwich at hers. Only when the girl behind the counter looks up and sees us, she looks mortified.

'I can't serve you,' she says, her eyes fixed on something invisible on the counter.

Next to me, Beth lets out an exasperated sigh.

'Oh come on, Becca, for God's sake don't be stupid. She just wants a packet of crisps and a Ribena.'

Becca lifts her chin defiantly to look at Beth. 'I've been told, Beth. And I don't know why you're defending her. You know who she is, don't you?'

'Yes I know.' Beth's voice takes on a slightly dangerous tone. 'I also know that what her dad did has nothing to do with who she is. Same as I know that when your dad took that money from the Christmas collection, it had nothing to do with who you are. We can't choose our family, Becca.'

Becca's face floods with colour. 'That's got nothing to do with this, Elizabeth Fisher, and it's not fair to bring it up either.'

She starts speaking in furious Welsh. I might still know the odd word, but there's no way I can follow this outburst. When she finishes, Beth tuts and shakes her head. She spits out one angry word and throws her things on the counter and grabs my arm.

'Come on, I've got food at mine that comes judgement-free.'

'Just remember, Beth,' Becca calls as we leave. 'You still have to live here after all this is over.'

Beth says nothing as we leave the shop. My teeth are clenched at the unfairness of it all. The determination and bravado I felt is long gone.

'What did she say in Welsh?'

Beth rolls her eyes. 'She says if she serves a Bowen her windows will be put through and her mum will do her nut.'

'And what did you say?' I ask, my fists clenching involuntarily. If Becca wants first-hand experience of the Bowen temper, I'm sure I can oblige. Give them something to talk about.

'I called her a coward,' Beth says.

I'm warmed by the fact that this woman who doesn't even know me is willing to risk making living and working here a whole lot more difficult just to stand up for me, but Becca is right, when this is over I go home to Manchester, Beth has to stay here.

'Thanks,' I say, because I don't know what else to say.

'I figured Miriam would kick my ass if I didn't say something.'

'She's going to kick your ass anyway,' I reply. 'Those crisps were for her.'

–

'Look,' I say as we get close to Beth's flat, where Miriam is waiting for us. 'Don't mention what happened back there to Miriam, okay? She's worried enough as it is. I think we should probably get out of here for a while, you know, until everything blows over with Abigail.'

Beth looks like we're about to have an awkward conversation. 'You can't go anywhere. You're our only lead to Abigail.'

'I told your boss, I don't remember anything more than I already told her. I can't hel—'

An unfamiliar ringtone cuts through the air and I realise after a second that it's the phone Beth loaned to me since mine has been missing. It can only be a limited number of people, I'm on a new number. Miriam, Jordan, Verity, or the hospital with news of Mum. I fumble in my handbag and answer with a breathless 'Hello?'

'Kat, it's Verity. Can I speak to Jordan?'

I'm so surprised to hear her voice that for a moment her words don't sink in. Then I say, 'Ver, I'm in Anglesey – don't you remember?'

'Of course I bloody remember. Can I speak to my husband, please?'

'He's at the hospital, with Mum.'

There's silence at the other end of the phone. Then… 'What?'

I'm not sure which part she's confused about, but I don't really have the energy for an 'I'm sorry what?'-off with my sister-in-law. 'Where are you?' I ask, going for an easier question.

'I'm at the hospital, where I've been since Jordan ran off to look after you.'

Now it's my turn at stupid silence. 'Ran off to look after me? I'm in Anglesey,' I repeat.

'Yes, I know that,' Verity says. She sounds like she's trying to stay calm. I still don't one hundred per cent understand what's going on. 'Jordan said you were in trouble and you needed him. He said he was going to Anglesey to meet you.'

'Oh, okay.' I get it now. Miriam must have called him to say I hadn't actually gone on a bender and was genuinely in trouble and he's had an attack of conscience and come to find me. 'He hasn't arrived yet. Sorry for the confusion, do you want me to get him to call you when he gets here?'

I'm glad Jordan's on his way. I've always relied so heavily on having him around, it will be good to see his face. Reassuring and strong, that's how I've always seen him.

Verity doesn't sound reassured. 'I think you're misunderstanding me. Jordan said he was coming to Anglesey to meet you on Wednesday morning.'

It takes me longer this time to comprehend what Verity has just said to me.

'That makes no sense. Miriam called him yesterday. If he was in Anglesey, he probably would have mentioned. He said he had to stay with Mum.'

'And every time I've spoken to him he said he's with you. I only stopped hearing from him last night. So if he's not with you and he's not here with me, where the fuck is he?'

Where the fuck is he indeed? I can't comprehend why my brother would tell Verity he was here with me. Unless, could he actually be on Anglesey? But if he is, why hasn't he come to meet me?

'Has he ever disappeared before, V?' I feel shitty for actually hoping my brother is having an affair.

'No, never. Not until Tuesday.'

'What do you mean, Tuesday? You said he came to meet me on Wednesday.'

'I don't know where he went, all I know is that he was gone for hours on Tuesday morning. I wanted to grill him about it, but then your mum... well, things happened with your mum. And then you ran off to Anglesey and he came after you and I figured I'd work it out when he got back. It was the anniversary and he probably wanted to have some space. I hoped he'd been to see you. Whatever's going on, he'll have a reasonable explanation.'

'How many hours, V? How many hours was he missing for?'

I can hear the cogs in her head turning. 'I woke up at sixish and he was gone. Then I got the call to meet him at the hospital when your mum...' she trails off. 'Why?'

I take a deep breath. Would he have had time to get back from Anglesey and straight to the hospital?

'Because,' I say slowly, not really knowing how to put it. If she hasn't considered it by now, then she's probably going to think I'm mad. 'Because Tuesday morning was the morning Abigail Warner went missing.'

Chapter Forty-Five

Maggie

Maggie took the piece of paper from DS Bailey and frowned. 'Where did this come from?'

'We have no idea,' Bryn said. 'We found it hidden inside of one of Abby's books. Mrs Warner says she's never seen it before, and she can't think of any way Abigail would know who Elsie was. It looks old. And it looks like—'

'It looks like Elsie drew it,' Maggie finished, understanding dawning. The picture she was holding depicted a woodland, basic brown trunks and green leaves, the sun in a blue sky and a small blonde girl holding hands with a tall figure scribbled in brown and black. The side that the 'monster' was on was coloured in darker crayons, the trees devoid of leaves, the sky a navy blue rather than the cornflower blue of the other half. It was quite an astute drawing, despite its childlike basicness. 'It looks like Elsie Button drew a picture of her with the monster in the woods twenty-five years ago. And labelled it with their names.'

'And if that's true?' She knew, of course, what he was getting at, but this was hardly evidence you could submit to a court.

'Then we know who the monster in the woods was. And probably who killed her. But there's no way we'll ever prove it.'

Chapter Forty-Six

Kathryn

Is it possible? Could Jordan be the one who has Abigail Warner? My wonderful, perfect brother, with his understanding nature and his eternal patience? Did he hurt Elsie Button? Did Patrick go to prison to protect his only son?

'Nononono,' I mutter, unable to comprehend how awful that would be. Worse, maybe, than my mum being responsible. Not Jordan, *please*.

'What is it?' Beth asks as I bend over, my hands resting on my knees. 'Is it your mum?'

I shake my head. 'I can't... I don't know where my brother is,' I say, my words coming out in a gasp. Is this a panic attack? Or a complete breakdown? I can actually feel my heart racing, my face is hot, but my arms have goosebumps running all over my flesh. 'I have to speak to Maggie Grant,' I say when I recover enough breath to speak. My knees feel too shaky to take me anywhere. 'Can you find out where she is?'

'Of course, but what shall I say? Do you know who has Abby?'

'I think I might,' I mutter. 'Oh God I think I might.'

'Okay.' She pulls out her phone and in minutes is speaking. 'Right,' I hear her say. 'Fine, great, I'll bring her there.' She hangs up and gestures towards her car. 'You'd better get in,' she says. 'DI Grant is at the Warners' house. Something to do with a picture of a monster they found in Abigail's room.'

A picture of a monster. Of the monster who played with us in the woods, who Elsie was afraid of. Had that been my big brother all along?

'Let's go,' I say.

I call Miriam as Beth drives, so she won't worry about how long we've been just to get some bacon sandwiches. I tell her that we've got to drop something off at the station and could she ring to check on my mum please? I can't face telling her anything else yet – not until I know the truth. I don't even know what I'm planning on telling DI Grant yet, or how she can help me, but I'm sure that if anyone can, it's her.

I don't get a chance though. As we pull up to the Warners' house, I see a familiar figure waiting for me on the edge of the woodland. The prodigal son has returned.

–

'Wait here,' I tell Beth, pulling off my seat belt. 'I have to speak to my brother.'

'Why are you here?' I call, as I walk towards him.

A few people turn to look and Jordan disappears down the side of the house. He's going into the woods.

He's waiting for me on the stone where I saw the vision of Elsie the first day I arrived. I shiver at the memory, the shade thrown by the trees around us making the day feel later than it is. I know, in this instant, that the monster is back in these woods and the realisation hits me like a train. My perfect, wonderful brother.

'Why are you here?' I repeat. 'Why have you come here?'

'Because you couldn't let it drop,' he says. He suddenly looks very old, and very tired. 'Because you couldn't just come home like you were warned to. Even after someone broke into your hotel room—'

'*You* carved that on my door?'

Jordan shakes his head. 'Nora did it. She wasn't happy about having to do it, but she understood why you couldn't stay. You're harder to scare than I expected. I should've known really. You've always been the tough one.'

'Me?' I scoff. 'I'm a mess. You're the rock, Jordan. You're the one we all look up to.' The one I look up to. The only constant in my life. The thought makes me want to cry.

There is a scream overhead and I jump before realising it was just a bird. This place feels charged with negative energy, with the stain of secrets and lies. I can't imagine why Abigail wanted to play in here, it feels evil. I wonder if it felt that way before Jordan killed Elsie, or only since. The trees seem closer together today, and taller, like they did when we were children. The gloom creeps around us like long fingers reaching out to wrap themselves around anyone who dares enter. Or perhaps that's just the way I feel about them now I know my world is in darkness.

'I remember you being there, on that day,' I say. 'I remember now. Elsie screamed that the Boggly was back and then I saw you. Was I there, Jordan? When you killed her? Is that why you kidnapped me, because you were afraid coming here would make me remember?'

Jordan looks pained. He sighs and rubs his eyes. 'I had nothing to do with that. I was frantic with worry but had to pretend I didn't think there was anything to worry about. Me and Kevin—'

'Kevin Wilson? Does he know you're here too?'

'Yes. I called him when you said you were on your way, and George Fisher. They were supposed to keep an eye on you, but that clearly went a bit wrong. I'm glad you're not hurt.'

'How are you still in touch with these men? I don't get it. What hold do you have on them? Did they cover up Elsie's murder for you?'

'They were Dad's best friends. It's hard to explain how close they all were. Kevin and George still help Mum out with money every month, and Will looks in on Helen. They just care. They're good men.'

'Good enough to cover up a murder? Is that why Mum tried to kill herself, because she heard a little girl was missing and knew you'd struck again?'

Jordan shakes his head slowly and lets out a sigh. 'You still don't understand anything, do you?' There's a pleading in his eyes. He wants so badly for me to see something, but I can't for the life of me understand what it is. 'Why do you think people have been telling you to go home, and trying to get you to stop digging up the past? You think that was to protect themselves? Or me maybe? Well, you're wrong, Kitty Kat. Your entire life people have been protecting *you*. This has all been about you, like everything in our lives, ever. *You're* the one Dad went to prison for. *You're* the one who killed Elsie.'

Chapter Forty-Seven

Kathryn

The laugh is out of my mouth before I can stop it, but I can't believe what he's just said. If he's going to find someone to pin this on, he's going to have to try harder than that. Next he's going to tell me I've got a split personality and I'm holding Abigail in my basement and I kidnapped her myself.

'You need help,' I say, pointing a finger at him. 'But first we need to find Abigail. Just tell me, Jordan, what have you done with her?'

Jordan takes a deep breath. 'I'm not kidding, Kathryn, and I'm not trying to shift the blame from myself. I've got no idea where Abigail Warner is, and I know you don't either. But the same person who killed Elsie couldn't have taken Abigail because *you* killed Elsie. I was there.'

The world seems to freeze around me. The trees, the rocks, then there's screaming – it's my mum, standing with Jordan, and she's staring at me. Why is she screaming? And I look down and my hands are covered in blood, so much of it. Have I cut myself? Nothing hurts – if there's this much blood something should hurt. And I begin to cry because I'm scared even though it doesn't hurt. I look down to see if there's blood anywhere else and there is

– it's all over the flat rock by my feet and all over Elsie – what's Elsie doing there? And why isn't she moving?

'Why isn't she moving?' I say, over and over. 'Why isn't she moving, Mummy? Why isn't she moving?'

'That's what you said, that day.' Jordan's voice brings me back to the present and I realise I've been speaking out loud. Now there is no blood, no dead Elsie on the floor, just me and my brother, standing where he stood with Mum all those years ago. 'That's what you said, over and over.'

'It was an accident,' I say, thinking of Elsie's tiny body lying on the floor. 'I… I didn't mean to hurt her.' I lean back against a tree for support, my legs feeling weak.

'The state of her,' Jordan says, as though the words cause him pain. 'It didn't look like an accident.'

Chapter Forty-Eight

Katy, 1994

Elsie runs out in front, her long blonde hair streaming out behind her. I love her hair, so soft, so silky. So unlike my wild orange curls. And cute-as-a-button Elsie says, 'Come on, slowpoke!'

She's not faster than me and we both know it – if I wanted to beat her into the woods, I could. I'm the fast one, the sporty one, the muddy knees and messed-up-hair one.

When we get to the clearing, she turns on me. 'I want to see the Boggly!'

She wants me to pretend to be a monster, like I do sometimes. It makes her laugh, like the boggart we saw in a book once, a nice pixie who gets angry and turns into an ugly monster, but I'm bored of that game, I'm tired of being the big ugly monster one. Let her do it for a change.

'It won't come out because you're here,' she says to me, jabbing a finger in my face as if the Boggly is a separate person who would only come if I could go away. 'I bet it would come and play if it was just me on my own. I bet it would like me best just like everyone likes me best.'

'They don't like you best,' I say, and my voice sounds sulky.

'Do too. Everyone says it. Because I'm pretty and you look like a wild feral. That's what my mum says, that you're feral. Even your dad likes me best, you know he does.'

And I do know it. Even though I know my dad loves me more than anything on earth, in that moment everything I fear about myself, that I am too loud, too ginger, too gangly and feral, it all comes rushing at me when Elsie says those words, 'Even your dad likes me best.' Because if that is true, if Elsie Button takes away my dad's love – well, that is the one thing I absolutely couldn't bear. Then I would rather die.

'You liar!' I explode, launching myself at her. She lets out a sound that is half scream and half laugh and begins to run away from me. I'm running after her – usually I'm much faster than her but today she has a head start on me. Until her foot snags on a tree root and she sails through the air, her scream louder and scarier this time. She hits the ground head first and I arrive at her side, throwing myself down next to her.

'Elsie, wake up,' I demand, grabbing her shoulder. Her eyelids flutter slightly and that's how I know she's faking. She's gone still now, but she's faking, I know she is. She's always doing it, pretending, then jumping up at me shouting, 'Fooled you!' She thinks she's so funny. 'Very funny. Get up, Elsie, you're just trying to get me into trouble.'

But she won't get up. She's like this sometimes, she always carries on with a joke even when it's not funny and I know she just wants me to get told off by my dad, so she can prove he likes her best.

Frustration prickles at me. 'Get up, stupid!' I slap her around the face harder than I mean to and the crack sounds loud in the silent woods, but still she doesn't move. 'Elsie, stop it! Stop it and get up!'

I pull her up by her T-shirt, almost to standing, but the sleeve rips where I have grabbed it and she slumps to the floor again. Why is she being so stupid? I poke at her with my toe and when she doesn't move, I kick her harder, leaving a dirty brown mark on her T-shirt where my muddy wellies have been. She still isn't moving. No one can be that still when someone kicks them... can they?

My heart starts to pound. 'Please, Elsie,' I plead, tears running down my cheeks now. I don't care if she laughs at me anymore, I just want her to get up and shout 'Gotcha!' But she doesn't. What if she's really hurt? I should run home and get Jordan, or Mum, but Elsie will be furious if I leave her in the woods on her own. She would never be my friend again. I'll have to take her with me.

I try to lift her again, managing to get her half off the floor, and begin to drag her back towards my house. Her T-shirt snags on a twig and rips again, but that doesn't matter now... her mum won't care about her T-shirt if I can get her back to the house and save her. She slides down again and I put my arms around her waist this time. She's smaller than me, and I can usually pick her up easily, but today she feels much heavier. There are leaves in her hair and marks on her arms from where the bushes along the path have caught her.

'Mum!' I scream. 'Jordan! Help!'

It's Jordan who finds us, me dragging Elsie along the path, panting and crying and unable to carry her any longer. I collapse on the floor next to our back gate and Jordan runs at us, calling for Mum, yelling at me am I okay and what's happened. I look up and my mum is next to him screaming. I look down at my hands and T-shirt which are covered in blood, and Elsie's silky blonde hair is all stringy and red and I'm screaming and I scream and scream until I can't remember anything else at all.

Chapter Forty-Nine

Katy, 1994

'Patrick, it's Kevin Wilson on the phone for you.'

Patrick glanced down at Harriet, who was gesturing towards the cottage with jittery hands. 'He says it's urgent.'

He navigated his way down the ladder and followed Harriet to her phone.

'Kevin?'

'Patrick, thank God I found you. You have to come home. Now. Jill has just called me, she's frantic. I'm on my way to yours. There's been some kind of emergency.'

'What emergency? What's going on? Why did she call you?'

'I have no idea, but I'm guessing it's legal advice she needs, which is why I want you there. I don't want to be giving any advice you aren't aware of.'

'Right, thanks, Kevin, appreciated. I'll meet you there.'

He pulled on his coat as he went into the kitchen where Harriet was standing, pretending not to have been listening.

'I have to go,' he said. 'Sorry, I'll try to pop back later, but I don't really know what's going on.'

Harriet nodded, wiping her hands on her tea towel. Patrick could tell she was disappointed, he should prob-ably stop stringing her along, but he felt sorry for her, what with being on her own and all that. Still, once this job was done, he'd probably tell her she had to find someone else to do her work for her. It was only best, Jill hated him going there anyway, she just didn't want to seem jealous. Maybe that's what this was all about, maybe she was just trying to drag him away from the charms of Harriet Tremayne.

He knew that wasn't the case as soon as he pulled up at the house. For a start, Kevin's wasn't the only car there – and both Kevin and the other two had parked in the field behind the house – it almost looked as though they were trying not to be seen. One of them was Doc Roberts, the other was George Fisher.

What were they doing here? What was going on?

Patrick hurried down the path, not bothering to lock his car. He shoved open the front door and called through the house.

'Jill?' he shouted, but there was no answer. The back garden then.

That was where he saw them. The three men – Kevin, Will and George – and Jill were standing at the bottom of the garden, gathered around something on the table. He marched towards them and, as he did, they parted, revealing something lying on the table. A little girl.

Kathryn?

But, of course, the long blonde hair told him what he needed to know, and as he got closer, he could see. Little Elsie Button lay on the table, her eyes closed and dry blood crusting over the entire right side of her face and staining her beautiful blonde locks. Patrick's face paled.

'What… How?' He looked at each man in turn, then walked over to where she lay, stroked her long blonde hair.

Silent tears began to roll down his cheeks. He saw Kevin looking towards his house. 'Not, Jordan?'

He was ashamed to even have thought of it, but Jordan was thirteen now, a time when boys become aware of the opposite sex… had a game gone too far? Had it been an accident, a shove…?

'Kathryn,' came a whispered voice, and he realised it had come from his wife. 'It was Kathryn.'

'Oh God,' he let out a groan. Not his little girl. Not his beautiful little girl. 'Where is she?'

'She's inside. Jordan took her away from…' Jill gestured to Elsie and let out another sob.

He instantly felt terrible. This was Rowley and Helen's girl, lying here, dead on his table, and all he could think about was what it meant for his daughter. 'Has anyone called Rowley?'

'Not yet,' George answered. 'We wanted to speak to you first. To find out what you wanted to do.'

'What I…' It took a minute for the words to sink in, but once they had, it was clear what he had to do. 'It was me,' he said, the idea taking root slowly. 'Someone has to take the blame for this, otherwise they will never stop looking for who did it. If I say it was me, they will stop looking.'

Jill let out a sob. Will shook his head.

'If you say it was you, you'll go to jail, spend the rest of your life labelled a child killer. Kathryn probably won't even be punished.'

'Maybe not. But she might be taken away from us, social services will be involved. She'll live with the stigma of this the rest of her life. The papers won't be able to print her name, but everyone will know. *She'll* know. I can't let her go through that.'

'Kathryn said it was an accident,' Jill said, moving forward to grasp at her husband's hand. Her eyes were pleading, but Patrick didn't know what she was pleading with him to do. This was the only way to protect Kathryn. 'She said Elsie fell.'

'Does it look like an accident?' he asked, gesturing at Elsie's ripped t-shirt, the bruises on her face and arms. Long scratches streaked her alabaster skin. 'Look at the state of the girl. Do you think anyone will believe those injuries were accidental?'

Jill couldn't seem to bring herself to look at the little girl who had spent so many meals at their table, so many summer afternoons playing in their back garden, nights sleeping in their daughter's bedroom. Who just a few hours ago thanked her so sweetly for the glass of ice cold juice she'd given her and sipped cordially at it whilst Kathryn gulped at hers and wiped the back of her hand across her lips. *Cute as a Button.*

'You can't do that, Patrick,' George said, his voice soft. 'You can't expect us all to lie.'

'I saved your wife's life,' Patrick said, the words he wasn't speaking more of a warning. Only Patrick and George knew that Linda had been attacked in retaliation for a man George had sent to jail based on planted evidence. The man had been guilty, but that didn't matter, George had fabricated the evidence that sent him down and Linda had paid the price. George looked at him with steely eyes, knowing that he must be serious to even bring that up.

'You have to be sure,' George said at last. He seemed to be the only one who accepted the gravity of the situation and what it meant for Kathryn. He was probably thinking of the daughter they were in the process of adopting,

Elizabeth, and what he'd already give up for a daughter he'd only met a handful of times. His freedom, his reputation, his life. There was no question.

'I am,' Patrick replied, and George's acceptance seemed to bring home to the other men that this was a very real possibility, that Patrick was going to admit to murder, that their friend was going to prison and that their lives would never be the same again.

Jill was the last to grasp what was going to happen next, and even then the realisation of everything that would mean didn't come until much later. That they were going to have lie, over and over again, that they were going to have to conceal the body of their best friend's little girl in case there was evidence that pointed to Kathryn as the person who had committed the crime. That their family was going to be ripped apart and that she was going to have to publicly denounce her husband if she was ever going to live a semi-normal life – if she even so much as visited him, she would be the woman who stood by a child killer. That his friends, his children, the entire country was going to think him a monster and hate him for the rest of his life. If he'd had a year to think it through, he'd still have done the same to protect his Kitty Kat.

Chapter Fifty

Kathryn

I open my eyes and for a second I'm not sure whether I'm still in 1994. The doctor is standing over me, a cold compress in his hand and my forehead wet. I know I'm in the present when I see Beth looking over me concernedly for the second time in as many days.

'This is becoming a habit,' I try to say, but my voice is croaky and my throat dry. From the corner of my eye, I see Jordan cross the room, but my head hurts if I try to turn towards him.

'Don't try to speak,' Will says.

Jordan snorts. 'Impossible,' he says, but I can see the relief on his face that I'm okay. I look at his face and can't believe I had accepted him as a killer, when all along the monster in the woods was me.

Miriam is standing next to him – I've never seen her so quiet. I wonder if she knows what I did. I wonder if they all know.

'Okay, everyone,' the doc announces, looking at me. 'Now you know she's fine, you can all leave her to get some rest.' He looks at Beth's mum.

'Oh she can stay here,' she says, and I realise that Beth and Jordan must have driven me here after I collapsed in the woods behind my old home. 'I'll bring up some soup when she's had another rest.'

The doc nods his approval and says to me, 'I'll come back and check on you later. No more traipsing around in the woods, okay?'

I nod weakly.

Miriam leans over and kisses my head. I must look awful for this show of affection. 'I'm not going anywhere,' she promises. 'Linda has said I can stay here too.'

'Doesn't know what she's letting herself in for,' I croak, but I'm immensely grateful.

Jordan is the last to leave, and his hand lingers over mine. 'I love you, Kitty Kat,' he says, his voice low. 'I'm sorry about how all this happened. I followed you down on Wednesday to try and stop it ending like this but I should have just told you the truth. We'll work through it, okay? We'll talk about it all later, when you're well.'

I nod, wishing that never has to happen. But it does, I know. The genie is out of the bottle and we have to figure out how to deal with the consequences. Which is something I should have done twenty-five years ago.

–

When they are gone, I take out the phone Beth let me borrow and scroll mindlessly for a while. I log on to ArmchairPoirot, but there are no new messages, Shakes is strangely quiet considering everything that's going on with their favourite case. Then again, I'm sure the same can be said of me, but I've been otherwise engaged.

I don't have a Facebook account under my own name – obviously – or even under Kathryn Starling, it would be more trouble than it was worth, but I've got a dummy account for whenever I need information on something that only the general public, aka Tracey from Scarborough, can give you. I log into that now and flick through the pages about Abigail Warner – there's hardly much more I can do.

There are dozens and dozens of comments on every link, on every picture. They all say roughly the same thing, that Abigail is better where she is, that the police should stop the search because she's fine, that she will be well looked after like Elsie was. *Like Elsie was.* And I remember that pink duvet and the little rabbit, the lifeless figure on the bed – Elsie's bed. Because that room had been furnished with Elsie's things.

I know where Abigail is. I know who has her.

Chapter Fifty-One

Maggie

'So am I the only one thinking from this drawing that Kathryn Bowen was the monster that Elsie was scared of?' Maggie slipped the drawing into the evidence bag and sealed it. 'And if so, what does that have to do with Abigail? Who gave her this picture? Not Kathryn.'

'The new friend her school pal was talking about,' DS Bailey said. 'Could they have given her the picture?'

'That would only make sense if *Kathryn* was her new friend,' Maggie replied. 'And I'm pretty sure she would have been noticed sneaking around Anglesey grooming young girls. I was tipped off the moment she drove over the border on Tuesday.'

'I wonder if she could have found it in the house. This might have been Kathryn's old room.'

'Except Kathryn didn't draw this picture, Elsie did. And I doubt she would have given her best friend a picture of her looking like a monster. Which would mean that the picture would probably still have been in the Buttons' house when Elsie was taken.'

And just like that the female DNA on the tissue, Abigail's new friend in the woods where Elsie was taken from and Dr Roberts being in the area when Abigail went missing all made sense.

'Helen Button,' Maggie whispered. 'Doc Roberts was looking for Helen Button that morning. Elsie's mum took Abigail.'

Chapter Fifty-Two

Kathryn

I know where Abigail is, I know who has her. I picture that lifeless form on the pink duvet, clutching Elsie's bunny rabbit and I pray to God I was wrong and that she's not dead.

Picking up the phone, I don't call the police, I don't even call Beth, which I probably should.

'Kevin Wilson's office.'

'I need to speak to Kevin immediately. Please,' I add. My mother would have said no emergency is too important to forget your manners.

My mother. She gave her whole life up to protect me. She lost the husband she adored, her home, her friends. I want a pang of sadness to come, but I feel numb, dead inside. How are you supposed to feel when you find out you are a murderer? Are you supposed to just go on with your life? Pretend like you're a normal human being? I used to be the girl whose father killed her best friend. It wasn't a common club to belong to, but it wasn't exclusive. Now, in the space of a few days, I've gone from a victim to a perpetrator, and how many people can say that? How many people are in my club now, a club of people who didn't know they were evil. It's an unfortunate fact that there are many, many people in this world who kill. Some who kill accidentally, some who kill on purpose, some who kill once, some dozens of times. But how many people can say they have killed their best friend without ever knowing they were capable of it?

Will I ever get over this? I honestly can't say – it's too soon for me to know how I am going to battle this particular demon. I don't just have Elsie's blood on my hands, I have ruined my dad's life, my mum's and Jordan's too. Everything we've endured is my fault, and what's worse is that they kept it all a secret to protect me and the way I repaid them was years of spoilt, selfish breakdowns and recklessness. That was a lot easier to explain away when it was all my dad's fault.

I'll probably take the easy way out, a bottle of pills or maybe a leap from the Menai bridge in the dead of the night. Give Helen Button and little Elsie the retribution they deserve. But first there is something I can do to make amends. I have someone else's life in my hands, the way I did twenty-five years ago. But this time I'm going to do the right thing. Because if she's still alive, I'm going to save Abigail Warner.

'I'm sorry, Mr Wilson isn't taking calls at the moment,' his secretary says in her perpetual bored tone. 'I can take a me—'

'Tell him Kathryn Bowen needs to speak to him. Right now. It's about Abigail Warner.'

I hear the secretary sigh and she puts me on hold without telling me. No sooner has the tacky music started, the phone is picked up.

'Putting you through,' she says, and the phone begins to ring again.

'Katy? Thank God, you're okay.'

'Hardly, Kevin, but that's a conversation for another time. This is important. I need you to meet me somewhere, and I need you to call Will Roberts and have him meet us there too.'

'Gemma said it was about Abigail Warner. What's going on, Katy, do you know where she is?'

'I think so. And I think Doctor Roberts does too, if he's being honest with himself. And we're going to rescue her.'

–

They climb out of their cars at almost the same time, these men who know my darkest secret, who conspired to throw Patrick Bowen in prison to save his only daughter from a lifetime of stigma. I wouldn't have even been punished, but he couldn't risk me being taken away from my mum and these men saw that and agreed to help. I owe them my life and I hate them.

I feel a small pang of recognition when I see the Button farmhouse. I'd driven past the actual farm five minutes ago, the barns full of livestock and machinery whirring and grinding, I remembered it all. I used to love coming to the farm, feeding the chickens, chasing the sheepdog, sitting and chatting to the cows. Elsie hated mud and dirt and anything that smelled bad; I sometimes wished we could swap lives.

Despite selling the farmland and the animals years ago, Helen still has a large barn to the left of the house, a wire enclosure attached that looks empty. I can just about see a stable beyond that – I'd forgotten she kept horses. That was how she'd known the best way to source and administer ketamine then. And how her upper body strength had still been enough to drag me into her car, despite the weight difference between us.

'Kathryn – are you serious about this?' Kevin Wilson looks up at the house, but Will Roberts doesn't speak. How much he knows, or has suspected, I'm not sure, but he's not surprised we're here. He's already accepted that my hunch is probably right, that Abigail is here some-where. I think he's known all along and was afraid that Helen has killed her.

'Perhaps you should wait in your car,' Will suggests, but I shake my head. I have to face this head on. I've avoided it for twenty-five years.

The shot cracks through the air like a branch splitting and the glass in the car window explodes. I scream and drop to the ground, hearing two thumps next to me and praying that Kevin and Will have done the same, that they are not hurt.

'Helen!' Will shouts towards the farmhouse. 'Helen it's me, Will! Don't shoot!' And then, in what is either the worlds bravest or stupidest move, Will gets to his feet and holds his hands in the air. There is another sickening crack and Will staggers backwards against the car, a bright red stain blooming on his shirt. He's been hit.

'No!' I scream. I don't know what to do, I'm not Lara Croft or John McClane. I'm terrified. I was expecting a broken shell of a woman, not an attack.

Another shot rings out, hitting the door of the car. I can hear Kevin shouting and Will is pulled away from me, around to the back of the car.

'Kathryn!' Kevin calls to me. 'You've got to try to get around this side! We have to get Will to hospital!'

Everything has gone quiet, there are no more shots… except I can still hear something. It's the sound of an engine running, a sound I noticed just before the first shot rang out. There's a truck in the driveway, the back is uncovered and there are bags piled up inside. She's going to try to get away. And if we let her go, Abigail disappears with her.

'Helen!' I shout towards the house, without standing up. 'Helen, you can't take her! You won't make it off the island!'

The front door to the house opens and I crane my neck to see Helen Button emerge. She looks nothing like the slack-eyed, broken woman she had been on the day we'd seen her at the search. For a start, her clothes fit properly now, she is wearing jeans and a vest, covered by a checked shirt that hangs open. She still looks rail-thin, but she doesn't look weak any more.

I know that in the house beyond is a pretty pink room, and that the Helen we are seeing now is the one who grabbed me from behind, drugged me and held me captive. She is stronger than anyone gave her credit for and she's been planning this day for a while, letting everyone believe she has retreated into herself, a broken, old woman, easily forgotten.

She's holding the gun pointed straight at me. A small figure draped in a blanket rests against her left shoulder. I can't see if the figure is moving.

'Is Doctor Roberts okay?' she shouts. 'I didn't mean to hit him, it was just supposed to be a warning shot.' She sounds so matter-of-fact that it's hard to reconcile with the fact that she's just shot a man.

'He needs a hospital,' Kevin's voice comes from behind the car. 'He's losing blood. I need to take him before he loses consciousness.'

'Take him,' she calls. 'I won't stop you.'

'We need you to hand over Abigail before we go anywhere,' I yell. 'We can't leave without her.'

'Her name isn't Abigail!' she screams, her face contorted with fury. 'She's Elsie! ELSIE! He thought he'd taken her away, but he hadn't!'

I hold my hands up and start to slowly push myself up from the ground. Helen is at her truck now, easing Abigail into the front seat.

'What about the chickens?' I practically plead. 'And your horse?'

'Dead,' she says, and I see the first stab of regret in her eyes. 'It was the only humane way. I wasn't sure how long it would take people to realise I'd gone.'

I can only hope that Kevin has called the police while he's been the other side of the car, and that they, and an ambulance, are on the way because Helen is determined to leave with Abigail. If she has gone so far as to kill her beloved horse, she is not letting any of us stop her.

'I'm sorry!' I shout, trying to delay her. 'It wasn't Patrick who killed Elsie. It was me, Helen. Me. I took Elsie away and I'm sorry. I didn't mean for it to happen, I loved her too.'

Helen takes a step back as realisation dawns on her. 'I knew it,' she whispers, swinging the gun at me. 'I knew they were lying to me. All this time they made me think I was mad, that I was the sick one. But I knew Patrick wouldn't hurt Elsie. Not his own daughter.'

His own daughter. So it was true, Elsie was his after all. That was why I always felt like he loved her as much as he loved me, sometimes more. And he knew I could tell, that's why he felt so guilty about what I did. He knew I had a reason to be jealous of Elsie.

'How does it feel to know you killed your own sister?' Helen spits. 'Just because she was prettier than you. Because you were jealous of her.'

'I didn't mean to!' I call out. 'It was an accident! I just wanted her to be quiet!'

'How dare you blame her!' Helen thrusts the gun at me and I close my eyes, certain she's going to shoot. Then we both hear it, the sound of sirens in the distance. This is it, her one chance to get away and she's not going to lose it. She walks backwards towards the driver's side of the truck, the gun trained on me the whole time. 'I played with her a few times in the woods,' she shouts as she walks. 'I gave her one of Elsie's old bracelets once and some money, and she liked that. Then, the other day, I realised – she didn't just look like Elsie, she *was* Elsie. It was like someone had picked her up and transported her through time to the place she had been lost from. No one was watching her. I was her friend, I was the only one she trusted! They never cared about her! I care about her. She'll be happy with me.'

'Then why was she bleeding? They found a tissue with blood on it. If you didn't hurt her, how did she bleed?'

'I got a nosebleed,' Helen said. 'And she was so kind. She gave me a tissue. Elsie would have done the same. It's how I knew for certain it was her.'

She's lost it, I realise. And if I don't keep her talking, she's going to drive away with Abigail and she might actually make it off the island. One last chance to do the right thing and I call a lawyer and a doctor instead of the police. *Always such a screw-up.*

'Why did you let me go when I was in your house? When you could have killed me? Why did you leave me where George Fisher would find me?'

'I didn't want to kill you then,' Helen says. 'I didn't know you'd taken my baby from me. If you want the truth, I thought it was your mother who took Elsie. I always thought she knew about mine and Patrick's one-night stand and she'd killed my baby out of revenge. I just wanted to stop you sniffing around.'

'So why let me go?'

'Because your friends were getting too nosy,' she says. 'I thought if I dumped you again, they wouldn't have any reason to come up here and find me and Elsie. I knew I was going to have to move on – I couldn't take you.'

Helen's hand is on the car door handle. She'll be gone any second, taking Abby with her and if there's a chance, however small, that she will get away, I have to try and stop her. I stand up and move slowly towards the truck, and as I do I call out to her, one last-ditch attempt.

'I can take you to her. I can take you to where they buried Elsie.'

She hesitates for just a second and lowers the gun. The sirens are getting closer, but if she goes now, they won't make it. I have a decision to make. I killed a little girl twenty-five years ago. I may not have meant to, but I did, and this is what it has led to – this was all caused by what I did on that day, and what my father and his friends covered up for me. If it's my life or Abigail's – well, I know who deserves the chance.

Helen shakes her head and reaches out to open the door handle and without stopping to think I rush towards her, knowing that even if she shoots me now, I might hold her up enough for the police to arrive. She looks shocked, but not shocked enough to stop her raising the gun, pointing it at me and pulling the trigger.

As I slump over the hood of the truck, I force myself to keep moving towards her, just to hold her up for a minute longer. My vision blurs and the pain is excruciating, but I see the blurry red and blue lights getting closer. Then the gun fires again and I know I have done my best, I just hope it was good enough.

Chapter Fifty-Three

Maggie

It was on the warmest day of the year that DI Maggie Grant, DS Bryn Bailey and Abigail's parents faced the press to tell them that Abigail had been found. Tears streaked Caroline's face and her husband held on to her as if she might run away at any moment. But they were tears of joy, the clinging together of a family that had been ripped apart and sewn back up again.

Maggie recalled the moment John Warner had heard her take the phone call to say that there was an incident up at the Button Farm and the missing girl was believed to have been located. She had shouted at Lesley to keep him at the house as she and DS Bailey had jumped into her vehicle, but there was no holding John back. He had jumped in his car and followed them to the farm before anyone could stop him. Luckily, he had been too far behind them to see the crash between Maggie's unmarked police car and Helen Button's vehicle that had almost killed his daughter, only arriving in time to see Abigail being loaded into the back of the ambulance. Alive and relatively unhurt, unlike Dr Roberts and Kathryn Bowen. Maggie herself had managed to sustain a broken wrist, while DS Bailey and Kevin Wilson had escaped unscathed.

The crowd outside Memorial Hall cheered and clung to one another when the announcement was made; more than half of them were crying. Grown men sobbed into their sleeves. Scott Marshall wiped away a tear.

'Abigail is still undergoing observation in hospital, but we are told she has no concerning physical injuries, no signs of sexual assault and is generally physically well. That's all I wish to say at this time, and we hope now that Abigail and her family can be left alone to come to terms with what they have been through.'

Dozens of hands shot into the air, but the journalists didn't wait to be asked to call their questions.

'Was Rowley Button thought to be involved in Abigail's abduction?'

'Is Helen Button implicated in her own daughter's disappearance?'

'How did you break your wrist?'

'Is it true two other people were rushed to hospital? Was one of them Kathryn Bowen?'

Maggie Grant held up a hand. Despite the amazing news, this was still an active investigation and she wasn't about to say anything that might harm it. She looked out at the crowd, sure that her exhaustion was etched onto her face. She felt at least ten years older than she had last week. No one could say she hadn't put her all into finding Abigail, and she had been thanking the gods ever since she'd had the call from the 999 dispatch that the little girl had been located. DS Bailey stood next to her, looking at her with something close to reverence. Bless him. She knew how much he had disliked her just a week ago; maybe she had managed to prove that she wasn't just a spiky asshole.

She answered the questions thrown at her to the best of her ability. These people had been out there all hours the same as she had – they deserved as much information as they could be given. They were questioning one adult male and one adult female in connection with Abigail's abduction. No, she couldn't confirm their names at this time. Yes, they still believed Patrick Bowen to be responsible for Elsie's disappearance. Yes, reports that two other people were taken to hospital were correct. No, we wouldn't be naming those people at this time…

She spotted who she had been looking for and held up a hand. 'No further questions at this time. We'll have another update for you tomorrow morning at eleven a.m.'

As she climbed down from the makeshift podium, she made a beeline towards the two women standing at the edge of the group.

'Ladies,' Maggie said. 'Congratulations on a job well done. Even you, Ms Pike.' She smiled and watched the crowds wandering around in the sunshine. The search was over but no one wanted to go home. It felt too significant just to go straight back to normal life.

'Kathryn should be here,' Beth said, her eyes filling up. Maggie closed her eyes at hearing the name. Kathryn Bowen had saved the life of Abigail Warner, there was no doubt about it, but what other involvement had she had?

Miriam sighed and placed a hand on Beth's arm. 'She made her choice,' Miriam said. 'Would you have made a different one?'

Beth shook her head. 'No, I guess not. I'm going to miss her though. And you.'

Miriam smiled. 'You come and visit me any time, PC Fisher,' she said. 'You can take care of my speeding tickets.' She looked at Maggie and winked. 'Leave your DI at home.'

Chapter Fifty-Four

Kathryn
Three weeks later

The visiting order trembles in my hand as I queue to have my possessions searched. The process is no different to every other time I've been here and yet it feels different in every way. Last time I came here, the monster was the one inside the cage.

Everything hurts – the doctors say there will likely be some long-term effects from the two bullet wounds I sustained. I'm not allowed to drive – I shouldn't be going out at all yet, but I had to make this one journey, so Miriam is in the car outside waiting to whip me home and lock me in my bedroom until I'm healed.

He is led into the room by the guards, like a dangerous animal watched closely by a zookeeper. It seems extraordinary now, that he is still treated this way when I know he is innocent, but there remains only a handful of people who know the truth. Maggie Grant thinks she knows, but she will be hard pressed to find any proof other than the child's drawing she clings onto like a talisman.

They sit him down in front of me and at once twenty-five lost years hit me like a steamroller. If only I'd known what he'd sacrificed for me. I remember the last time I was here, telling him I hoped he'd rot.

'Hello, Dad,' I say.

He begins to cry.

We sit for a few minutes in silence, the amount there is to say overwhelming the space in-between us.

'How is your mum?' he asks, even though I know he spoke to Jordan from the hospital just this morning.

'She's stable,' I say. She woke from her coma two hours after I returned from Anglesey. We haven't yet told her that I know. 'Thank you. For what you did for me.'

'Thank you' doesn't seem enough to cover the sacrifice he made, but he knows that. The legal system would have been kinder to me than it has been to him, I was five years old. But he also knew that what happened didn't look like an accident, and my dad made a choice to shield me from the repercussions of that. I understand his decision, even if I'm not sure I agree with it. Part of it was certainly fuelled by the guilt of the secret he and Helen had been carrying for nearly six years.

'Was Elsie really your daughter?' I ask.

He puts a hand over his eyes and nods. 'It was a stupid one-night stand,' he says. 'I loved your mother. I still do. Would have done anything to take it back, anything. When she told me she was pregnant...' he lets out a sigh. 'If I'd stayed faithful to your mother none of this would ever have happened.'

'But Elsie would never have existed,' I say gently. 'And she deserved to exist.'

He lets out another sigh, like the effort of speaking after all these years is too much.

'The evidence against you,' I say. 'Fabricated? You burned Elsie's clothes? Put hair and blood on the barrel? Hid her underwear in our house?'

'I had to make the charges stick. Without a body... they might not have accepted my confession. They needed enough evidence to convict me, so it could just go away.'

Except it never went away, not for any of us.

'We redressed her,' he says quickly, as if that makes it better. 'In some of your clothes. She was wearing that dress of yours she loved when she was buried. We chose such a beautiful resting place for her, on a coastal heather heath, looking towards Holyhead Mountain. It's peaceful there.'

'I appreciate what you've done for me,' I say, knowing that what I'm about to tell him will hurt him as much as the last twenty-five years in prison has. 'But I'm going to tell the truth.'

I watch his face contort in pain.

'No,' he whispers, 'please no, Katy. All these years I've protected you.'

'But I'm a grown woman now,' I say. 'And I need to atone for my actions. I think on some level I always knew – it's why I self-destructed while Jordan built himself a life. I didn't feel worthy of a life. All these years you've got through this by feeling that you made the right decision. I can't live the rest of my life knowing I had the chance and didn't. And Elsie should get a proper burial. Rowley and Helen should know where their child is. I'm not going to screw this up anymore.'

Dad hangs his head, but I see him nod.

'What about the others? George, Kevin, your mother?'

'I'll keep them out of it,' I promise. 'I'll say you were the only one who knew.'

'What has happened to Helen?'

I take a deep breath in. I knew we'd have to talk about his sooner or later. About how the decision to protect me all those years ago nearly lost another little girl her life.

'She's been charged with kidnapping and false imprisonment of a minor. Beth says they can't find any evidence that Doctor Roberts was involved.'

He hesitates. 'And Abigail?'

'Still in hospital,' I say. 'She was given a lower dose of the sedative than I was, and Helen made sure she drank water, but she was still very weak when they found her. She's going to be okay, physically at least.'

'Kathryn, you don't have to tell anyone what you discovered,' he says gently. 'I'm an old man, comfortable with the choices I've made. It doesn't make you a bad person if you just leave things as they are.'

'I'm done running, Dad,' I say. 'My whole life I've felt sorry for myself because these things happened to me, because they were done to me, but Elsie was the real victim, she always has been. She deserves the truth.'

The world deserves to know the truth about what happened to Elsie Button. I just hope I'm brave enough to tell it.